I0743642

The Four Of Clubs

Part 10 of the Red Dog Conspiracy

Patricia Loofbourrow

Copyright © 2023 Patricia Loofbourrow
Cover design by Patricia Loofbourrow
All rights reserved.
ISBN-13: 978-1-944223-56-4

This is a work of fiction.
No part of this work may be reproduced or transmitted in any form or by any means without the express written consent of the publisher.

Published by Red Dog Press, LLC
Printed in the USA

Praise for the
Red Dog Conspiracy

"Melancholy and loyalty. Blood and love. Violence and tenderness. They're all tangled together in this powerful series ..."

— OLIVIA WYLIE

"This very well thought out world is created with incredibly believable and realistic scenarios based on the best of steampunk, mafia family organisation, 19th century English living (not the nobles, but the real world of real people, similar to Dickens or Swift) and an intriguing dystopian future."

— LIN CRAN

"Rival gangs, dishonest wealthy, and the grubby poor — all trying to make a living amidst a life-style that has fallen into ruins."

— MARILYN COATES

"Although it's an easy read there are twists and turns, dead ends and hidden meanings that help provide a wonderful dangerous complexity. For me the greatest meanings are in relationships and cultural distances. Things that are the heart of Jacqui's problems. That and love. A brilliant portrayal of flawed people caught in their own suspicion-based traps."

— KAY MACK

"Even if you aren't a fan of steampunk, this series is a fun read! The author has created a unique world set far in the future where Victorian culture and steampunk technology are the norm. It is in this world that Jacq must try to make her way. Surrounded by enemies, married to a man she doesn't love, and every action by any person in her world could be an act of betrayal that will cost Jacq her life!"

— KEVIN SIVILS

For clues, backstory and more, visit JacqOfSpades.com

FICTION BY PATRICIA LOOFBOURROW

RED DOG CONSPIRACY

Part 1: The Jacq of Spades

Part 2: The Queen of Diamonds

Part 3: The Ace of Clubs

Part 4: The King of Hearts

Part 5: The Ten of Spades

Part 6: The Five of Diamonds

Part 7: The Two of Hearts

Part 8: The Three of Spades

Part 9: The Knave of Hearts

Part 10: The Four of Clubs

Part 11: The Jack of Diamonds

Part 12: The Death Card

THE PREQUELS

Gutshot: The Catastrophe

The Alcatraz Coup

Brothers

Vulnerable

THE COMPANIONS

Drawing Thin

OTHER FICTION

Weird Worlds: Science Fiction and Fantasy Flash Fiction

More Weird Worlds: Science Fiction and Fantasy Flash Fiction

Homa

The Paramour

My dressmaker Tenni Mitchell and I stood in my former bedroom at my apartments on 33 1/3 Street, Spadros quadrant, as she fitted me for a new gown.

The event? The opening of the Spadros Castle Museum tomorrow. The day marked one year since the murder of my father-in-law (the former Patriarch Roy Spadros) and the burning of his home.

I didn't like to think of that day.

I'd found my own front garden red with the blood of our men. I think that for a while, the terrible time afterwards broke me.

But I put the thoughts from my mind — daily, hourly. I had too much to do.

Like prepare for this event — which of course, meant a new dress. Emerald green silk, to match a vest my husband Tony had specially made for the event. Tony wanted green, to signal a new beginning.

Tenni was the only one I trusted for the task.

But for a Clubb quadrant citizen — as Tenni now was — to visit Spadros Manor involved a great deal of fuss, so here we were.

I stood on a fine wooden crate, on display like a store-front doll. But the sturdy metal screens were still in place outside my windows, the curtains shut. No one might see.

Outside, the day was overcast, pleasantly cool. Birds sang.

I was safe. Six of my men stood guard, encircling the building. More guarded the other side of the duplex.

For a while, this had been my home. I loved being here. And it was much better to do these preparations here than all the fuss for the Spadros Queen to visit Tenni's dress shop in Clubb quadrant.

Things were about as good as they might get, all things considered.

Tenni, however, was in tears.

"She moved **out**! She won't tell me what's wrong, only that she can't be with someone keeping secrets from her. Can you believe it? **Her!**" Tenni began sobbing once more.

The "her" in question was Tenni's paramour, Cheisara Golf, with whom she'd just bought a home on 93rd Street, Clubb quadrant. From all accounts, it was a nice home, with a lovely fenced yard where Tenni's younger sisters might play, or even one day receive suitors.

Cheisara's father, Mr. Ferdinand Golf, had married one of Alexander and Regina Clubb's daughters. And until Alexander Clubb had the man killed a few years earlier, Mr. Golf had been a vital part of the Clubb syndicate.

Cheisara had approached Tenni at Madame Biltcliffe's funeral and confessed her love. The two had been together ever since, and up to now, all seemed well.

The Clubb Family was well-known for their trade in secrets. Their vast network of spies. So for Cheisara to leave Tenni on **that** account sounded ... different. "What does she think you've kept from her?"

Tenni wiped her eyes, her face downcast. "We had men there moving the girls' rooms, and they asked about my sewing room." Tenni glanced round. "You know."

I smiled at her. "Yes." The room where Tenni kept the sewing machine that Madame Biltcliffe had left her. The machine was tech forbidden by the Cultural Correctness Committee, because it ran on electrical power.

Strange, that we might have electrical lamps, but not an electrical sewing machine.

"And after the movers left, she asked what lay inside. Why I kept it locked. Why I never let her see. I told her it was only my sewing supplies, with dresses that customers wished kept hidden. But she pressed the matter." She glanced at me then. "You told me never to tell anyone, mum."

Oh, dear. "I did."

Tenni shook her head. "I thought it was settled! But last night, with the girls in bed and the boxes around us, she said she couldn't live with secrets. Just like that, she got up and called for a taxi-carriage." Tears streamed down Tenni's face. "She went back to Clubb Manor!"

I wanted to hug her, but her tears would have quite ruined the dress I wore. So I rested my hand on her arm. "I'm sorry."

"I don't know what to do! I —"

"It sounds as if you don't trust her. Not to tell anyone else."

Tenni nodded. "Especially that grandmother of hers."

Regina Clubb. The woman was insufferable. "I think Mrs. Clubb already knows. She must. Don't you see? When Madame Biltcliffe was murdered, the police went everywhere. They had to have seen your machine. But they didn't ask for bribes to keep it quiet. So she must have put you off-limits."

Tenni nodded, took a breath. She was five years younger than me, but right then she seemed even younger than that. "Okay."

"I don't wish to pry." I hesitated. "But surely a locked door isn't reason to leave. Is it?"

Tenni looked despondent. "I don't know! She's always asking about things I'd rather not speak of. I love her, truly I do. But ..."

"There are things you don't wish to speak of."

She threw her handkerchief on the floor. "**Yes**! Why does she need to **know** everything? Why won't she just let it **be**?" She turned away, hands to her face.

I wasn't sure what counsel to give her. My choices in relationship matters had hardly been successful.

I stepped off the box. "Perhaps she just needs time to think about what's important." My handkerchief lay on the tea-table, so I offered it to her. "I recall how uncertain I felt when I bought this place. She's made a big step." I struggled to find the words for her. "Perhaps this time apart will help her see why she feels as she does."

Tenni glanced over, a bit more hopeful.

I thought a change of subject might help. "How are the wedding plans?" Tenni's younger sister Oma was set to marry a Spadros quadrant Detective Constable in a few weeks.

Tenni scoffed, rolling her eyes. "His mother's a fright! She wants to dictate every part of it. Yes, she's helping to pay, but what Oma wants is just as important." She let out a laugh. "Leone doesn't seem to care one way or the other about any of it."

I chuckled. "Men just want the time to be done with, so they can bed their wife."

Tenni giggled.

Lifting my skirts slightly to clear the edge, I stepped back up onto the box. "What else needs doing?"

Whilst Tenni fussed at the dress, pinning it here and there, I thought about my dearest friend Josephine Kerr's aborted wedding.

The murder of her betrothed, my half-brother Etienne Hart, had seemingly put her into melancholy. By all reports, she'd kept to deep mourning. She'd never acknowledged the cards and gifts I'd sent her. The bridge guards told me she'd see no one.

I worried for Josie, across the city in that dreary brownstone bordering the Hart slums, with only her dying grandfather, her elderly servants, and that scoundrel of a brother for company.

No. I would **not** think about Joseph Kerr. He'd caused quite enough trouble.

***

Tenni left with the dress, her mood somewhat brightened. Back in the royal blue linen walking dress I'd started the day with, I went to my office to prepare my Family fees.

Oh, the irony: the Queen of Spades paying fees that mostly returned to Spadros Manor. But whilst I was held exempt, my business wasn't. Tony said it was good for the quadrant to see me follow our own law.

My butler (and Tony's distant cousin) Blitz Spadros knocked on the door. "Mrs. Spadros, your carriage is here."

"I'll be out in a minute."

I now paid my Family fees by check. Looking over the numbers, I signed the check and put it into an envelope, which I sealed. Then I made sure my pistol lay in my pocket. Since witnessing my brother's murder by his own men, I'd not gone anywhere without it.

And it reminded me of Jonathan Diamond, who'd given the gun to me. Who also lay dead.

Gods, I missed him. I still miss him, to this day.

I fetched my green and gold carpetbag and went into the hall.

Ariana Spadros toddled down the hall, arms wide. "Jacqui!"

I picked her up with one arm and kissed her chubby little cheek. "How's my girl?"

"Mama make sannich."

I laughed. "Well, that's good: it's almost tea-time! What kind of sandwich did she make?"

"Chick-in."

"Very good!" I set her down. "I have to go home now. I hope you like your sandwich!"

Ariana rubbed her left eye with the back of a chubby fist. "I wish you live here."

So do I, sweet girl. I kissed her forehead. "Now off with you!"

Mary Spadros appeared at the end of the hall. "There you are!"

Ariana took off towards her, arms wide, her little house shoes clacking on the floor.

Mary smiled at me. "Sure you can't stay for tea?"

"I wish I could, but I promised I'd be home."

Mary's husband Blitz held the door, but the carriage wasn't there. Instead, a man barely taller than I with a big bushy beard stood at the bottom of the steps. He tipped his gray tweed cap when he saw me.

"Why, Mr. Howell," I said. "Whatever are you doing here?"

Mr. Eight Howell was my personal secretary, as well as the owner of the Backdoor Saloon down the street. "It's time we take a stroll."

***

Mr. Howell made it clear this wasn't a request. Which surprised me enough that I went down the steps and alongside him towards his establishment without a word. I was the Spadros Queen, after all.

Since I'd almost been abducted by Trey Louis over a year earlier, I went nowhere without a stout guard. Tony's men stood at intervals along the street, tipping their caps as Mr. Howell and I passed. My footman Skip Honor, Blitz, and his oldest brother Mr. Theodore Sutherfield took spots ahead and behind, as if we all strolled along on a nice spring day. Which, other than being overcast, it was.

I didn't fear anything with these men around me; they'd saved my life time and again. But I did feel curious. "What's happened?"

Mr. Howell twitched, as if he'd been thinking of something else entirely. "Happened? Nothing, mum." He lapsed into silence, most unhelpfully, which was out of character for him.

Unenlightened by his reply, I figured that the answer to whatever this was about would turn up shortly.

Mr. Howell said, "How's our little Heir?"

I smiled to myself. "As well as ever."

Acevedo's cast had come off months ago. But although the surgical scars had healed well, part of his inner left thigh had withered. Dr. Salmon said this was due to lack of blood after the shooting.

My son was late to crawl, but it was never from any mental impediment. Acevedo wanted to crawl. He wanted to walk. But he'd begin, then his face would spasm in pain. After one such time, he put his face on the floor and sobbed.

The doctor rayed him; Acevedo's bones had healed well. He didn't know what pained the boy so.

Acevedo's nursemaid Daisy and I spent many of our days devising things to amuse him. He loved Yuletide, with its bright lights and colors. He used to love sitting out front watching the carriages drive past. Yet now, he screamed in terror if brought out front, particularly when carriages went by.

I didn't blame him. He'd been almost killed on his own front porch, the one place he should have felt safe.

I should have been there.

I should have died instead.

At the end of the block, Mr. Howell's men opened the doors to the Backdoor Saloon.

All those lovely bottles ... I drew back. "I shouldn't go in there."

Mr. Howell let out a breath. "I know, but I couldn't think of anywhere else that I knew was safe." He gave me a warm smile. "Your husband's waiting for us."

The Husband

I was so surprised that all I said was, "Oh."

I let the group escort me in. Blitz took my arm and led me past those warm golden bottles to Mr. Howell's office in the back.

Mr. Howell had removed the portraits of half-clothed women. But otherwise the office hadn't changed much: small, untidy, dark-paneled, and smelling of cigars.

My husband Tony was a pale, ordinary-looking man with straight black hair and deep blue eyes. He sat behind Mr. Howell's desk, his piano-black cane tipped in silver leaning on the arm of his chair.

He didn't rise. But that didn't bother me.

After the New Year, Tony had another surgery on his leg, which had begun to swell and pain him. Another drainage, with more weeks of healing. A year after being shot, he still walked with a cane, as he did the rest of his life.

Matters had been quiet since Tony's ascension to Patriarch. I suppose it helped that we spread far and wide that Master Seven Bresciane, the dreaded Knife Man, once again stood beside the Spadros Family.

Of course, this made many on the island of Market Center hate the Spadros Family even more. But Tony's first cousin, right-hand man, and former chief enforcer Ten Hogan (also known as Sawbuck) advised a public announcement.

I say former because Sawbuck's back, struck by a bullet in the spine, never healed well, and troubled him until the day he died. So whilst the quadrant still reported to him, he chose others to do the actual dirty work.

Seeing Sawbuck injured gave me pain of my own. I never wished any of this upon him, not once. Not even though he only wanted my husband's love.

Tony had been changed by the attack on his home. The injury of his son. The death of his sister. Learning the true nature of the man he'd always thought of as his father. The cutting words of his nephew. The betrayals of his mother. Over the past year, he'd spoken little and spent much of his time on the veranda, even meeting with his men there as winter came and went.

When he wasn't on the veranda, the servants told me he'd been out in the meadow with Sawbuck and some of his most trusted men. Learning to wrestle.

Wrestle? That didn't sound like Tony at **all!**

And when he wasn't at Spadros Manor, rumor had it that he spent his days in Diamond quadrant, presumably with his son Roland's mother, Gardena.

I didn't like to think of that, either.

I recalled what Sawbuck said once, and I'd have to agree: Tony's eyes were his best feature. I curtsied low. "Good afternoon, sir."

Tony's eyes turned amused, in a sad sort of way. He gestured across the desk. "Please, sit down."

Two chairs sat on the side of the desk closest to me: I picked the right-hand one.

The rest left, shutting the door.

I recalled when Roy had me brought in here, and I felt annoyed. "How's Gardena?"

Tony acted as if I'd not spoken. "Have you seen Master Rainbow?"

I normally thought of the man by the first name he ever gave me — Morton — so it took a second for me to reply. "Blaze Rainbow?" I shook my head, wondering why Tony asked. "Not for some time."

Morton and I were both investigators. After retrieving little David Bryce from his kidnappers, we became business partners.

The arrangement had gone well; it was nice for us both to have another set of eyes at our backs. Yet since Morton had moved to Clubb quadrant, the times I'd seen him had been few and far between.

I pictured Morton, all in brown, strolling down the street. His hands in his pockets, with his round-topped Derby hat tipped back as he whistled a tune I didn't recognize.

Then I saw his pale horrified face in the alley behind the Twenty-Eight tavern on Market Center, the instant he realized what sort of man he'd helped. "The last time I saw him was the day your man Sheinwold was killed." I shook my head. "Almost a year ago."

"Odd," Tony said. "Master Rainbow was supposed to meet us here. I asked him to come a half-hour early."

"That **is** odd. He's normally so punctual."

Tony nodded, his eyes far away.

Where could he have been? If he'd been in the quadrant, why had he not contacted me? And what possible business might he have with Tony? "I hope he's well."

Tony took a deep breath, let it out, not looking at me. "As do I."

"Is there a reason we're meeting here, rather than at home?"

Tony chuckled quietly. "It was your Mr. Howell's idea."

I crossed my legs, folding my hands upon my knee. It wasn't like my husband to be so cryptic.

"Well," Tony said finally, "I suppose he's not coming." He leaned forward, arms on the desk, hands clasped in front of him, his eyes boring into mine. "I want you to learn who killed my sister."

The Caution

I peered at him in confusion. Seventeen-year-old Katherine Spadros had hung herself after the death of her father. "What do you mean?"

Tony leaned back, looked away. "I don't believe her death to be suicide. First of all, how did she get on any bridge without the guards seeing her? And why would she wear a dress? Throw flowers in the water? No, for them to be floating around her when she was found, she'd have had to release them at the moment she went in. Which meant she couldn't have hung herself." He turned towards me, face skeptical. "**Flowers?** Why would she even **do** that?"

He had a point: the whole scenario was much too dramatic, even for Katie.

"And why would she dye her hair back to its original color? She **hated** it." He shook his head. "Even as a young child, she asked why her hair was auburn, yet her Mommy's and Daddy's and mine were black. Even then, she knew something was wrong." He shook his head. "She spent time, money, and effort to change her hair. She would never have changed it back." Then he sighed. "None of this makes sense."

I nodded. These things had bothered me, but at the time, so much was going on ...

"What made me suspicious was the way that Constable kept looking at those river-men. I felt at once that the three hid something important. So after Katie's funeral, I sent for them to be brought in." He leaned forward. "All three are missing."

A bolt of shock went through me. Then I felt even more confused. Why had he never said anything?

"And their families, too. Their neighbors and friends can't account for it." He leaned back, shaking his head. "We've searched for them this entire year. They've not left the city. It's as if they've vanished."

I realized my mouth was open, and I shut it. "This only proves it."

Tony blinked, staring at me. "Oh, gods. Do you think —?"

"That the Red Dog Gang killed Katie?" It took a moment to compose myself. I had to think. "It's possible. But if I remember right, there were no cards on her."

"No, there wouldn't be," Tony said. "Not if they wanted it to look like suicide." He put his head in his hands, ran his fingers through his hair. "I have to know what happened to her, Jacqui. Who did this. She's my sister. I was supposed to protect her, and I've failed miserably. Whatever it is, no matter how terrible ... I need to know."

Suddenly, I needed to know, too. But first, there were a few other mysteries I wanted the answers to.

I rose, intending to go.

"Jacqui," Tony said from behind, "you **will** be at the museum opening. Will you not? Please tell me true."

I turned to face him. "I'll be there. You have my word."

"Forgive me for not trusting you. But I can't get that scene of blood and death at my doorstep from my mind. And tomorrow I have to — have to face what my father's done. I need to know you won't go out a window at the last moment and leave me standing at this horrible ... museum alone."

I felt ashamed. "I'll be there. I promise."

Blitz, Mr. Theodore, and Honor stood in the hall; they brought me out front.

Feeling troubled, I asked to speak with Mr. Howell.

Honor went in to get him. As we stood there, Mr. Theodore looked around. "We shouldn't stand out here like this."

I smiled at him. "This should only take a moment."

Mr. Howell arrived, and my men retreated a bit to watch the rooftops. I said, "Why do you feel this place is safer than my apartments — or Spadros Manor?

Mr. Howell pursed his face: part hesitation, part amusement, part dismay. "My father and I built this place. I know its secrets." He glanced aside, hesitant, and spoke quietly. "There were two spies inside Spadros Manor."

I nodded, emotion swelling within me. *Peter and Amelia Dewey.*

Both had served our Family their whole lives. Peter had been the Spadros Family stable-man for over a decade. Amelia had been my lady's maid since I was sixteen. She'd served me, cared for me in sickness, kept my business secret, and traveled with me many a time.

But she and her husband betrayed us to our enemies, and now they were dead.

"And like rats, where there are two, there are always more." He took a deep breath. "But your apartments ... now, they were designed to spy. I have the men rotated out of watch duty on the other side of the duplex so that no one man does a second duty within a year. I personally verify each. Neither knows the other well. And I debrief each one separately, to make sure their stories match."

I nodded. A good plan.

"But for someone to have gone to the trouble of building that duplex — over twenty years ago, I might add —"

I'd forgotten that.

"— well, they might have had a second plan for listening, should that first one be discovered." He shrugged. "It's what I would do."

***

My men and I strolled back to my apartments. The narrow way along 33 1/3 Street could barely admit a carriage, so few drove down it.

Women swept their porches, men carried burdens or loaded carts. A sign advertising artist supplies graced one doorway. As we went, people bowed or curtsied, crossing the street to avoid us.

When we reached my steps, I stopped Blitz before he might go in. "Have you seen Master Rainbow?"

"He came by the other day. Sounded in a terrible hurry to be somewhere, but he wanted to let us know he was alive."

This surprised me. "Alive?"

"Yeah," Blitz said. "I thought it strange. I asked if anything were the matter, but he denied it."

In a terrible hurry to be somewhere? Wanted to let us know he was alive? Never showing up to an appointment?

None of this sounded like Morton at all.

Just then, Mary opened the front door. "I was wondering where you'd taken to." Then she seemed to realize I stood there. "Aren't you supposed to be home by now?"

I laughed. "I got overbid. Where's Ariana?"

"Down for a nap." She closed the door behind her, leaving it open just a crack. "What's happened?"

Mr. Sutherfield turned to look at us. I went up the steps to her, lowered my voice. "Mr. Howell believes people still listen here. In these apartments."

Mary exclaimed, "For goodness sake!"

"Heh," Blitz said. "Not sure where someone could hide themselves. I've been over every inch of this building, inside and out, and haven't found so much as a crawl space."

Mary said to me, "Do you believe him?"

I shrugged. It didn't matter if I believed him; the fact that he'd considered this and I hadn't was what bothered me. "Just be careful what you say inside."

Mary frowned. "Why should we even stay, if we can't speak freely in our own home?"

I felt surprised at her tone. "I don't have anyone else I trust." I glanced at Blitz, then back at her. "Should I sell it?"

"No," Mary snapped. "We'll make it work." She went inside and shut the door.

"Forgive her," Blitz said. "She's with child again —"

"Oh! Congratulations."

Blitz smiled to himself. "This one has been more difficult than the last." His smile faded. "We plan to name the child John, after her father. If the Dealer grants us a boy."

John Pearson had shielded my son with his body, giving his life to save Acevedo from the Red Dog Gang's assassins. "I heartily approve."

A small smile returned to his face. "I thought you might."

"Go to the city and get the blueprints to this place. I need to know what's going on here." I left him then, and returned to Spadros Manor. But on the way, I wondered about the apartments, and about Katie.

Tony had made complete sense. Nothing about that scenario with Katie felt right, now that I looked at it.

But I hadn't looked at it.

Why?

***

Spadros Manor was quite some way from my apartments. It was just a half block over to Scoop, but then all the way up to 192nd, in the day's traffic. So I had time.

It was in those times, just sitting by myself with nothing to do, that I most wanted a drink.

More than one.

The carriage passed a liquor store, and I drew the curtain shut.

I felt so tired all the time, both in my drained still-recovering and often painful body, but also in my mind. Every little thing — a word, a color, a sound — reminded me of someone I'd lost, someone I'd hurt.

Someone I'd loved.

I carried two handkerchiefs in my pocket, along with the pistol Jonathan Diamond had given me, long ago. I took the gun out, gazed at the smooth black and silver in my lap.

I had very little of the man left.

This gun. The letters he'd sent me. Memory.

Why had it taken him dying to make me see how much I valued him? How terribly I'd miss him?

I put the gun back into my pocket. It'd been over thirteen months from the night Jon died whilst my little Acevedo was being born. I grieved for Jon every single day.

Some days, I felt like I couldn't breathe.

I often chided myself for carrying on so. He'd never once said he loved me, even when I said it to his face, there near the end.

But he called me "my love." He begged me to leave with him.

Why had I refused?

For a while after Jon died, the Red Dog Gang and everything they'd done to me, to my friend and family ... it just seemed too much to tackle. So I didn't.

And now, Tony's request. It made Katie's death real again, piled on another heap of guilt.

I loved Katie. She'd loved me. Why had it taken Tony giving me his sister as a case — of all things — for me to go after the truth?

***

When I returned to Spadros Manor, Tony's men were all smiles. Relieved smiles.

A pit formed in my stomach, and I felt shaky. Their smiles reminded me of little Acevedo's terror of the front porch. When would the fear of sudden attack ever leave us?

As usual, Honor moved ahead of me to knock. As usual, Alan Pearson opened the door.

Alan was older than I, perhaps even as old as Blitz, sharing the light brown hair of his sister Mary. He strongly resembled his father, but the two men were entirely different. For one, Alan smiled when he saw me. "Welcome home! What can I get you?"

I handed Alan my coat and hat. "I've completely missed tea-time. Would you have something brought to my study?"

"At once, mum."

"And have Shanna sent to my rooms."

I went past him and up to my bedroom, where it turned out, my lady's maid Shanna stood dusting my dresser.

Shanna was just nineteen, yet the time so far had matured her. She stopped to curtsy low when I entered. "Afternoon, mum." She rose, pointing to my tea-table. "Some mail came for you."

"Thank you. Would you get me changed? I'll take tea in my study."

"Of course, mum."

Being the Queen of Spades wasn't quite as advertised. Sure, I had power over the whole quadrant. But going even to my own apartments meant a great deal of bother. I needed suitable clothes, and my special carriage, and a guard around me. I couldn't visit anyone that I needed help from — that would show weakness. No, they must come to me. And if I formally summoned them, that entailed even more trouble and fuss. And of course, everyone would know.

Everything I did now meant something, was remarked on in the press, was scrutinized.

I hated it.

But I loved being with my son. "How's Acevedo?"

Shanna was putting my house shoes on me. "I'll fetch Daisy."

Daisy was my son's nursemaid. Around the same age as Shanna, and fiercely protective of "her boy."

The thought made me smile. If anything should happen, at least he'd be cared for by someone who loved him. "Send her to my study, if you will."

I scooped up the pile of mail, almost tossing it into the overflowing basket of things I must get to one day.

But I stopped myself. These were letters Mr. Howell felt I must attend to personally. And no one dared send mail to their Queen without there being no other choice.

I couldn't ignore these people. I might only be six and twenty, but I was their Queen, the mother of my quadrant. I must care for them.

Carrying the mail, I went out my bedroom door, down our grand sweeping stair, then along the hall to my study.

My beautiful cherry-wood desk sat in front of the window overlooking our side gardens. Next to the window were some new filing cabinets of the same. A piano-black box sat in the center of my desk, with THE QUEEN carved in silver lettering on the top.

Every day, I touched it reverently, in awe of its beauty. This had been my mother-in-law Molly's box, before Tony had banished her to her rooms. Before that, it had belonged to Roy's mother.

I made myself remember, every day, so I might understand. I must not run my affairs as they had. I must not let this place, this box, this power turn me into them.

I shut the curtains, as my advisors urged. No one must see me here.

Every day I sat at my desk, I surveyed my room. Thank you cards from the Grand Ball on New Years' Eve were propped up on my desk. Jonathan Diamond's pressed daffodils hung framed upon the wall to my left, next to a portrait of baby Acevedo. A dressmaker's form stood in the right corner. The beautiful green shantung silk dress Madame Biltcliffe made for me before she died hung upon it, a dress I'd never worn and never would. It was all I had left of her.

Tony's portrait hung upon my right wall above my sofa, beside a small stand with fresh flowers. It wasn't his best portrait, but I liked to have him close, even though every day he seemed further away.

"I love you," I whispered to the portrait, as I did every day.

Of course, Tony didn't reply. But at least he didn't become angry, like he did when I spoke those words to him in reality.

I was safe here. This was my refuge, where I might sit and relax, think and plan.

And I needed to plan before doing anything.

Someone abducted the teenage sister of their King then murdered her, making it look as if she'd taken her own life. By doing so, they'd not only smeared her name but put dishonor on our entire Family.

For a moment, grief choked me. Who would do such a thing?

The Red Dog Gang came first to mind. Katie had run with them more than once, and had seemed devoted to one of their men, a scoundrel named Frank Pagliacci.

But we had many enemies, both in our city and beyond. Any one of them might be heartless enough to do something like this to a girl.

But how might I learn who did this when Tony himself could not?

A knock; I rushed to wipe my eyes. "Come in."

Daisy came to me, holding my son in her arms. When he saw me, he struggled to get free of her grasp.

I didn't rise, but I smiled, taking Acevedo into my hands. "How's my boy?"

A big toothy grin. His eyes were deep blue like Tony's, shaped like mine. I kissed my son's cheek, careful not to jostle his leg, which tended to hurt him, then settled him on my lap and smoothed his dark brown wavy hair. "It'll be time for your first haircut soon!" I looked up at Daisy. "I hope he's well."

"As well as ever, mum. He's trying to walk, but it pains him."

I nodded, taking a deep breath to settle the emotions this raised. I hadn't been here when the Red Dog Gang killed twenty of our men, including Mary and Alan's father. When my baby was shot in the hip.

Would he ever recover?

Acevedo looked up at me, and I gently drew my son close, heart full of anguish. I'd betrayed him, his father, everyone, to run after a man who didn't love me.

I felt Daisy's hand on my shoulder. "He gets stronger every day, mum. I'll try giving him a drop of medication before he tries to walk. Maybe it'll go better for him."

I nodded, unable to speak, unable even to open my eyes. I'd done this. I'd destroyed everyone who came near me.

Acevedo began to cry, but a sad, heartfelt cry, sharing my grief.

I drew him closer, kissed his hair.

"I'll take him, mum," Daisy said. "He probably needs changing."

Once she left, I pushed the box aside and put my head on my arms on my desk, sobbing. What had anyone done to deserve this?

After a few minutes, I had the distinct feeling someone stood outside my door. I wiped my face and called out, "Who's there?"

Honor, now dressed in his black and silver Spadros livery, peeked in. "Sorry to disturb you, mum. Your tea service?"

I sighed. "Yes, bring it in."

Honor had two of Alan's younger brothers with him, and they set up a small tea-table beside my desk. Small sandwiches, tea, and so on.

Once that was set up, the three bowed and went to go, but I said, "Honor, please stay, if you will." I don't know why I said it; I think I just wanted company.

He glanced at the other two, and said, "Certainly, mum."

The other two left, leaving the door open.

Honor glanced behind him, then at me.

Even though I was Queen, I could never have privacy. "Leave it; it's fine."

Honor moved before my desk and bowed. "How might I help?"

He clearly felt uncomfortable, even after all this time. What could I have him do? "Perhaps some tea. And make up a plate for me?"

This seemed to make the man more at ease. He filled a plate, poured my tea, then stood on the other side of the tea-table.

I sat drinking my tea as Honor stood at attention facing me, and for some reason Peedro Sluff came to mind. I'd thought about Peedro's murder a lot over the past few months. How Tony's manservant Jacob Michaels killed him, and why he did so. I couldn't fault the man: Peedro had murdered a man Michaels loved. But at times, I still wept when I thought of the man who'd called himself my father for so many years.

Why would I cry over him? The man had sold me into this life. But it seemed he'd cared about me as well.

Peedro's binder still lay on top of that huge basket filled with items, notes, and letters I needed to look through upstairs in my room. Information about the Red Dog Gang I didn't know what to do with yet, the pack of letters my friends had stolen from me.

It wasn't anything I needed right then, but it wasn't anything I cared to throw away.

I was grieving, I was exhausted, I didn't want to look at any of it. But if I had, I think this would have ended much differently.

I looked up at Honor, and I realized something. "I never thanked you for your help. The day of the attack. The days following."

He smiled to himself. "It's nothing, mum. Happy to be of service."

So much had happened, so much duty thrust upon me ... the event tomorrow seemed to be bringing all that I'd not done over the past year to my mind. I sat, eyes closed, willing away the guilt, the grief. Then I opened my eyes. "I imagine you have many questions for me."

He twitched, a startled look upon his face. "It's not my place to question you, mum."

I took a deep breath. "Very well — I have one for you. Peedro Sluff. You learned who murdered him the night you and Master Michaels fought. True?"

Honor got very still. "Yes, mum."

"That was almost two years ago, was it not?"

"It was."

"So why the fight?"

Honor hesitated. Then he faced the door, so I might only see his profile. "At first, I was furious that he'd betrayed you. His Family. And he had only excuses for why he did so. That's why we fought."

Oh. "I see."

I took a bite of my small sandwich, chewed, swallowed. It was good. "And yet your Master Michaels only spoke to me last year."

"Yes, mum."

I set the sandwich down, took a sip of my tea. "Why did you never say anything?"

"I wanted Jacob to confess on his own."

Honor had been outraged enough to fight with someone he loved, even a man of smaller stature. Yet he wanted Michaels to own up to what he'd done, even if it meant losing him.

He turned to face me. "And Sluff was protected by Mr. Roy. I couldn't let anything happen to Jacob."

That made sense. He feared Roy, and rightly so. Yet Tony would have been within his rights to kill Michaels for his unauthorized murder of a Spadros man.

So Honor didn't fear Tony, not in that same way.

But now I knew where Honor's loyalties lay. "So if Jacob Michaels and I were in equal danger ..."

Honor gasped, falling to his knees, clasping his hands in front of him. "Forgive me, mum. I was foolish and weak." Something came to his voice then, something real, something haunted. "Please, mum. Please. Don't send me away."

I felt surprised at this. "Don't be silly; I'm not going to send you away." When he didn't move, I said, "Get up." Once he'd done so, I said, "But I need the truth from you, right now."

Honor blinked. "Um ... I don't know. I serve **you**." He seemed to be seriously considering the matter. "You both can defend yourselves ..."

I nodded. But if it came down to it, he served me. He loved Jacob. I took a deep breath. "Thank you. This makes things easier."

A slight frown came over his face. "How?"

I smiled. "Now I know I must never put your Jacob into danger. Not if I don't want to have to send you away."

A laugh burst from him. "I never considered such things."

A bleak feeling came over me. "Well, now that I'm Queen, I must." I needed to know how much he knew. "What questions have you about my father?"

His eyes narrowed, his head drew back. "Which —?"

I chuckled. "So who told you? Mr. Theodore?"

"No, mum. I didn't know he knew of it. I suppose I guessed it." He shrugged. "From ... everything."

Very good. Theodore Sutherfield hadn't actually pledged himself to me. But it was nice to know he hadn't spoken of what he'd overheard in the warehouse after Etienne Hart's murder.

"I had two daughters and a son," Mr. Hart said, "and I've lost you all."

"Not all, sir," I said.

At least, he hadn't spoken of it to Honor.

"Um, mum, I really have no questions. About that. It's said many great men dishonor themselves. But I see no fault upon **you** with it." He shrugged. "Most in the Home were orphans, but many were left upon some doorstep by a woman in trouble."

I never considered such a thing. But then I recalled Acevedo's nursemaid Daisy, who'd been put upon by a rich man and paid to keep the matter quiet. She'd sent her little daughter to that same Home in Dickens where Honor and his Jacob had been brought up, long ago.

I, on the other hand, had been left with my mother in the Pot. Mr. Hart had insisted my Ma refused to leave, or to let me leave. Why?

I recalled the package my lawyer Doyle Pike had received with letters for me and others inside. "I may need to send some messages. But I can't write directly. And I can no longer trust these messenger boys. Would it impose upon you to —?"

"Of course, mum. I'd be happy to." He hesitated. "Forgive me for taking offense that one time."

I smiled to myself. "It won't be today. I've got to figure out who to send to first."

"Very good, mum."

"That'll be all for now."

Honor left, and I sat musing over what Tony had said in Mr. Howell's office.

We'd been fools to trust the police in Katie's death. Clearly, it'd been a Family matter, and we'd let her down. Now the men who knew the truth were likely to be dead, and their families with them.

I specialized in the missing. But how might I learn the truth when Katie had been in the ground almost a year?

I put my face in my hands, feeling exhausted. There was so much I hadn't done.

Taking a deep breath, I rang for Alan, and in a few minutes, he arrived. "Yes, mum?"

"How's the Business coming along?"

"Mum?"

"Well, Mr. Blitz and I estimated that your father was secretary to the entire Family. It's been a year since his death. I presume you've gone through his ledgers and gotten yourself apprised of things."

He looked uncertain. "Um ..."

"Very well: I want you to schedule a meeting with Ten Hogan."

"You mean Mr. Anthony's man Sawbuck?"

"I do. If anyone knows what's going on here, it's him. The two of you must work together."

Alan hesitated. "Must I, mum?"

"You must." I felt amused. "He's not going to bite. And I want those ledgers of your father's read." I shook my head. "I'm surprised my husband hasn't spoken to you about the matter already."

"Well, mum, with all this ... it's been quite a shock for everyone. And I only lost my father." He sighed. "I don't think I could bear to lose my sister, too."

And for Tony to learn his mother Molly betrayed his father over and over, and the circumstances around Acevedo's birth ... and his own birth ... and reliving the murder of his older brother ... and with his son so terribly injured ...

I nodded, feeling weary. "We've got to put our own concerns aside if this Family is to survive. You're telling me that for a year now, you've had no idea what's gone on —"

Alan flinched.

"And for a year, we've had only what Sawbuck's managed to learn to guide us." I shook my head. "This won't do." If he hadn't done the obvious in all this time, was he ready for the challenge?

Alan straightened. "Mum, forgive me. I've fallen in my duties." He hesitated. "But I — I don't know what to do. Who to speak with."

"It's in those ledgers, I know it. I watched your father; he kept records of everything here."

"There's a whole room packed full of them. He did show me that." His gaze grew distant, as if recalling. "We'll need another room soon — there's not even space to go inside."

I sighed. "Well, get your brothers together. If it takes an hour each day until the Dealer collects your cards, I want it done. Start with the most recent, just before he died." I took a deep breath. "I want a report one week from now on your progress. I hope I won't have to burden my husband on this matter."

His face turned pink. "Yes, mum." Then he peered at me. "That wasn't what you called me for, was it?"

A small laugh rose in my throat. "No, it wasn't. I need the report from the coroner about Miss Katherine's death. And I need it done **quietly**." His father would have had it here the week she died, but I didn't want to say that.

"Yes, mum. But I don't know which coroner."

"What was the name of the Constable who brought us the news?"

Alan stared at me blankly. "I don't recall."

I tried very hard not to laugh. "That's why your father wrote everything down. My husband's men went to bring him in, so one of them knows the man's name. I'd start with his precinct."

"Right."

I felt as if I were teaching an investigator, minted new. "You may always ask. Mr. Blitz is also good at this sort of thing."

"Yes, mum. I'll get on it at once." He disappeared from the room as if chased out.

What was I going to do? I couldn't do **his** job as well as mine!

Speaking of which, I had work to do. Pushing the newest letters aside, I opened the box of letters already opened for me by Mr. Howell and read through them whilst I ate.

They were mostly petty matters — would I donate to this? Would sponsor that? Which one of two events on the same day and time would I attend?

Mr. Howell and I had a correspondence: I'd send the box back with my notes in the evening. It felt tedious, but so far it seemed to work. And I felt a little less dragged off my feet with this system in place.

At the bottom of the pile was every tabloid in the city printed the day before. They filled half the box.

Mr. Howell had read them, apparently, because things he felt I should know were circled. One such was:

DIAMOND KING ATTENDS CHARITY EVENT

The article spoke about some dinner Julius Diamond went to which benefited orphaned children. Near the bottom, a passage was circled:

Mr. Moretti also attended, with his wife and sister.

I didn't particularly want to be reminded of Gardena Diamond. But Mr. Howell seemed to think I needed to know of her doings, because he'd sent items like this many times over the past year.

Beneath the tabloids lay a note:

Joseph Kerr went to your apartments again, looking for you.

Ugh. Joe.

My carriage with the mark of the Lady of Spadros on it had been seen at Joe's home before the attack on Spadros Manor. I can't say if it was fortunate or not, but the massacre at Spadros Manor and the attack on Spadros Castle did push the matter from people's minds ... for what it's worth.

But it didn't matter. I'd loved Joe. I'd **loved** him.

And in return, he'd given me womb fever.

Even with the most urgent care by the best healers, womb fever was the main killer of women in the brothels. Which was why all men who went to Ma's Cathedral were checked before being allowed to have a woman there.

I was foolish. I'd been drugged. I was too enamored with Joe to see the signs until it was too late.

Joe's attentions so far had gotten me almost dead. The doctor said I'd likely never have another child. My monthly bleedings since I'd recovered had lasted longer than usual, and come with terrible pain. The first one had been the worst; each one after was shorter and less painful than the one before. But I had a dull pain now, low in my belly, that never left me.

I'd been very lucky to have survived; everyone said so.

But since last we met, Joe had been coming round every month or so, either at the Manor or at my apartments.

Joe and his twin sister Josie lived with their grandfather in Hart quadrant. I'd told the bridge guards not to let him pass, but somehow he'd appeared anyway. Again.

Of course, by now Tony's men wouldn't let him close to the Manor. But with all the alleys and places to hide around 33 and 1/3 Street, it'd been difficult to keep him away from my apartments.

And every time they spotted him, Tony learned of it. I always knew by the way his mood changed. He'd become even more distant, surly, for several days refusing to even look at me.

A knock at the door. "Mum," Shanna said. "Your tonic."

Now I was on two daily tonics. The thick green morning one was for my liver, ruined by years of drink. The second, I took in the late afternoon to help strengthen my body. This second was much thinner, the color of cream, and tasted of garlic.

I drank them dutifully, every day. And every day, after Shanna left, I cried. These tonics were a penalty for the horrible choices I'd made. Drinking them reminded me, every day, of every one of them.

At dinner, all was beautiful. We were finely dressed. A magnificent electric candelabra hung above us. Fine silver and delicate plates held delicious food.

But Tony never so much as glanced at me. He never once smiled.

I would've given it all away to have Tony smile at me again.

During the last course, the front door-bell rang.

Alan went to answer it. After a few moments, he returned, his voice shaking. "M — Master Seven Bresciane, sir."

Tony nodded. "I'll meet with him in my study."

So he'd been expecting the man?

"Sir," Alan said, "he insists on meeting with both of you."

***

Master Seven Bresciane was a spindly pale elderly fellow with a grayish tone to his sallow skin. His big, deep gray eyes peered at us from a large balding head as we entered, yet his gaze was kindly and full of humor.

He looked like you might knock him over with a feather. Hardly the sort of man you'd expect to haunt the nightmares of an entire city.

But he was also the Knife Man. Mothers warned their children: *keep silent, or the Knife Man'll have out your tongue!* His very name made strong men shrink back in fear. Mr. Eight Howell had gotten sick in my parlor at the thought of being in the same room with him.

So any visit from the Knife Man urged caution.

The Treasure

Master Bresciane stood in Tony's study holding a piano-black box a foot wide and four inches thick with a reverence I'd never before seen in him. "Come in," he said. "I have something for you."

We entered, Alan shutting the door behind us as he left.

Master Bresciane straightened. "I have been charged to perform this service twice in my lifetime." He took a deep breath. "This box has passed through eight generations of the Spadros line. Tomorrow marks the first year of your ascension. You have survived it well."

Tony and I gaped at each other. Then Tony took a deep breath, voice shaking. "Is this what I think it is?"

Master Bresciane smiled warmly at him. "I suppose we'll see. You may want to sit down."

After a quick glance at him, then at Tony, I sat. Tony sat more reluctantly, glancing at the box, then at the strange little man, then back at the box, placing his cane beside him.

Master Bresciane didn't sit. Rather, he opened the box by grasping the front of it, drawing the sleek shiny lid back for us to peer inside.

There, under glass, each in their own recessed deep brown velvet-lined cubby, sat the Holy Cards: the King and the Queen of Spades.

"Oh, my gods," I breathed. Seeing the actual Holy Cards there, right in front of me, made me feel faint, and I was glad for Master Bresciane's warning.

Tony gripped my hand tightly. "How —?"

Master Bresciane closed the box. "I was brought in by Mr. Acevedo's own Knife Man and charged to carry this box when I was called to stand at Mr. Roy's side." He smiled to himself. "Well, he was Master Roy then. But I recall the look on Mr. Roy's face upon seeing it, a year minus a day after his father's death, as if it happened yesterday. I never thought I'd live to have the honor of presenting it to you."

I felt slightly confused. "So who will carry it now?"

"The task now passes to Master Hogan, I presume. Or whoever else you might deem worthy. But for tonight, it is yours, for you to safeguard as you will."

I frowned. "It sounds like Ten should've had this for a while now."

Master Bresciane gave a slight shrug. "Perhaps. I don't know the motivation for keeping it from him."

It was well-known that Sawbuck and Roy had bitterly hated each other. But who knew why Roy did what he did?

Tony said, "I want you to keep it safe for now. But you and I must meet again, with Ten present." He peered at Master Bresciane. "This is too important for only one man to know its whereabouts."

I hadn't felt as if Master Bresciane had been tense before, but the man visibly relaxed. "Thank you, sir; I'm most grateful. I'd not like the knowledge of this treasure to be lost."

I said, "There's one thing I don't understand. Why do you wait a year minus a day?"

Master Bresciane gave another slight shrug. "That's how it's always been done. But I think it a good idea." He let out a quiet sigh. "The first year of any transition is a rocky one, and many a Patriarch in past generations didn't survive to receive their honors."

A shock went through me. *They didn't live even a year?*

Tony nodded. "We have been most fortunate."

Master Bresciane fixed Tony with an even, kindly gaze. "You surely have, sir. And I'm glad of it." He hesitated, just for an instant. "You're the third Patriarch I've served under, and you have the makings to become one of our greatest."

Tony seemed taken aback. "Thank you! But I can't say that it's my own doing!"

Master Bresciane smiled warmly. "And that statement proves my feelings to be right."

***

Tony was quiet that evening, and didn't come to my bed. Since his confession in the meadow almost a year ago, his visits to my bed had become rare, and never once had he actually bedded me. I'd gone to him a few times, only to be rebuffed.

It seemed clear to me that he'd given his heart back to Gardena Diamond, as I'd wished him to, and she to him.

And yet I felt torn. I'd fought so hard for the two of them to become a family, for him to be with his son. But now that it seemed to be happening, I hated it.

I hated it because I loved him, and he seemed not to care for me.

Perhaps that's too strong a phrase, because he did care for me in many ways. I still lived under his roof. He provided all I needed. He noticed my moods and wanted to help. But any affection or desire for me seemed to have vanished.

When he said I might go that night in the meadow, he meant it.

I've never slept well — even to this day, the nightmares come and go. But that night, I didn't sleep at all. I couldn't stop crying. Like those Holy Cards, the greatest treasure in the world stood right there in front of me, yet I couldn't touch it.

Jonathan Diamond told me as he lay dying to find a way to be happy. I'd had a chance at real happiness. But in that one horrible afternoon with Joseph Kerr, I'd let it slip through my fingers.

***

When the sky began to lighten, I got up to sit on the side of my bed before Shanna even opened the drapes, feeling weary. It seemed pointless to try and find any rest that day.

Honor brought my morning mail and paper as usual; I skimmed the paper first.

The news was full of the museum opening. In no way did I want to go. But no new catastrophes had happened, thank the gods.

Downstairs, I heard the front door-bell.

29

I missed Pearson's heavy tread, his deep voice. His calm assurance that all would be well, that all would be taken care of.

I missed him. I needed him here.

But alas, he lay dead.

Alan knocked. "Mum, there's a Memory Boy to see you."

At this hour?

I put my robe on and followed Alan down the hall. But instead of taking me to the front door, he took me to my parlor.

I stood outside the open parlor door for a moment, confused.

Then I realized that the Queen of Spades didn't sit on the front steps to speak with anyone, not even a Memory Boy.

It was only then I understood how very powerful I was, if I might only grasp it.

The Memory Boy Werner Lead had changed since last I saw him over a year earlier. Now thirteen, the boy's formerly pale hair had darkened to golden brown, and he'd grown taller. He stood in the middle of my parlor looking around, and I had a sudden memory of Roy Spadros doing much the same. But where were Werner's brothers? I'd never seen the boy without them.

Werner's face brightened. "Mrs. Spadros! So good to see you."

I nodded to him. "And you as well."

He glanced at Alan, and I turned to my butler. "Master Alan, you may leave us."

Alan bowed. "Yes, mum."

Once he'd gone, I faced Werner once more. The boy's face contained many questions, but he seemed content to stand there. After a moment, I said, "Well? Why are you here? What's happened?"

He took a deep breath. "I bring urgent message from Master Blaze Rainbow: *The Four of Clubs are after me.*"

The Guilt

I felt surprised, not only at the message but who it was from. "Do you know who the Four of Clubs might be?"

Werner's face held no guile. "No, mum."

"And did Master Rainbow seem well?"

For the first time ever, Werner looked afraid. "No, mum. He seemed nervous, always looking round. And he was hurt bad. Like he'd been fighting."

Fighting. With who? "Did he ask for a reply?"

"No, mum. I did ask, and he said he hoped he'd not be so easy to find as that." The boy let out a chuckle, then sobered. "Sorry, mum."

I shook my head. The turn of phrase did seem funny, unless you meant it seriously. "Where did he send this from?"

"Madame Biltcliffe's Dress Shop, mum. In Clubb quadrant. It was in Spadros when we first met, if you recall."

Yes, I recalled that day well. "Thank you."

"Do you have a message for Miss Tenni, then?"

Did I?

Morton visited when she and her sisters stayed with me after their home had been attacked. If Morton had gone into a dress shop for long enough to fetch a Memory Boy, then either half of Clubb quadrant knew about it, or she'd hidden him. "Where in the shop did you meet with him?"

Werner smiled to himself. "In the back alley, mum."

Werner Lead didn't normally go to Clubb quadrant, so far as I knew. Which meant Morton wanted to make sure I got the message from someone I'd trust. "As a matter of fact, I do have a message for Miss Tenni: *It's time for another fitting.*"

I didn't want to go to the museum opening. We had to find Morton, and soon. It sounded as if he most desperately needed our help, and I didn't want to lose even a day in getting him to safety. But I'd promised Tony I'd be there.

What should I do?

*****

Morton's message was in my mind as Shanna got me dressed.

As I had my breakfast, waiting for Tenni's reply, I picked at my food. Wondered where Morton might be and why he'd run. What had happened to him. Who he'd been fighting.

Clearly he intended to go into hiding.

But was he safe? Was he well?

Morton had been at my side for so long that he seemed one of my Queensmen. Inventor Etienne Hart had never let go of his hate and suspicion for long enough to become the older brother Morton had been to me all along.

The thought that Morton might have come to harm, might be in serious danger ... it frightened me.

Tony sat at the other end of the table, clearly curious as to what might be wrong yet unwilling to ask in front of the servants. But afterwards, he told Alan to run the morning meeting and asked if we might stroll the gardens.

The morning was overcast, but warm. A fine mist lay in the air. We walked, side by side, not touching. And as we walked, I was reminded of Gardena.

After Tony's confession of betraying me with Gardena Diamond, I'd told the bridge guards I was never to be "at home" when she came to call. But she'd come anyway, the week earlier, to see Tony.

Of course, it wasn't that way at all. Tony had summoned her brother Beloty Diamond, now Keeper of the Court, on what matter I never learned, and his younger sister had arrived with him.

Tony had insisted I accompany him to the parlor to greet them. He'd said we must, no matter how I felt, so as not to cause an incident between our two Families. So I went.

They'd brought a gift: daffodil bulbs from Gardena's mother. Gardena and I had discussed the bulbs oh, perhaps a year before. But whilst I'd been glad to see Mr. Beloty, and to be reminded of their mother, and even to have the bulbs ... I'd preferred to imagine Gardena not there.

Tony took us to the veranda, where we sat at the table. Took tea. Sat at the table, Tony trying to make small talk.

I hated small talk. "I think I'll take a turn in my garden."

Gardena had risen. "I'll go with you."

I'd stared at her. Then at Beloty, who'd seemed confused.

No matter how I felt about Gardena, I hadn't dared offend the Keeper of the Court. And he was blameless in the matter. "Very well." I'd gone down the steps, Gardena trailing behind.

Once we were out of earshot, I'd said, still walking, "What could you **possibly** have to say to me? You stood in your Country House, saying how you **regretted** what you'd done. And now, to find out you've been bedding my **husband** this whole time?"

Gardena had followed silently for some time. "You told my sister-in-law this wasn't a problem —"

I stopped, faced her. Yes, I'd wanted them together. But not like this. "Unless it be hidden with lies. You **lied** to me, Gardena, more than once, to my face. And I can't forgive that."

"But Jacqui —"

"But nothing. What is it? You want another **child**? Your father wants more money from Spadros **Manor**? My husband is so besotted with you that he might not know or care how he's being treated, but I won't go along with it."

I'd continued on, left Gardena standing there. After I'd done the turn round the gardens and returned to the veranda, Gardena and Beloty had gone.

Tony had dragged me back out to the gardens, furious. "What did you say to her? She came back in tears!"

I'd shrugged. "What did you want me to say? Oh, yes, keep bedding my husband and **lying** about it?"

I'd expected Tony to show embarrassment, or even remorse, but for the first time I had known him, he'd shouted at me. "You chastise her for **lying**? How **dare** you? You have done nothing but lie since the **day** I met you." He turned away then, hand to his forehead. "And now you wish all to be forgiven, yet you offer **none** to anyone else."

Oh. "It's not like that, Tony —"

"It is **exactly** like that."

As I again walked alongside him in my gardens a week later, his words gnawed.

I hadn't forgiven him. He hadn't forgiven me.

The look on Gardena's face when I spoke those cutting words to her ... they lingered in my mind, made my emotions close.

"Jacqui?"

I took a deep breath, not willing to look at him. "Yes?"

"What's troubling you? Has something happened?"

I nodded, unable to speak.

He moved his cane to his other hand. "Come." Taking my arm, he drew me to a tea-table along the path sheltered by an arbor, where we sat. "Tell me what troubles you."

In my mind, the list lay as long as I stood tall. But at the time, those seemed less vital. "I got a message from Blaze Rainbow today."

Tony nodded; he must have been notified of Werner's visit. "And?"

I took a deep breath. "He's in trouble. He said, 'The Four of Clubs are after me.' And the boy said he looked like he'd been fighting."

Tony leaned back, mouth open, for several seconds. Then he leaned forward. "You're sure that's what he said — the Four of Clubs?"

I nodded. "It can't be a person; he said they '**are** after me.' Besides, I can't see him going to all this trouble if only one man pursued him."

"No." Tony sounded as if talking to himself. "He'd just come here. Why didn't he come **here**? We would've sheltered him —"

"Unless he feared to cause us trouble. What if this is some rogue group within Clubb quadrant, like those Ten of Spades?"

Tony let out a breath, looked away. Most of those "Ten of Spades" had been his cousins. All were now dead. "I've been worried ever since he moved there, him being a Hart and all."

For some time, even though Morton said he was from Hart quadrant, he'd been working for Tony. And a year after Tony's ascension, the Clubb Patriarch, Mr. Alexander, had yet to formally acknowledge Tony's rule here.

It didn't matter, really, as far as the workings of our quadrant were concerned. But for months, every day in every tabloid, someone mentioned it. Up until the death of Roy Spadros, Spadros and Clubb quadrants had been allies. Alexander Clubb doing — or rather, not doing — something like this ... well, he could be preparing for war.

And Mr. Alexander had himself told me he didn't trust the Harts.

Why had he told me that?

If my day footman Skip Honor had figured it out, Alexander Clubb had to know Charles Hart was my father. Not that I thought Honor would betray me, but the clues had been there for anyone to see.

I'd been named for Mr. Hart's mother. And other than her heavy straight orange-red hair, pale skin, and narrow eyes, the woman looked just like me.

Mr. Clubb was past eighty, and had been Patriarch well before the Bloody Year. He had to have known the former Queen of Hearts.

So what could the motivation have been for Mr. Clubb warning me about Mr. Hart? Was he warning me not to trust Morton? If so, why?

Tony said, "I'll look into it." He got up and left me sitting there.

I went upstairs to put on the gown Tenni made for me, which had arrived overnight. And then Tony and I set off.

Spadros Castle was ten miles south of us, along 192nd. Many rows of horsemen in black and silver Spadros livery carrying white flags edged in black with the black Holy Symbol of Spadros on them rode ahead and behind Tony's carriage.

Acevedo and his nursemaid Daisy, of course, were at home. Spadros Manor lay ringed with armed men. His kin guarded the inside of every entrance, and Tony's most trusted men guarded the way to the boy's rooms. Sawbuck himself sat in Ace's room, armed, to watch over the boy.

If I had any say in it, my son would never be in danger again.

Tony never said a word the entire way. His public mask for the crowds lining the way appeared once we'd cleared our block.

Yet at breakfast, he'd eaten little. And from his words to me the day before, I knew he felt unhappy to be here.

We arrived precisely at noon. A wide space had been cleared around the entry to the home Roy Spadros had built for his family. A band played and the crowd cheered as we stopped.

A microphone had been placed at the top of the steps. The Acting Mayor, a mousy little man, stood to one side next to the Chief of Police. The City Clerk, Mrs. Brenda Trex, stood beside him, smiling when she saw me.

As we exited the carriage, the Chief of Police spoke into the microphone. "The King and Queen of Spades, blessed by the Dealer to reign over Bridges as highest of the Holy Suits. We welcome you."

It sounded insincere, yet we ventured up the steps as if called.

Despite the name, Spadros Castle wasn't. It had obviously been intended to serve as a fortress, yet on the day of the attack, it hadn't earned that name, either. The stone had been scrubbed and whitewashed. But if you knew where to look, you could see the scorch marks, the chipped rocks, the bullet-holes imperfectly patched.

We faced the crowd. Tony, leaning heavily upon his cane, went to the microphone and spoke. "My Family, my friends, and my people: today marks one year from the death of your Patriarch, Roy Spadros."

The crowd glanced at each other, unsure how to respond. In the quiet, someone off to the left shouted, "Yeah!" and was promptly removed from the area.

Tony continued as if nothing had happened. "We are here to present this museum, both to honor him as your Patriarch and to lay bare his life, good and bad. We have nothing to fear from the truth. We have only to learn from it."

Scattered applause.

"Our sincere thanks go to the Hart Family for their generous donations to this effort —"

It was then I noticed that although a few of the Clubbs had arrived, all dressed in mourning, not one of the Harts were there.

"— and to those of you who have worked countless hours in restoring Spadros Castle. In cataloguing, cleansing, and framing the items and documents we've recovered —"

Mr. Charles Hart had paid the entire expense for the building's restoration, the cleaning and framing of documents about Roy's life, and the dredging of the basement pit Roy had used to dispose of his victims. By all accounts, it'd been a ghastly mess.

Why wouldn't he be here, when Tony meant to honor him?

"— your donations to enter today will go entirely towards ensuring this work continues in perpetuity. Thank you, all."

Applause, and the band started playing — a bit too brightly for my taste, given the circumstances. The doors opened, and we went in.

Guards stood at every corner. The inside of Spadros Castle had been repainted a greenish-gray, and changed to look much as any other museum. Lettering upon the walls explained the history of the place. Portraits and other items hung framed under glass with inscriptions below them. Suits Roy had worn, placed on dressmakers' forms and enclosed in glass, stood near framed photos of events he'd worn the suit to. Memorabilia. The pencil portrait he'd drawn of his daughter Katie.

A timeline of Roy's life ran along the walls, with portraits of some of the thousands of people he'd killed. One whole room was dedicated to the Bloody Year, and spoke of Roy's part in the fighting. Another room was dedicated to his father's assassination, along with speculations as to who might have done it.

Tony looked very pale the entire time, gripping my hand the whole way. When we got to the stairs down to Roy's torture room, I thought Tony might be sick. "I don't think we'll go there."

We left then, going straight to the carriage, our guides gaping at and calling after us as we went.

The lines stretched all the way down the block. Once we got into the carriage, the guards allowed the others to enter.

Tony pulled the curtains. His cane thumped to the floor as he slumped back into the seat. "It's over," he panted. "Oh, gods, it's finally over. I don't ever want to go there again."

I nodded. "You don't have to."

The carriage started off. He leaned his elbow on the window's edge, his forehead upon his hand. "Right before the shooting began, we were arguing. About something that seems so utterly stupid now." He squeezed his eyes shut. "And then I was so completely useless. **He** got up and fought the men, covered with his own blood and riddled with bullets as he was. It was John Pearson, of all people, who gave his life protecting my mother and my son, with his own body." The words burst from him. "How I **wish** it might have been me!"

"Oh, Tony." I took his hand, feeling grieved. "Please don't think this way. We **need** you. Your sons need you."

He let out a bitter laugh. "My sons. I fear I won't have them for much longer."

"Tony, Acevedo grows stronger every day. Roland is entirely well, under the best guard in the city." I squeezed his hand. "Take heart."

A small bemused smile touched his lips then, but his lashes were moist. "I'll try."

The carriage continued on. I wondered at Tony's mood, his sudden vulnerability, and why not even Charles Hart had arrived. Mr. Hart was the one who'd wanted this museum in the first place.

The bridges into Hart quadrant had been barred for a full month after Inventor Etienne Hart's murder by his own man. Not even shipments of food from Clubb quadrant had been allowed to pass.

Charles Hart had closed his beloved Racetrack and moved to Hart Manor to be with his wife. From all reports, over eleven months later, Hart quadrant still lay draped in black.

The bridges into Hart quadrant lay open now. But they closed at nightfall, and the Racetrack had only recently re-opened.

How had the Hart Family fared with that loss of income, on top of paying for Acevedo's surgery and the restoration of Spadros Castle?

I looked out at the homes moving past, feeling melancholy.

Mr. Hart and I being at the scene of his Heir's murder had been a huge scandal. Rumors had flowed like water: that I'd killed him — or had him killed. That his father had killed his son with his own hands.

The fact that Mr. Hart had come out with his son's blood all over him only gave credence to that speculation.

But the police saw the evidence: my half-brother Etienne's most trusted man lying dead, the pistol he used to take his own life still in his hand. The Inventor — also dead — held by his sobbing father. Nine more stood in the room, all giving the same report.

But everyone knew that the police would say whatever the Families told them to say. So of course, few believed what the police said. Once more, Family violence had come onto Market Center, and the swarm of candidates for Mayor took that to heart in their speeches.

Over six hundred men had signed up for the Mayor's race so far, with more applying every day. But with Hart quadrant in mourning and the City Clerk's office overwhelmed, it was unclear when — or if — the election might actually take place. Mrs. Trex had hired dozens of helpers, but searching the City records by hand to verify each candidate had turned out to be a formidable task.

In the meantime, disgraced former Mayor Chase Freezout — or his lawyers — occasionally appeared to give a speech. By all reports, the Mayor looked thinner and more pained with every event. Inevitably, there'd be some backhanded statement sniping at the Four Families.

The people on Market Center loved it. Even after the scandal of the Mayor allowing a murderous villain to walk free, unhampered, and as yet, uncaught, petitions circulated for the Mayor to be reinstated.

But most of the murders had happened in Spadros quadrant. I do believe the people on Market Center hoped the Bridges Strangler would kill the entire Spadros Family and be done with us.

It frightened me when I thought of it that way: Tony faced men who wanted to exterminate his people. And I'd abandoned him to — nay, caused — the most excruciating ordeal he'd ever faced: the rebellion of his own men. He'd had to kill his cousins, men he'd grown up with. And now to be confronted with the shame of what his father had done to this city ...?

I knew Tony. He blamed himself for not putting a stop to it.

Filled with compassion, I kissed his hand. "I won't leave you, Tony. I won't. Never again. No matter what."

The Need

Tony had chosen to eat luncheon in our dining room. In Bridges, no one might eat until the host had done so. But after an obligatory bite of potato, done only for me, Tony sat slumped in his chair, staring.

I worried for him. He looked gray and drawn, utterly exhausted. "Maybe you should rest. We don't need do anything more today."

He shook his head. "Ten will be back at two to report on what's been done regarding Master Rainbow's plight —"

In the last three hours?

"— and he has the monthly figures, and —"

"Let me meet with him. You're barely staying awake. And I have my own inquiries out about Master Rainbow." I wished I sat beside him, rather than down the long table. "Please let me help you."

Rather than offer encouragement, my words only seemed to give him pain. But then he sighed. "Very well." He rose, leaning heavily on his cane, Alan hurrying to pull out his chair.

Alan's youngest brother Rob Pearson stood as waiter, and I gestured to him. "Make sure Mr. Spadros gets safely to his rooms."

Rob nodded and followed Tony out.

I finished my luncheon, feeling weary. How much more of this could Tony take?

***

Sawbuck arrived at two; Alan put him in the parlor.

Ten Hogan was Tony's mother Molly's nephew, a huge man of two and thirty without a bit of fat upon him. When I entered instead of

Tony, Sawbuck leapt to his feet, fear and pain upon his face. "What's happened? Is he well?"

I went to him, rested my hand on his lower arm. "No, Ten, he's not. I fear today was too much for him; he's ready to drop from exhaustion and grief. I insisted he take to his bed." I smiled up at him. "And I shall be vexed if you disturb him."

He let out a slow breath, fear draining away. "I should be glad he listens to you. I've been telling him this for months now." He sat on the sofa, wincing. "And now I must report to you?"

I sat in an armchair facing him. "I suppose you must."

To my surprise, he didn't hesitate. "Well, the Button Men have Master Rainbow's description, and they've been instructed to send the situation down the lines. Many of the men know him, so they'll be motivated. But it'll take days to get anything back."

"Very well. Has Master Bresciane contacted you?"

Sawbuck's eyebrows rose, and he looked more than a bit afraid. "The Knife Man? What would he want with **me**?"

"Nothing bad; he has something to discuss with you. I think you'll find it very interesting."

This seemed to relax him, even put him into a good humor. "I await his summons, then!"

"And I take it you've met with Alan Pearson?"

"I got a message this morning that he needed to meet with me." He shrugged. "Didn't say what it was about." He glanced at the door. "Strange — he didn't mention it when he let me in."

I suppose I shouldn't have been angry; it was just yesterday that I'd commanded the man to do so. "He's not gone over his father's records." I shook my head. "A whole year now!" Had we made a mistake in promoting him? "I don't know if ... "

"Hmm," Sawbuck said. "He'll have to do. I don't see a line of people clamoring for the position." He gave a thin smile. "I'll get his deck in order."

"Do it gently, Ten. I think he's afraid of you."

Sawbuck laughed, preening. "I **am** rather fearsome, aren't I?" Then he grinned. "I'll treat him as kindly as a boy's first tutor."

I wasn't sure if this was good or bad. "So what else does my husband need from you?"

He reached into his jacket's breast pocket and handed over a rather thick, sealed envelope. "This month's cut."

Impressed by the weight of the thing, I set it beside me.

Then he drew out a second sealed envelope which appeared to only hold a few sheets. "And here are the quadrant reports."

"How are we doing, Ten? Tell me true."

He shrugged. "Everyone's being paid, no one's killed each other in a while, and the trains run on time. I'll take the win."

I laughed. "And how are you?"

He sighed. "Mornings are the worst." His gaze softened, turned inward. "But I'd do it again in an instant, even knowing this was to follow." His voice shook. "He's alive. That's all that matters."

I nodded. "We have to keep him that way." I took a deep breath, feeling shaky myself. "So what else does he need to know?"

***

The museum trip, being confronted with pictures of the man who'd tormented me most of my life, learning of the horrors he'd done ... it'd affected me as well. After Sawbuck left, I locked Tony's envelopes in my cabinet and sat at my desk, dully trying to get through my daily box. So many letters and tabloids and things I must answer that for a time I felt close to tears.

I never wanted to be Queen. I didn't know the niceties of the game, whilst being confronted with one finesse after another. A hesitation at the wrong time, the play of a wrong card ... it could lose us everything.

And the one man I might trust in this, Mr. Howell, had no real experience in dealing with high-cards. I hoped he hadn't missed anything important.

I opened a note from one of my informants. It was coded, of course, so Mr. Howell wouldn't know what it was about. But I'd told him any mail from that address should go straight to me.

And I read the note with horror.

For a long time, I'd wondered of the circumstances around Jonathan Diamond's death as my son Acevedo was being born. There were fanciful tales of the Dealer's light in the window, or the ghost of Jack Diamond scaling the delicate wooden trellises to Jon's second-story bedroom. Both supposedly happened the moment Jon died.

At the same time? I immediately discarded those stories. I'd seen those trellises; they could barely hold up the white roses in front of Diamond Manor, much less the weight of a grown man.

After repeated attempts over the past year, my informant had finally learned part of the truth. Jon's sister Gardena had left the room to get something for him, and returned to find him dead.

I put my head on my arms and cried for most of an hour. Jon died alone. Alone, not knowing if I lived or died.

Jon deserved so much better. He deserved so much more.

Why hadn't I gone with him when he asked me to leave the city with him during my trial? Even if nothing at all might be done to stop his death, at least I'd not have left him, no matter how much he pleaded with me to do so.

I needed Jon. I needed his counsel. He could always make me laugh, always knew the right path, never hesitated to tell me when I was about to make a bad play.

Why had it taken his death to make me see how much I loved him?

***

Tony slept through dinner, so I ate in my rooms, ordering his plate to be kept warm. As I was dressing for bed, I heard him ring for his manservant Jacob Michaels. No doubt Tony was famished.

I hoped the rest had done him good.

I worried for him so. What I'd told him wasn't just to soothe him. We did need him. Ace needed him. The quadrant needed him.

I needed him. Even though he ignored me, snapped at me ... I had hope that one day we'd overcome all that I'd done to us both. But if he died ... At the time, I thought I might die too.

***

I stood in the Old Plaza, that rectangular mile-long field of weeds in the Spadros Pot, broken 'scrapers all round me. It was night, the Plaza lit by a blood moon.

Jack Diamond stood before me all in white, holding out a knife, the moonlight giving the scene a deep red glow. But he just stood there, holding the knife, its tip pointed slightly down.

I wore a dress from my childhood. Some of the plants around me had been uprooted. Yet nothing about it seemed strange. I held a knife, too. I wasn't afraid. I was angry. "How dare you come here?"

Jack's voice came forth without his lips moving, that deep, rich voice so different from his twin brother Jonathan's. "Beware."

I felt confused. "Beware of what?"

Suddenly, I stood in a strange field, one I didn't recognize. People were everywhere. Joe stood nearby. The sun blazed round us, but its light was harsh, glaring, more green than golden. Joe said, "Kiss me."

I felt a great sadness, yet an equally great passion. The light disturbed me, he disturbed me, the people frightened me, yet my body wanted him desperately. I moved to kiss him ...

... and I woke, light streaming in through the open curtains. The sadness lingered, yet I wasn't sure why.

Why would I dream of Jack Diamond? Why dream of Joe?

I thought of the look in Joe's eyes the afternoon he bedded me and shuddered.

I got up, put on my robe, slumped onto the toilet, body still tingling. I hated Joe. But it'd been so long since someone kissed me, touched me ...

After brushing my teeth, I crept through our closets to Tony's room. He lay sleeping.

Lately, he'd startle at the slightest thing, so I hesitated to enter. But his chest quietly rose and fell. So I tiptoed to his side, placing a chair beside him.

He looked so young, so exhausted, so forlorn, that I felt moved.

I didn't dare touch him, though I longed to. I wanted to hold him. I wanted him to make love to me like he used to.

What were we going to do? Would Tony never trust me, never love me ... for the rest of our lives?

For a moment, I felt dismayed.

Then I decided: it didn't matter. **I'd** done this. I'd caused this. He'd loved me with everything he had, and I ...

The memory of me spitting in his face in the courtroom, in front of everyone, brought me such shame that I put my hands over my face so as not to let out a sob.

I did this. I ruined everything, like I always did.

Then I felt Tony's hand upon my knee, and he spoke kindly. "Be at peace: all is well." He'd sat up, swinging his legs over the side of his bed, though somehow I'd not heard nor seen it in my grief. He put his arm on my shoulder. "Come here."

I had to move from my chair to his bed so as not to fall over, and for a moment he held me. Oh, gods, he held me.

I didn't want to cry in front of him, but I did anyway.

He spoke gently. "What's wrong? Has something happened?"

I felt very small. "No."

"Another nightmare?"

"No." I didn't know what to make of that dream. But he was very close. "I suppose I should be glad of it."

He chuckled. "As should we all." He put his other arm round me, and rocked me for a moment. Then he let go, peering at me. "So why the tears?"

I shrugged, dejected. "I should never have spit on you in the courtroom. I don't ask you to forgive me. But I am sorry." How could he forgive, when I'd humiliated him in front of everyone?

He seemed lost in thought for a moment. "I'd honestly forgotten about it." He shook his head. "But I don't blame you. You thought I'd murdered someone you loved!" He laughed. "I'm glad you only spat at me, rather than tried to shoot me."

"Oh!" I'd never even considered it. Then I recalled the entire thing. I touched the pale bullet-graze scar on the side of his face from the time his cousins rebelled against him. "I'm sorry about that, too."

He got very quiet. Then he shook his head. "I was foolish, and I was wrong. I regret it all."

He'd tried to help me learn who killed Marja, the woman who helped raise me, and ended up making a mess of it. I took a deep breath and put a hand on his knee. "Well, it's over now. You survived it, and for that I'm grateful."

Tony placed his hand over mine, moving it away. "It's time we get to our duties."

I returned to my rooms in a miserable fog. I'd ruined everything. I held the highest position a woman in this land could, and yet right then, I felt like I had nothing.

***

Fortunately, in my mail was a notice from Tenni, asking if we might fit my Midsummer gown.

I did the morning meeting with our servants. As Alan went over their tasks for the day, I looked at their upturned hopeful faces, their weary eyes, and it reminded me of the most recent New Years' Eve, when the Spadros Family hosted the Grand Ball.

Tony's mother Molly didn't attend the Grand Ball with us. Tony had stripped her of her title as Queen Mother and locked her in her rooms as punishment for all her betrayals and defiance.

We came down that grand staircase first, as hosts, to the applause and cheers of our servants. We raised the first toast to our people.

We had hoped the Grand Ball might ease some of the suspicions, the tensions between our four quadrants. It was the one night where we might relax together in peace.

But none of the other Patriarchs arrived. So we turned off the clockwork dais, and greeted the guests ourselves.

Most of the aristocracy refused to come, but those that did surprised us. The man whose wife had died of cancer after knitting a blanket for Acevedo. The woman whose husband and sons had died for the Family. All people I'd gone to see, those weeks before everything went so wrong.

"It was good of you to see them," Tony had said to me that night. He spoke to me so infrequently back then that every word stayed in my mind. "You helped us, and we won't forget it."

To this day, I'm not sure who else he meant. The Family, perhaps. Strange, if so.

In any case, we had many, many cases of food and drink left over. Tony had some food and all of the drink sent to his men. Then he sent the rest to the Dealers, to distribute as they wished.

At least our people ate well that year.

I felt touched at seeing our people now, five months later. How hard they worked, how much they wanted to be of service. If anything ever happened to us, we needed to make sure they were cared for.

As Shanna got me dressed yet again, it seemed that beyond the food and drink, our people needed the encouragement.

The Bridges Strangler still hunted, though men walked the streets of the Spadros slums in groups, carrying cudgels to stop him. If anyone knew who the fiend was, they weren't talking, but many a disliked man, particularly a man with strong hands, might find himself beaten, or even killed.

Yet the deaths continued. We'd stationed men every few houses along the slums at night. This seemed to deter the villain; for several months, no strangulations had occurred.

Somehow, this unnerved me more than the deaths. What was the fiend planning next?

The Silence

My appointment with Tenni was at three, which meant I had to leave immediately after luncheon to arrive at my apartments on time.

On the way, my carriage passed a group of older girls and their chaperone. One wore a wide-brimmed hat and she turned to speak to another, her long thick brown hair spilling around her shoulders.

She reminded me of Nina.

My vision blurred; I swiped at my eyes angrily. Why think of Nina Clubb now?

She was gone. She'd died alone, just like Jonathan had.

I'd vowed not to let Jon suffer and die alone. Yet I'd failed him, just as I'd failed my poor Nina.

Why did I fail everyone? What was **wrong** with me?

***

Tenni looked much improved from our last meeting. "I know you're here for something else, mum. But I brought over your dress for the Midsummer Eve celebration. It's hung long enough: I might as well get it hemmed."

I smiled at her. "Good thinking!"

I changed into the fine creamy-white linen, trimmed in black cording. It really was a lovely dress. "I hope you're well."

The question seemed to sadden her. "Yes, mum. The girls also."

Tenni's little sisters had grown up under much turmoil. The death of their mother, attack by men upon their home, having to flee to my apartments, and constant moves. For Cheisara to have left must have distressed them greatly.

"And how is Calcutta Clubb?"

Tenni blinked. "Why do you ask?"

Calcutta was Cheisara's much younger first cousin, born "under the table," as it were, before her mother's marriage when the girl was ten. "We had an event yesterday. You might have read about it in the papers. I got a glimpse of her parents there, but ..."

Tenni's eyes widened. "Have you not heard? It's quite the scandal."

"Heard what?"

"Miss Calcutta ran off, oh three years back. A search was done, but when she was found, she said she'd not go back. Can you believe it? A spinster, refusing to return to her father's home!"

I shrugged. "Cheisara has lived with you. How is that different?"

"Cheisara's well-past marrying age, even if she wished it, and with her own fortune. Calcutta's just barely of age, and they've let her run wild! She's taken up with some rake —"

Suddenly, I recalled something Katie said: *I'm not the only girl.*

Tenni said, "What is it?"

Dread crept into my belly. "Do you recall the name of that 'rake'?"

"Seth something."

I felt relieved. *Not Frank Pagliacci.*

"I never saw the man. Cheisara says he's nice looking, if you like that sort of thing. Flashy. And too overly flattering for her taste. From the sound of it, I'd not be surprised if he has other women as well."

"Oh, dear," I said. "I suppose her father's unhappy with that."

Tenni began pinning my hem. "Her father challenged him to a duel, but at the appointed time, the man never arrived!" Tenni giggled. "Cheisara called him a coward."

I chuckled. "Well, if he were an honorable man, they'd not be in this situation." How many scoundrels were **in** this city?

***

After the fitting, I brought Tenni out front to ask about Morton.

"Yes, mum, he came to me there. He was so badly hurt that at first, I didn't recognize him. I had Oma handle the customers so I might wash and bind his wounds. He was ravenous — he hadn't eaten in some time. I kept him in my parlor several hours, until the Memory Boy he'd asked for arrived."

"Did he say what had happened? Who hurt him?"

Tenni shook her head. "I asked. But he'd tell me nothing. He didn't even want me to stay outside with him when the Memory Boy arrived. And when I went to see if he needed anything, they both were gone."

What could have happened to him? I lowered my voice. "Do you know anything about a group called the Four of Clubs?"

"No, mum, never heard of them. Should I ask?"

I shook my head. If this was some rogue group inside Clubb quadrant, I didn't want Tenni involved. "But there is something you might do. Could you arrange an invitation from Karla?"

Tenni looked away.

Karla Bettelmann was as good a friend as any I had in Bridges. But she was also Cheisara Golf's older sister. I suppose mentioning Karla might have been awkward for Tenni right then. I said, "Don't worry about it; I'll find a way to contact her."

Tenni faced me. "No, mum, I'll do it. You don't want to bring attention to yourself, not being Queen now and all. You've put your trust in me, more than once. I won't let you down."

***

When I went up the steps at Spadros Manor, several of Tony's men came out, tipping their hats to me as they went.

Once I'd changed into my house-dress, Tony called me to the veranda, where he sat watching the birds hop along the dirt path. "Come with me," he said, so I followed him once more out to the gardens. It was mid-afternoon, and the sun was hot, so we returned to the tea-table, now under the shade of the arbor.

Tony said, "I've contacted Mr. Hart, and had him contact Mr. Diamond. Neither have heard from Master Rainbow in some time. And Master Bresciane knows nothing about the Four of Clubs."

"Thank you," I said, and meant it. "He'd gone to Tenni's shop —"

Tony let out a laugh. "The sudden need to have a dress fitted. And at your apartments, of all places. I trust you spoke with her outside?"

"Heh. You even ask? I may be foolish at times, but I'm no fool."

I didn't mean it as a slight on him, but he seemed to shrink within himself, just a bit. "I never meant it that way."

I waved him off, yet I felt bitter. "It's of no consequence. What she said, though, is that Master Rainbow was hurt badly enough to warrant binding his wounds. And he hadn't eaten in some time."

"He sounds as bad as when he washed up on our doorstep a few years back."

"Tenni said she didn't recognize him, he'd been beaten so badly."

"Good gods." Tony looked stunned. "I can't see that he's ever done harm to anyone! What's this all about?"

I didn't know, and it bothered me. "Did either of them know what the Four of Clubs meant?"

"No." He let out a breath. "I hesitate to contact Mr. Clubb. He's not responded to any of my inquiries, and other than send his men that one time, has kept himself silent."

Right after Spadros Manor had been attacked and Spadros Castle burnt, Mr. Clubb sent a letter denying any involvement. He'd sent five men to help us restore order. Once we'd sent them home, though ... "It's strange. And did any of his men say anything to indicate why?"

"Not a word." He lapsed into silence.

"I had Tenni set up a meeting with his grand-daughter Karla Bettelmann. Perhaps she knows something that no one's telling us."

"Not the wife of that miscreant causing us so much trouble at the station ... ?"

A laugh burst from me. Mr. Mikhail Bettelman, money-grubbing extortionist extraordinaire, the man — unfortunately — set in charge of the zeppelin station. "The same. But I've never met the man, and I don't think I ever should have cause to." Then I recalled Karla's father had been killed by Mr. Clubb for rising in revolt against him. "To be honest, I think Mrs. Karla Bettelmann might know more about this than anyone."

The Illness

After several days, Karla Bettelmann arranged for us to have luncheon at the Kournikova, a rather nice restaurant on Market Center. I'd been there many a time with Mr. Charles Hart, so I knew the place well.

Instead of booking the entire room as Mr. Hart always did, the place was half full. Eyes, some unfriendly, followed us as we went. We made our way to the left back corner booth and sat, our men surrounding us on all sides possible. Fortunately, Karla had retained the presence of mind to book two booths. Her men sat behind me. Honor and Mr. Theodore stood along the wall beside Karla, watching everything but us.

"I'm so happy to see you," Karla said. "I hope all is well."

"It is." I now felt glad the room was so full; it was barely possible to hear her, which would prevent our own men from doing so. It was then I noticed she wore mourning garb. "I hope you're well also."

Karla shook her head. "My aunt has died of apoplexy."

"I'm so sorry to hear that. But I don't understand." I wished I had my dictionary with me. "What's apoplexy?"

Karla shrugged. "A sudden illness in the brain. My cousin Lori says it's like a fuse blows inside your head. But I don't quite understand what a fuse is." She thought for a moment. "I've known several who've suffered it. In some, it leaves them void," she tapped her head, "or crippled. In others, it's like the Dealer instantly captures their hand." She seemed downcast. "Like my great-grandfather, Johnny Clubb. He was tending his garden outside the Manor one summer's day, and just ... folded." She sighed. "It was long before I was born. But I would have liked to have known him."

First her father dead, now her aunt. And she couldn't refuse a Queen's summons. "Good gods," I said, "I hope I'm not taking you from anything important."

She smiled to herself. "The funeral was two weeks ago. We'll be in our forty days for a bit yet."

Now I felt entirely confused. "Forty days?"

She shrugged. "It's a Clubb thing, I suppose. Forty days of mourning is our people's tradition."

"I see."

The waiter came, took our orders, left.

Karla seemed hesitant to speak. "Is this about my sister?"

I shrugged. "It can be, if you wish. I admit that particular situation distresses me."

Karla spoke so quietly I had to lean forward to hear her. "She told my sister she must choose where her devotion lay: to her, or to being a Clubb spy." She sat back. "Can you believe it?"

I laughed to myself, shaking my head. Tenni did have a way with words, when she wanted to. But I was beginning to see the picture. "I fear I may have worsened the problem. I told Miss Mitchell to tell no one of her findings, and she took the matter to heart."

"Exactly," Karla said, annoyed. "Now my sister feels she cares for your good opinion over hers."

This explained why Karla set this up so quickly. "Please let your sister know that I have no designs here." At this, I felt sad. "Miss Tenni is very young. I only wanted to protect her."

Karla nodded, her passion seemingly cooled by my words. "So what did you want to speak of today?"

Our food was set before us. I let the waiters leave and took a bite before answering, considering how to begin. "The Four of Clubs."

Karla froze, staring at me.

I sighed. "So the name means something."

"It used to." Karla seemed ready to cry. She set her fork down. "But they're all dead." She shook her head, eyes on her plate. "My father was one of its members."

I nodded, trying to make sense of what she'd said. I knew that some of the "Clubb husbands" — the sons-in-law of Alex and Regina Clubb — had banded together to try to assassinate Alex and his son Lance, the Clubb quadrant's rightful Heir.

Apparently, this plot began over Tony's son Roland, who was born "under the table" with Gardena Diamond. Somehow, the Clubb husbands had learned of the boy during the negotiations over Gardena's courtship with Lance. If this courtship went through, and Lance took Roland as his heir, these men didn't want a bastard one day ruling over their true-born sons.

Or that's what Morton told me.

Had this group somehow been re-formed? Then both Lance and Gardena were in danger, and possibly Roland as well. "I'm sorry to distress you. But I got a message that this group was in pursuit of one of my men —"

Karla looked up at me, startlement upon her face.

"— so if you know anything, I'd be greatly in your debt."

I said that in the way that I said it to make her stop and think. The Lady of Spadros being in your debt was one thing. The Queen of Spades being in your debt was something entirely different.

I watched as she thought it through, worked out the ramifications.

She nodded. "I'll tell you what I know."

The Misread

Karla Bettelmann's father, Mr. Ferdinand Golf, had indeed been part of the plot to kill Mr. Alexander and Master Lance. And it'd been over what Morton told me it'd been over: Roland.

But as the boy still used the name Roland Diamond (instead of his birth name, Roland Spadros), it seemed they misread the table. They believed Roland was **Lance's** son! No one had told them differently.

It was a bold move, and brilliantly done. The alliance between Diamond and Clubb now made sense. And it made Cesare Diamond's motives behind the seemingly foolish closing of his quadrant after hearing of spies inside it clearer.

For any of this to work, the name Roland Clubb must become an undisputed fact. A boy named Roland Anthony Spadros had to be a boy who never existed, nor was even thought of. Or else one day the child could become a target.

If the Clubb husbands couldn't even accept Lance's bastard as their Heir, well, they'd never accept Tony's! So when his father Julius Diamond refused to act, Cesare cut off contact, sealed his quadrant, and purged any spies until the matter was more firmly in hand.

Which made the fact that the group seemed to have re-formed rather disturbing. I might have quarrel with his parents, but I don't think I could bear any harm coming to little Roland.

"Jacqui? What is it?"

I sighed. I wished I could tell her the truth. "It's plain that the group has re-formed, or someone wants us to think so. Do you have any idea who might be involved?"

She shook her head. But she didn't meet my eye.

So she suspected her husband, or someone else close to her.

Lance once had ten older sisters. One was dead — my beloved Nina, who took her own life rather than live in a cage, even one that might keep her alive. Her younger sister Kitty was now with the Dealers, having never married. Four of his sisters' husbands — three of Karla's uncles and her father — were dead, killed by her grandfather for betraying him. So Karla had four uncles who might be suspects in this.

But I surely couldn't expect her to betray her kin. "Never you mind; you've helped more than I expected. We'll say no more."

***

Now that I understood the situation better, I needed to consider how best to contact Lance. Learning who the Four of Clubs were was my only real hope of figuring out why they would want to hurt Morton. And that might lead me to where he was hiding.

There are only a few people the Queen of Spades might ask for counsel. I'd pushed the limits as far as I could with Karla.

I felt sure the news that the Spadros Queen met with the grand-daughter of the Clubb Patriarch was spreading throughout the city like wildfire. I owed Karla, not least of all for the myriad questions she'd be getting the rest of the day, especially from her husband.

So I had no choice: I had to go to the person I least wanted to speak with on the matter.

***

Molly Hogan Spadros sat upstairs at Spadros Manor, at her tea-table, by the window overlooking the street. When I opened the door, she seemed surprised. "I thought you were the maid."

"Not even so useful as that," I said. "May I come in?"

Molly shrugged. Since Tony had banished her to a life of semi-imprisonment for her betrayals of ... well, just about everyone, I don't suppose she felt she had much control over things anymore.

56

I sat across the tea-table from her. "I hope you're well."

"No, you don't," Molly said mildly.

It was a good reply, actually. "Very well." I leaned back, crossing my legs. "If you needed to speak with one of the Heirs, how would you contact him?"

Her face turned scheming: she'd gain any advantage she could from this conversation. "I suppose it'd depend on which Heir."

"No, it doesn't. Tell me true, or I walk out of here and announce myself at the bridge."

Molly burst into laughter. "I do believe you might." She eventually wiped her eyes. "But it's ever so much easier than that."

I sat waiting for her. "And?"

"He's a man."

"What is **that** supposed to mean?" Did she want me to seduce him? I needed to get to the man, not betray my husband again.

"So you want me to tell you **everything**? Spell it out so you see the whole, **entire** picture?"

Oh, she was enjoying this, making me wait. Making me her supplicant. "If you would. If it wouldn't take too much of your time." I smiled, feeling smug. There was more than one way to motivate her. "But perhaps your surroundings are too much of a distraction for you to focus on the matter at hand. We do have other quarters, if these aren't suitable." She'd have a poor time down in Roy's torture room.

Molly snorted. "Jacqui, you are such a blunt instrument. It's a wonder Roy ever bothered to try and sharpen you." She let out a breath. "Even Katie could have figured it out by now."

The hairs on my arms raised. She spoke of Katie as if her daughter were still alive. I peered at her: was she ill?

"Oh, very well," Molly said, evidently annoyed at my failure to play. "He's a man. A high-card man. Like every other high-card man in the city, he has a manservant. The menservants all go to this tavern called the Twenty-Eight —"

"Yes. It's on Market Center."

"Oh, so you know of it. I'm sure Tony's manservant knows this Heir's manservant, or can figure it out. He's reticent, not a dullard."

I nodded. "Very good. Thank you." I rose.

"I would **never** have threatened you, Jacqui."

I shrugged and went out, closing the door behind me. I didn't have time for her jabs. I had a friend to find.

***

But first, Tony's manservant.

I found Jacob Michaels in front of a row of Tony's shoes, polishing the middle pair. When he saw me, he bowed low. "Mum. Mr. Anthony's not here as yet."

I left the door open. "I wished to speak with you."

Michaels was quite a short man, about as tall as I. Although he was much older than I, he looked younger. His bearing only made it seem so in truth. "How may I help, mum?"

I considered who might be listening. "I need to send a message, and I believe you to be the person I can most trust with this one."

I thought he might be offended, or even refuse. But his gaze turned inward, as if recalling some conversation. Then he nodded.

I'd written Lance's name on a slip of paper. "I must meet with this man. I hear you know of a way to arrange it." At his blank look, I added, "Upon Market Center."

"Oh," he said. "Yes. Yes! I know exactly who you mean." He smiled. "I've been meaning to take Skip on an outing."

I handed him twenty-eight dollars.

He was so surprised by the gift I thought he might drop it. "That's too much, mum. By far."

I shrugged. "I thought it might help you recall. I'll be at my apartments until tea-time tomorrow."

He smiled to himself; I could see in his eyes when the gears clicked into place. "No need, mum. No need at all. But it is truly appreciated."

***

After dinner, Tony asked if I might join him in his study. We'd dressed for dinner, as we did most nights, and I suppose we made a fine pair going down the hall, Tony in his dinner jacket and I in my red taffeta and jewels.

Sawbuck sat in the corner, smoking a cigar, his leg over one arm of his stuffed chair. And I was reminded of the day Tony and I had visited Joe and Josie and their grandfather. Joe had been smoking a cigar, and sat the same way.

Sawbuck quickly stood when we entered.

Tony seemed amused. "Take your ease, Ten." Looking in my direction, Tony gestured at one of many armchairs in front of the desk. "Sit." Tony took the chair behind his desk, leaning his cane upon it.

Sawbuck moved the aforementioned chair next to Tony, stood behind it until I sat, then returned to his stuffed chair in the corner.

I felt intrigued. Why was I here? What had changed?

Tony said to me, "I wanted to thank you for taking care of things when I was unable. This is thrice now —"

I'd almost forgotten the night Tony had been beaten in his own warehouse.

"— and I wish the two of you to confer more, so as for you to understand the entire situation we face."

"Situation?" I felt puzzled.

Tony let out a small laugh. "Perhaps I spoke too strongly. We need clear communication to ensure a coordinated play."

I nodded. "Whatever I might do to help."

Tony gave three tiny nods. "Ten, what about Pearson's ledgers?"

I stared at Tony. How did he know about that?

Sawbuck gave me an amused smirk. "I moved the ray cannons to one side of the storeroom, and set up shelves to the ceiling on the other." He took a puff of his cigar. "Not sure why Mr. Pearson didn't do this long ago. Everything is there now, arranged by date." He gazed to one side, suddenly pensive. "The earliest ones are personal; I plan to give them to his wife."

Tony nodded. "And? What have you learned?"

"Well, we've only read a few. But the Clubbs could take lessons from the man. He had spies in places I didn't even think of." Sawbuck gestured to me with his chin. "Mrs. Brenda Trex, the City Clerk —"

I felt a shock of surprise. The lady who'd helped me find Jack Diamond's clues in my search for Jonathan!

"She was one of his. Perfect place to find out what's going on in the city. Pity the man before her wasn't — we'd know a lot more."

"Contact them all," Tony said. "If any balk, you have permission to pay them up to twice what they'd gotten before. But make sure to investigate them first. I'll have no horses at my table."

Sawbuck snorted. "Way ahead of you, sir. This'll keep our men busy for some time."

Tony grinned. "Good."

A knock, and Monsieur Sabacc peered around the door. "Is this a good time to speak with you?"

Sawbuck and I rose.

Tony smiled at Monsieur, but did not rise. "Please! Come in."

Monsieur was the Chef for Spadros Manor, who though he was on his own quite a large man, seemed short next to Sawbuck. Behind Monsieur came his wife, Mrs. Anne, our Mistress of the Kitchens. They'd married ten months earlier, and seemed very happy.

Tony gestured to the armchairs in front of his desk. "What might I help with?"

Monsieur and Mrs. Anne glanced at each other, but did not sit. "Sir," Monsieur said, "we're here about Mrs. Jane. Your housekeeper."

Tony seemed amused. "Yes, I know who she is. What about her?"

The two glanced at each other, hesitant. Then Monsieur said, "There are two matters, sir."

Tony said, "Might you please sit?"

Monsieur seemed taken aback. "If you command it, sir."

"I do."

Monsieur and Mrs. Anne gripped each others' hands and then sat. Monsieur ran a finger around his collar. "I must say, sir, you are nothing like your father."

"Good," Tony said. He leaned forward, resting his arms upon the desk. "What troubles you?"

Monsieur hesitated. "The position of butler, sir, is by tradition the highest of servants. But Master Alan still sleeps in the male servants' dorm. He deserves his own rooms, sir, and the respect of being called Mr. Pearson. I've approached him on both matters, but he demurs."

Tony said, "Modesty is a virtue, for certain."

"Yes, sir." Monsieur hesitated once more. "This brings me to my second thought: Mrs. Jane —"

"Ah," said Tony. "Who still has Pearson's quarters."

"Yes, sir. She —"

Mrs. Anne broke in. "She's melancholy, sir. Deeply so. The whole staff is worried for her."

Tony drew back, peering at them both. "I've not noticed any problems with her work."

Mrs. Anne let out a bitter laugh. "Her work would be spotless until the day she died. I just don't wish it to be at her own hand!"

Tony leaned forward. "Good gods." He gestured to Sawbuck. "Send for Alan and his mother, please."

"Yes, sir." Sawbuck's heavy tread went down the hall, then back, and he returned to his chair.

Tony said, "Have the two of you any suggestions?"

Monsieur said, "Perhaps the doctor should see to her."

Mrs. Anne said, "The staff has talked of a holiday for her, or so as not to single her out, perhaps for the entire staff. Like when we had the picnic."

I smiled to myself. I'd had them all out, giving them pins and necklaces cut from Dame Anastasia's fake necklace. They did seem to enjoy it.

Then I thought about how lonely I'd been, how much I'd missed Tony beside me. "Do you think it would help for her to remarry?"

Tony scoffed at my idea, which stung.

Monsieur seemed taken by surprise. "I don't know! She's getting on now. Perhaps so. I'd not be sure how to —"

Sawbuck spoke lazily. "Well, if you need someone to marry the widow, I'll do it."

There came a sudden commotion outside Tony's door. The door flung open; Mrs. Jane Pearson held the handle, her son Alan trying, it seemed, to stop her.

Jane stormed in. "**No!** I mourn because I loved my John!" She pointed at Sawbuck. "I know what you are, sir, and I'd rather sleep in an empty bed than with someone who neither loves nor wants me."

Sawbuck's eyebrows lifted, but he said nothing.

She turned to Tony. "And **you**! I've seen you grow from a boy — and now you do **this**? I'd thought better of you."

I felt embarrassed that she'd overheard us, upset that she blamed Tony for my words. "We meant no harm; we're only concerned."

"Well, you need not be. If my work doesn't please you, reprimand me to my face! Don't have this ... **discussion** ... behind my **back**!

Tony suddenly stood. "No one's unhappy with your work! We care for your welfare. We want to help. Tell us: what do you need?"

"A moment's peace! I've lost the only man I've ever loved," her voice broke, "and it was just a year since."

Tony spoke gently. "Forgive me: I've been so focused on my sorrows I've seen none of yours."

Jane curtsied low. "There's no need —"

"Yes, there is. Stand up, and look at me. This is my command: take the rest of the week off. Surely the girls and Mrs. Sabacc can manage things. And if you ever need a day to yourself, you have only to ask."

Jane curtsied to the floor. "You're very kind, sir."

Tony said, "Master Alan."

Alan had been standing there, mouth open. "Um, yes, sir?"

"Monsieur tells me you've been sleeping in the servants' dorm. Surely we have —"

"So **this** is the meaning of the gathering," Jane said bitterly. "I've kept for myself what rightly belongs to my son."

Alan turned to her. "Mama, no. I'll not take you from your home on my account. I'm glad for you to be there, truly I am."

I said, "Surely we have enough rooms for you both?"

"We will make room," said Tony, as if I'd not spoken. "Peter and Amelia's quarters lie empty. They're not as close to the kitchens as Miz Jane's, but they're expansive enough for any butler and his family." He smiled at Alan. "Mr. Pearson."

Alan gaped at him. "That'll take some getting used to. Mr. Pearson was always my father."

Tony smiled. "Then it's settled. Have the servants clear and redo the rooms in any way you like."

Jane ran around Tony's desk and knelt before him, clasping his hand in both of hers. "Thank you for your care of my son."

Tony bent to touch the older woman's cheek and spoke fondly. "My dear lady. Please, get up." As she did so, he said to Alan, "Mr. Pearson and I have something in common; we've both lost a father. Surely if I'm here for any reason at all, it's to care for those who the Floorman has given me to serve in his stead."

I felt stunned. This was more than I'd heard him speak in a year, and yet ... he had grown, in ways I'd not ever seen in him.

And yet the whole evening, he'd barely so much as glanced at me.

***

I asked Alan to give the entire household the next day off and took our breakfast out in the gardens. Over our reheated leftovers from dinner, I could tell Tony was curious as to why.

After we ate, we walked in the gardens as I told him all that Karla had told me, including my suspicions about the Four of Clubs.

I also told him about my conversation with his mother.

He scowled at that part. "Be careful, Jacqui: she's one of the most dangerous people in this quadrant."

I found this hard to believe. "Truly?"

"She's only out to consolidate power for herself. Look at what she's done. Every day, she tries to learn what's going on outside, subtly questioning her maids, trying to pit one against the other."

"Wait. You're questioning her maids **daily**?"

"I must. She commanded enormous forces before. I've stripped them from her, but clearly she's trying to find a new army. If it hadn't saved your life, I'd regret letting her out long enough to see to you when you were so ill."

She **had** saved my life. Funny, that she never brought that up as a way to put me in her debt. "Well, I should have a meeting set up soon for you and Lance Clubb. Maybe he knows something about this Four of Clubs that Karla didn't."

Tony peered at the path. "If it's his own uncles, though ... would he want to tell us? He has to consider how that might look."

"I don't know. But if these ... I can't imagine it's anyone else but their underlings, or perhaps sons, wanting to avenge their deaths. Even if these **are** his uncles, well, he may not know."

Tony let out a breath, still looking down. "I should hate him, but I can't. Even though he's taking the woman I love."

I gaped at him for his brazen honesty. *The woman I love ...* Why did him saying that hurt so?

He shook his head and turned away. "He's a better man than I am."

My people would have been happy that he'd found yet another to love, that he loved more. That his life had become more, not less.

But I knew what it meant to **him**.

His people didn't see it this way. Here, when you loved someone, you didn't love anyone else. He'd cut his heart-ties with me to fix them on Gardena Diamond, and the cutting hurt.

I turned away so he'd not see my eyes. "I'm going to my apartments. Your Master Jacob is to meet me there later today, to confirm he's made contact with Master Lance's manservant."

"Good thinking." Tony sounded surprised, proud.

Still with my back to him, I shrugged. "It was your mother's idea." *You're such a blunt instrument ...* "Don't count her out. She plays better than I do. We may be able to use her one day."

Tony said nothing.

I knew he still hadn't forgiven her for any of it: her betrayal of Roy, her betrayal of me, her defiance of him and Roy both. "I'm going now. The servants should be back after tea." I gave him a glance; he still stood turned away. "See you at dinner."

But he never moved, and I went into the house, got changed, and left for the day.

***

Most everyone would be scandalized by the scene when the doorbell to my apartments rang. I, the Queen of Spades, sat on the floor legs spread, skirt hiked up around me so my knees showed!

Little Miss Ariana Spadros sat the same way, as we rolled a ball back and forth in the parlor.

At the sound of the bell, Ariana cried out, "Ugh! I don't want you go way."

"Maybe they're here for someone else." Thankful that the parlor doors were closed, I tucked my feet under me, making sure my legs were covered. I rested my hands in my lap. "Let's sit here a minute and see."

On the other side of the door to the front hall, Blitz said, "What the hell? No. You are not welcome here. Get the fuck out. Go, before I call for her men."

Ariana giggled. "Daddy cuss-ted."

I turned to Ariana. "Stay here." I hurried to the front window, but could see nothing. Then I saw Joseph Kerr, of all people, going down my front step!

He must have seen the movement of the curtains, because he began banging on the door: bam-bam-bam.

"For gods' sakes," Blitz muttered, now in the back hall.

I told Ariana, "Hurry. Go find your mama." I ran out of the parlor door, closing it behind me just as Blitz came up. He fixed me with a "I don't fucking believe this" sort of glare.

I took a deep breath. "Let me see what this is about."

Blitz grabbed my arm. "He can't keep demanding to see you. You're the Spadros Queen, not some wench he can call on for favors whenever he pleases."

That stung. But it gave me some resolve. "I'll take care of this." I flung open the door, the pistol in my pocket hitting my leg.

Joe almost fell in. But he recovered quickly. "Good afternoon."

I put my hands on my hips. "What is this? Why do you come here, harass my servants and disturb the neighborhood?"

Joe frowned. "Why can't I see you? Are they keeping you trapped?"

"It's nothing of the sort! Now what do you want? What is so urgent that you make all this commotion?"

Joe glanced at Blitz, who still stood there.

"Whatever you have to say, you can say with him here."

"So I'm out and he's in. Is that it?"

"**What?**" A laugh burst from me. "That's not it, and you know it." I had reached the limit of my patience. "Say what you want, or go."

Joe glanced at Blitz again, and I sighed. If I drew on Joe, he'd only laugh. "Blitz, fetch your pistol."

Blitz said, "With pleasure."

I turned to Joe. "You have until he returns.."

Joe scowled. "I'm leaving the city."

The Suffering

"Leaving?" I felt surprised. Confused. "But how? Why?"

"Mr. Hart is allowing me to take my grandfather to Azimoff. Maybe they can help him —"

Azimoff had the best medical care in Merca. Things must be dire for Mr. Hart to pay the enormous amount to send them, particularly with how he felt about Joe.

"— and the way things are here, I don't think I want to come back."

Really? Whatever would Joseph Kerr, of all people, do in Azimoff?

"But he gave me a ticket so Josie might come along." He shook his head. "She won't leave the house, not after what happened. So I thought to take you with me instead."

I felt so surprised that I laughed. "What makes you think I would go **anywhere** with you, after what you did?"

"Jacqui, you keep saying that, but I don't understand. What did I **do**? Josie said you were angry that she put Party Time in your tea, but what are you angry at **me** for?" He put one hand high on the doorpost, and his eyes were wet. "It'll be days with him in the hospital. I don't want to be there alone. Please, just tell me what I did, so I can make this right."

I snorted. Leaving Bridges was what I'd wanted my whole life. But not with him, not anymore. "You know what? Get out."

"But why?"

"**Why?**" The woman sweeping her porch across the street looked up, and I lowered my voice. "You drugged me, seduced me, then gave me womb fever, that's why. After swearing you'd never been with **any** other woman than me."

His face was all innocence. "But Jacqui, I haven't. Never."

"I almost **died**! And even though I've been through so much suffering, you've not once in all these years so much as sent a card."

Joe looked confused. "What's been going on? You've never told me anything of it."

"My friends, my brother —"

"Wait. Something's happened to Benji?"

Benji, my friend in the Pot, had always called me his sister, but we weren't related, not really. "No ..." Should I say it? "Inventor Etienne Hart was my brother. Well, half-brother."

Joe's mouth dropped open. "Really?" He glanced away, then back. "My grandfather said something like that once, but I thought he was joking." Then he shook his head. "You had womb fever?"

"Yes, and if it weren't for my Ma, I'd be dead now."

"But why do you think **I** gave it to you? I don't understand. Why, it's ... that's **impossible**!" He let out a breath, scowling. "Why don't you ask your **husband** about it, anyway?"

"**What?**"

"Well, everyone's saying he's having affairs in Diamond, so —"

A surge of shame: *everyone was saying it?* "You are unbelievable. To accuse my husband of such a thing!

"— so why do you accuse **me**? I love you, Jacqui. No one else. And I'm perfectly well! Besides, I'd **never** do anything to harm you."

"Really? Really. Because I saw your dripping. I'd just had a child. I'd only bedded you. Only you, and then I get womb fever. And you know what? My Ma had the doctor speak with the others, to look for any kind of women's fever in the city. What man the woman was seeing right before."

Joe drew back, just a bit. "And?"

Ma had insisted on it, if only to perhaps save some. The investigation had gone on for months. The answer I'd gotten was the most humiliating thing I'd ever experienced in my life. "Over a hundred named you."

He put his hands on his hips. "Now wait just a minute. There are hundreds of men named Joe —"

I scoffed, pointing in his face. "Named Joseph Kerr? With your exact description? That fucking ... horse-shoe on your belly?" I grabbed his coat, shoved him back. "Dozens of women are **dead**! And you want me to believe you've had no one **else**?"

He stepped forward. "I do! And who asked them? How did they ask? Did they say, 'Were you with Joseph Kerr?' A woman looking for someone to blame is going to say yes, specially if she don't recall."

"My Ma's smarter than that. You want me to bring her here to ask?"

An instant of alarm, then his face turned sly. "Well, no matter what she says, you can't prove a thing. And you haven't exactly been celibate yourself."

I was not going to let this scoundrel make me feel ashamed for bedding my own husband. "Get out, and don't you dare try to return."

Blitz stood a step behind me, pistol in hand, his face stricken.

"Make sure he leaves," I said loudly. "If he comes back, shoot him."

A look of grim resolve came over Blitz then, but Joe had left.

***

My mood had been entirely spoilt by Joe's visit, and I went to my office to be alone. But Mary knocked on the door. "Mum, what is it? Ariana said you needed me in a hurry."

I smiled to myself at the image this brought forth. Then I sighed. "Come in." When she closed the door, I said, "I owe you an apology."

"For what?"

"You were just trying to help me last year at Vig and Natalia's wedding, and I was so angry with you." At her obvious confusion, I said, "The man? In the alley?"

Compassion filled her voice. "Oh, mum —"

"You were right to be wary of him." I put my elbows on my desk, my face in my hands. "He's no good, no good at all. How did I come to **love** a man like that?"

I heard Mary approach. "Mum, don't blame yourself. You can't help who you love." She let out a soft breath, and her voice was fond. "I've been very lucky."

I smiled to myself. "You have." I wiped my eyes, looked up at her. "Tell Ariana thank you for following my command. I didn't want her to see any of this."

"I will, mum. And thank you for caring about her."

"I do care for her, like she was my own child. And she's smart, Mary. She remembers things." Should I say? "I don't know how old you have to be, but I'd get her tested."

Mary blinked. "You think she could be a Memory Girl?"

I shrugged. "It couldn't hurt to ask. And if she is, her school would be paid for." That was the only good thing about Bridges — if a child had a talent that helped the city, they didn't skimp on exploiting it.

Mary's jaw dropped. "My girl could go to **school**? Oh, mum, that would be incredible!"

"Well, we won't know anything until she's tested. If there's a fee for the tests, I'll be happy to pay it."

Tears stood in Mary's eyes. "Thank you, mum. You don't know what this means to me. To all of us."

***

At tea, both Blitz and Mary had questions, most of which I couldn't answer. "Any of the Memory Boys should be able to tell you more."

Memory Girls didn't tromp through the streets delivering messages. Not only was it unseemly, it put the girls into danger. No, Memory Girls were amongst the city's Computers: those people who took information and found the patterns in it. Many could do calculations in their heads at incredible speed. Some ended up working for the Dealers, others for the Clubbs. But we in Spadros had our own set of Computers, mostly men too old to be messenger boys who had ties here. Tony had long wanted to recruit little Werner Lead to join them once he got old enough.

And of course if Ariana did test well, someday she might become one too.

I didn't understand much of what the Computers did, only that it was quite secret. Few even knew where they met. If I had to guess, my money would be on Master Bresciane having the knowledge, and perhaps Sawbuck.

Tony had wanted Inventor Maxim Call to create an adding machine as fast as a Computer which ran on power. The intent was to free the Computers for questions only a man might answer.

But Inventor Call had been murdered.

I had no idea what the new Inventor, Montgomery Arrow, had been working on. At the time, I supposed Monte (as he'd asked to be called) had taken up Inventor Call's lifelong work on how to fix the Magma Steam Generators.

I hadn't seen the man since Maxim Call's murder, and I wondered how he fared.

We were almost through with tea when Master Michaels arrived. I told Blitz to invite him for tea, but Blitz told me the man had refused. So I greeted Jacob Michaels in my parlor.

He'd been looking around, but he quickly composed himself and bowed when I entered.

"Master Jacob," I said. "I hope you're well?"

He took a step backwards, eyes on the floor. "Indeed, mum."

"How do you like my parlor?"

"It's not my place to say, mum."

I smiled to myself. "Even so."

He gave me a quick glance. "It's just as Skip said. Except you've done the place over." He nodded quickly. "I like it."

"I'm pleased you do!" I guessed that asking him to sit would make him feel even more uncomfortable than he was already. So I said, "Have no fears; all that happens here will be relayed to my husband."

He relaxed then, letting out a breath. "Thank you, mum. I'd not like to fall under his anger."

I chuckled at that. "What news?"

He raised his head then, looked me in the eye. "Master Lance's manservant has agreed to speak with him tonight. I did notify him you were 'at home' on Wednesdays."

"Thank you," I said.

"A plain letter will come for Mr. Anthony, thanking him for his invitation to meet but declining due to a prior engagement."

"But —"

Michaels smiled to himself. "There was never an invitation, mum. The nature of the engagement will tell us the place you're to meet. The place they were to meet is a code for what time. And the date will tell you whether the meeting takes place in the morning or evening."

"I see. And did he give you those codes?"

"He did. But I'm to deliver them to you personally." At that, he handed over a slip of paper.

I put it into my pocket without opening it. "Very good. I'll see you to your carriage, sir."

A wry look came over his boyish face. "You're very kind, mum."

Blitz, of course, had heard everything, and was ready with the door when we emerged. "Have a safe trip."

Michaels had arrived in the plain carriage; my carriage of the Queen stood ready. Glistening piano-black, with the arched Crown of Spadros encircled with roses raised in real silver upon its side. Since I'd left Spadros Manor in the plain carriage, to see mine there also confused me for a moment.

Everyone on the street stopped to curtsy or bow as I went down the steps. I was no longer their neighbor. I was their Queen.

I hated it.

Honor stood by my carriage, dressed in the black and silver of Spadros livery. He and Michaels exchanged a glance as Michaels got into his carriage. Something passed between them in that glance, and I wondered how much Michaels told Honor in their pillow-talk. More to the point, who might be listening.

I'd have to speak to Honor about this.

I hated all the formality of being Queen, the way people's faces changed when they saw me as Queen rather than as me. But I loved my carriage. The black velvet was so soft, the cushions so comfortable.

I could get used to this.

But this life couldn't help but change people, and I must be wary of it. Like Roy's mother, it had made Molly complacent, feel entitled to lay claim to everything, everyone. To twist and control even the fruit of their wombs. They'd done it in different ways, but I never would. I wanted my little Acevedo to become his own man.

***

When I reached Spadros Manor, Alan met me at the door with a large envelope. "I have the report you requested, mum."

"Oh! So soon? Very good."

Alan lowered his voice to speak in my ear. "They bring all drowning cases in the city proper to the coroner's on Market Center."

Ah. So at first, Katie's death wasn't considered suicide. I took the envelope from him. "Is Mr. Anthony home as yet?"

"He's upstairs with Master Acevedo."

I went to my study, locked the envelope in my filing cabinet, then went upstairs to change. I put the slip of paper Michaels had given me under my left foot inside my soft house shoes and went to find Tony.

A quilt lay upon the floor. Tony sat tailor-seat, his shoes, cuffs, and collar laid upon Acevedo's dresser. He wore a dark blue house trousers and vest with a subtle check pattern. Not a navy blue, but the color reminded me of Jonathan Diamond's uniform when he was Keeper of the Court.

Acevedo Spadros III sat wearing a white baby gown, tilted onto his good hip, playing with a set of blocks. His eyes met mine. "Mama."

Tony looked up at me. "Did you find what you needed?"

I sat to Tony's right on the quilt tailor-seat, my house shoes still on. "I did." I leaned over to my right to kiss Acevedo on his forehead. "You two look to be having fun."

Tony grinned. "We are."

Acevedo picked up a block and handed it to me.

"Thank you," I said. "Is this your block?"

"Bock," quoth he.

Tony beamed proudly at his son. "He's a smart boy." He smoothed Ace's wavy brown hair. "He'll make a fine Patriarch one day."

For some reason, emotion rose within me, and my eyes stung. Was my boy destined to one day run this place? Order men's deaths?

Tony glanced at me and smiled. "As you once told me, not everything must come to ruin. He's a strong child, and one day, we'll get him well again."

But how? He clearly needed another surgery for his hip. But the doctors in Azimoff were adamant: it would be too dangerous for him to have it done here.

A Family Heir couldn't dare leave the city until he had Heirs of his own. What would happen to the Family if assassins were to find him? And if we were to take him to Azimoff anyway, and the doctors had to put a mechanism into him, the Cultural Correctness Committe would forbid him to return. Tech like that was illegal here.

So I had to watch my baby suffer. Because of me.

Acevedo was watching me. "Mama?"

Tony put his hand on my shoulder. "All will be well. You'll see."

So I tried to smile for my little Ace, and kissed him once more. But I hadn't been there for him when the assassins came. I'd been off betraying his father, and I could never forget it. "He came by after Michaels left."

Tony sat still for a moment. "Oh?"

"Mr. Hart is sending him and his grandfather to Azimoff. Joe wanted me to leave with him. I told him to go. Not come back, or I'd have Blitz shoot him."

Tony let out a laugh. "Oh." Then he said, "Are you certain?"

I leaned on my left arm. "I am. Why would I want to go anywhere, when I could sit here on this lovely soft quilt with the two of you?"

Tony said nothing.

At the time, I meant it. The day was warm, my son was happy, and we were safe. No one could harm us here.

But that reminded me for some reason of Katie. And yet I didn't want to spoil Tony's happy mood with talk of her death.

"What is it?"

I shook my head. "Nothing for now. But I'd like to speak with you privately after dinner."

He smiled to himself. "Always Business. Just one day in my life, I'd like to not have to consider it."

"I'm sorry. I should've never —"

"Don't fret." He sighed. "I don't sit in this Manor for nothing. I must consider my quadrant, daily, or by rights the job should be given to someone who will."

***

After dinner, Tony told the servants he wished to walk in the garden.

The sky still held the very last wisps of day. The moon had not yet risen. Low candles had been hurriedly placed along the garden path.

I gave Tony the slip of paper Michaels had given me, with the codes he'd mentioned. Tony seemed impressed. "So this is how the Clubbs pass their messages along. Very good."

Heh, I thought. *We learn from our enemies,* the Eldest once told us. I'd been just a child then, but her words stuck with me.

We continued to walk along the hard dirt path. Tony said, "I want you to come with me when I meet with Master Lance."

This surprised me. "Whatever for?"

Tony kept walking as if nothing had happened. "You see things I do not. You ask questions I don't think of." He turned to face me. "Why would I **not** want you there?"

I shrugged, not having an answer. It just didn't seem like something a Patriarch would do.

"I still value you," Tony said. "Never doubt that."

I nodded, once more feeling close to tears. He'd allowed me to stay, but some days he didn't even so much as touch me.

Then I straightened, my resolve firm. It didn't matter. He was right to be angry, to doubt my words. I loved him, and I'd not leave him ever again. One day, he'd see that I meant to stay, and not because anyone forced me to.

We returned to the house then, and each to our rooms. But when Shanna came to dress me for bed, I told her to go about her business. "I'll ring for you later, if I need you."

Shanna curtsied and left.

The house was quiet, dark, chill. I put my too-large green wrapper over me, the one Tenni had made for me when I was with child. Taking a lit candle in its holder with me, I went down the marble back stair to my study.

When I'd closed the study door, I turned the light on, blew out the candle, and set it atop one of my filing cabinets. I unlocked the drawer with the envelope in it and brought the package to my desk.

Alan had brought me the entire coroner's report — including photographs. After seeing it, I felt glad I'd obeyed my instincts and not told Tony of this.

Her maidenhood had been taken. Violently. And from the photos of her neck, she'd been strangled, not hung.

I closed the report. The Bridges Strangler had found her.

And in his perversity, he had made his deeds look like suicide.

My poor Katie! To end her days at the hands of this fiend! I felt sure this was Frank Pagliacci, a man she'd defended, nay, loved. To learn what horror she'd supported, then to be murdered!

It was too much.

And the policeman who stood in my parlor had supported him, forced those river-men to participate in a lie. The coroner let the papers publish the lie. Let the girl be abandoned by everyone who thought her to have put her Family into scandal. Let her be buried without one of her friends at her side.

A soft knock came at the door. "Mum? Is all well?"

I wiped my face. "I'm here."

Alan's youngest brother Rob peeked in, glancing about. The man was a year or so older than his sister Mary, with the same light brown hair, but he resembled his father more than she did. "Sorry to disturb you, mum. I thought you were abed."

I shook my head, trying to compose myself. I couldn't. "I won't be up much longer."

Rob gently closed the door without another word.

How could I tell Tony about this? What could I possibly say? He was sure to hear I'd been down here in the middle of the night crying. I didn't know what to tell him.

Or Molly, for that matter.

They'd both be devastated.

No, now was not the time. I'd say nothing, not until we'd met with Lance. Not until we found Morton, safe and well. Tony didn't deserve to receive yet another shock.

Katie had been dead for almost a year now. Surely the truth could wait a few days longer.

***

I woke when Shanna opened the curtains for the day. "Good morning, mum," said Shanna. "I have the dress you wanted ready."

"Thank you." I got up, put on my robe, waited at my tea-table for Honor to arrive with my tray.

And so he did, like every morning. Like clockwork, right on time.

He gave a start of surprise to see me there. "Good morning, mum."

I smiled at him and gestured to the tea-table.

He set my provisional tray — tea and toast, paper and early mail — in front of me, then stood, hands behind him, not looking at me.

"I have questions for you, sir."

He didn't answer, so I continued. "You and Master Michaels have been together, what, some twenty years?"

"Since we were boys, mum, so yes, at least that."

"I expect that in the servants' dorm there's not much privacy."

His stance became guarded. "No, mum."

"So where do you go?"

He licked his lips. "We set a ... um, cot, mum, behind the stair in the store-room. The one by the stables. It folds away so no one might see."

"And so what if you're needed?"

"Um, we rigged the bell so it rings there. When one of us is called."

"Ingenious." The store-room wasn't near most anything but the stables, so only the stable-boys might hear anything.

"Then we go to the staff room to see which one got called."

I wondered who was caring for the boys, now that Peter Dewey was dead. "I don't care where you go or what you do. I only have two concerns: that you not leave yourselves open to blackmail —"

Honor's eyebrows rose.

"— and that you be mindful of what you say, and more to the point, who might be listening."

Honor took a step back. "I never considered that."

"Well, you must." I lowered my voice so that only he might hear. "Mr. Howell believes at least one spy remains in Spadros Manor."

He looked dismayed. "Oh."

"You won't be harmed. But I want you both to think on anything you might have said that might harm the Family."

Honor gave three little nods, face pale.

"And my husband and I must know if you suspect anyone."

He spoke just as quietly. "I — uh — I don't know. Me and Jacob, well, we're low-cards, mum. Orphans, or born under the table, like the stable boys." He smiled fondly. "Tommy and Listy are really getting too old for it, but now Mr. Dewey's gone, we like to put them to bed. Tuck them in, read them stories. Before we — you know."

I chuckled. "I wondered about that."

"They know about us, mum. They aren't all that young anymore. Older than Master Pip. Almost men. Anyway, none of us know nothing of any spies. If we did, we'd tell you straightaway." He looked down. "We all miss Pip something terrible." His head raised. "How is he?"

"You'd have to ask Monsieur. Master Pip has never once written."

He looked crestfallen. "I'm sorry, mum."

I shrugged, looking away.

"We'll keep our eyes open, though, mum. Anyone not right. You can trust us on that."

I surveyed him. They'd been taking care of these boys, all on their own, despite their numerous other duties. They seemed good, honest men. "I do believe I can."

***

Tony advised me to dress in something quiet and plain. So I took off my makeup and jewels. Shanna brought out my old patched and mended charcoal dress.

Katie was the last to wear the dress, so seeing it brought a sharp pain of grief.

Our housekeeper Jane Pearson loaned me her black mourning bonnet, and I affixed a bit of old veil to it to hide my face.

To my surprise, Tony wore workman's gray tweed, the jacket and trousers a bit too long, with a cap to match. "I never would have guessed it: Honor is about my size!"

I hadn't really considered the matter, but here stood the proof.

Daisy brought Acevedo downstairs to see us off. Leaving through the side entrance to the stables, Tony and I rode in the plain carriage towards Market Center. Only Tony's driver knew the destination.

Something in that comforted me.

We arrived at — of all places — the Twenty-Eight tavern, just as Lance climbed onto the street from a taxi.

Lancelot Clubb was a tall, quiet man with thick golden hair (now covered by a brown cap) and a sprinkling of freckles across his nose. He seemed surprised to see me, moving to the back alley where Morton and I had found Albert Sheinwold dead as he gestured us to follow. In the alley, he and Tony shook hands. "I've got a place for us in back," Lance said.

Tony and I followed him to a rusty metal door, which opened onto a short hall. A kitchen lay straight ahead, but Lance took us right, to a small office. We pulled three chairs together and sat facing each other.

"My manservant is friends with the owner," Lance said, "so we shouldn't be disturbed."

Tony had an uncertain look on his face. "May we speak freely?"

Lance snorted, amused. "Not if you wish your words to stay here. But we can certainly speak."

Tony and I glanced at each other. Not knowing Lance's involvement in all this, I hesitated to bring Morton's name into it.

Tony took a sheet of paper from his breast pocket and handed it to Lance. "We've recently heard of this. Do you know anything of it?"

Lance took the paper, glanced at it, and shook his head. He folded it closed then peered at it. "I don't know." He let out a breath, not looking at us. "It pains me to say it, but there's been some ... well, dissension. In my Family."

Tony nodded. We'd learned of it a couple of years back, right before Gardena's oldest brother Cesare closed Diamond quadrant. "I know the feeling all too well."

Lance gave Tony a quick glance. "I suppose you would." He returned to peering at the folded page as if it might tell him something. He said to Tony, "And I suppose you know of the conspiracy to attack us, my father and I."

I nodded. "You told me so at the Diamond Country House. Don't you remember? But Master Rainbow told me of it before that."

Lance glanced at me in surprise. "Oh?"

Tony put his hand on mine. "We've known of it for some time."

Lance handed the paper back, most pointedly not looking at me. "Those conspirators are dead. So I don't know what this is about."

Tony stood. "We're sorry to trouble you."

"Wait," Lance said. "You wouldn't come all this way just because you heard of some group. What's really going on?"

Lance knew more than he said. "One of our men is in trouble —"

Tony snapped, "Jacqui!"

"— and he said these men were after him."

Lance looked down. "Well," he said, entirely ignoring how Tony reacted, "that makes things different." He shook his head as he took a deep breath, let it out. "I'd not worry too much about it. If I hear anything more, I'll contact you."

We returned to the alley. I faced Tony. "He's hiding something."

Tony snorted. "Can you blame him? His uncles have tried to murder him and his father once already, and it looks as though the group — with different members — is at it again." Then he looked away. "Why did you say anything? If he's involved with Master Rainbow's disappearance, now he knows the man has gotten a message to us."

I hadn't considered that. "That has to make him take pause, though, that we know. Surely he'd be eager not to harm him for fear of what we'd do."

"I suppose," Tony said. "But you mustn't blurt things out like that! You're Queen now! Act with some decorum."

I felt stung by his words, and I turned away.

A voice behind me, ten yards down the alley. "Jacqui? Is that you?"

I turned to see Joe coming towards us.

Tony grabbed my arm. "We have to go."

I shook my head. "He won't hurt me." I felt curious to see how he found us here. "You can wait in the carriage if you prefer."

"Like hell I will," Tony growled. "Go then, if you must."

Joe had stopped a few paces away, face confused.

I looked back at Tony. "It's not like that at all. Stay then, if you must. It'll only be a minute."

Taking a deep breath, I went a few steps towards Joe, heart pounding as I recalled my dream. "However did you find us here?"

"Find you?" He let out a laugh. "I came out for a smoke. I'm friends with the bartender."

Who likely told him important people were meeting here today ...

"But I'm glad I saw you." He took a deep breath. "I didn't want us to part like we did, Jacqui. I never, ever meant to hurt you."

I didn't know what to say.

"And it hurts me to not even know why you distrust me so. I thought you loved me."

It felt as if a knife went through my heart.

"I thought we had fun," he glanced over my shoulder, "you know, that afternoon together."

I shook my head, not daring to look back at Tony's face. "I thought you loved me, Joe. But when we ... were together, all I saw in your eyes was triumph. Like I was some grand chip you'd finally taken possession of. I felt used." It came to me. "I felt violated." I shook my head. "It wasn't fun. It was **terrible**!"

Joe's face softened. "Oh, Jacqui. To put yourself in such turmoil and distress, throw away all we have had together, give up the one chance to get away from here ... simply because you thought I **looked** at you wrong?" He shook his head, tucked a curl behind my ear. "My poor girl. What are they **doing** to you? Your mind is in such a state you can't even think straight."

Was it true? Had I only imagined it? "I don't know ... the whole thing felt wrong."

"This isn't like you at all," Joe said. Then he took my hand. "I'm glad I saw you, if only to warn you. You're in serious danger."

"I don't understand. From who?"

He shook his head. "There is so much you need to know. But this is neither the time nor place." He let go of my hand. "I won't beg you to love me. I won't beg you to come away with me. And I won't ask again. Do you want me? Or not?"

The money he'd stolen from me, the sickness he'd given me, the look in his eyes. The young woman at her window, still waiting for him to return to her, that little boy with his eyes at her side ...

I shook my head, took a step back, feeling shaky. "No. I'm sorry. I just can't." I took a deep breath, willing myself to believe it. But in that moment, I couldn't face his eyes. "I have a life here."

I glanced up; he was nodding, peering at the ground. "Then I suppose this is goodbye."

I turned away. "Yes, Joe. This is goodbye."

The Longshot

Tony stood glaring past my shoulder.

I walked to Tony without looking back, and we rode in silence.

I felt discouraged and afraid. We hadn't learned anything from Lance. If Joe had found out we were there, others surely knew as well.

Morton was missing, badly hurt, and in terrible danger. Clover, the only one who knew how to reach him, was dead, murdered by the Bridges Strangler. I had no way to know the identities of the friends who'd saved Morton before.

Why hadn't I at least asked? Morton had been wary of letting anyone know who his informants were, but surely it wouldn't have hurt to ask.

"All is not lost," Tony said. "Master Rainbow knows he can come to us if need be. We wouldn't betray him."

I nodded, just to show Tony that I'd heard him. But what if he couldn't get to us?

"What did he want?"

I shrugged, feeling surprised it'd taken Tony that long to ask. "It doesn't matter. He's leaving."

Tony took my hand, and I got the feeling he wanted to say something, yet hesitated to.

"Why were you glaring at him like that?"

Tony shook his head. "I hate everything he's done to you. The look he gave me ... it was devious, gloating." Then he shuddered. "The man makes my skin crawl."

That seemed rather dramatic, but I said nothing. Tony's feud with Joe didn't matter.

Shouts outside to the horses' hooves striking the cobbles. A policeman's whistle.

"Protestors," Tony's driver said through the speaker tube. "Police got it handled."

Tony took my hand. "They don't know it's us going past."

I didn't answer. Nothing mattered. Morton was still missing.

Who else might Morton have gone to, if he couldn't get to us?

By the time we were coming up on Spadros Manor, I had the solution. "I need the carriage."

Tony frowned. "But the horses need rest, and I promised my driver he'd be off-duty after this."

"Switch out the horses. Call Zeus and Honor. I know two places Master Rainbow might go, and I can't rest 'til I've been to them."

Tony nodded gravely. "I understand." Then he hesitated. "Should I come with you?"

Picturing Tony in Vig's saloon, I almost laughed. "Not unless you have business in the Spadros slums. But I can go by my apartments first and have Blitz accompany me, if it'd make you feel better."

Tony let out a breath. "It would. We can use the Telephonic Telegraph to contact him."

And so we did. Blitz agreed to meet us at the Pocket Pair saloon.

As Tony turned to go, I caught his arm. "Thank you for caring about my welfare."

He gave me a sad smile. "Of course I do." It seemed as if he wanted to say more, then just patted my hand. "Have a safe trip."

I smiled at him. "Thanks."

"When will you return?"

It was at least an hour there and back, maybe more if there was traffic. "I can't see being so late as dinner."

Tony nodded. "See you soon."

My driver Zeus, Honor, and I got into the carriage, now equipped with fresh horses, and set off. But I wondered at Tony's sudden changes. First angry with me, then caring for my welfare, in the course of an hour. What was this all about?

***

The Pocket Pair saloon filled the corner of 19th and Broadway in the Spadros slums. The area wasn't bad, really, especially when you compared it to my home in the Pot. Just more than a bit disreputable.

And the Pocket Pair thrived on being the most scandalous part of it. Bar, restaurant, dance hall, women dancing half clothed on stage, and live music. Rather less-clothed women entertained customers in the back, for a price. Which wasn't entirely legal, not here amongst the quadrant-folk.

I had my carriage park a few blocks down. The reason was that the man who owned the place, Vig Vikenti, hated the Spadros Family with a passion — and let everyone know it.

So it wouldn't do at all to have me publicly waltz in.

But I knew a few tricks.

I went round on Broadway towards the side door to Vig's rooms (which he now shared with his wife Natalia), sending Blitz in through the front. Cheers and Vig's booming voice emanated from the building.

Vig's door was almost to the end of the block. I went up the steps and gave my old signal: triple-knocked, then rattled it, stopped, and rattled it again. Then I gave two thuds with my fist.

No answer.

But I didn't expect an answer at this time of day, which is why I sent Blitz in the front. I leaned gingerly on the rusted wobbly railing, not trusting my full weight to it, until the door slowly opened and Natalia peeked outside.

Natalia was a bit shorter and older than me, with curly dark hair. She gave me a warm smile. "Ah! You **did** come to visit us!"

I went in, raising my veil to look round.

Vig's room had become a real bedroom. Their bed filled the end to my left, with a lovely white coverlet embroidered in gold and red. Red curtains edged in gold covered the walls, with fishtail swag curtains of the same atop them. Glittering golden tassels ran along every edge. A thickly embroidered woven rug in red, blue, gold, and green covered the floor.

It reminded me of being inside a canopy. "This is beautiful."

Natalia beamed proudly. "Happy you like it."

We went through the door across the room to the back hall. Vig and Blitz stood there.

Vígharður Vikenti, a huge burly man, raised his chin in greeting. "Hey there, my buddy friend. What trouble you in now?"

I chuckled. "Let's talk somewhere private."

I thought he'd bring us down the hall to one of the side rooms, but instead he went back to his bedroom, turning up the lamp. "This as private as it gets!"

Blitz and I exchanged a bemused glance, then went back in. Whilst Vig and Natalia pulled over two chairs, I got a better look at the room. The shelf above their bed was full of portraits, with an icon of the Blessed Dealer in the center. The area across from his bed had a small tea-table set in front of a book-case covering the wall, with many a book and portrait there.

A large chest sat at the end of the bed, with several afghans folded atop it. Vig and Natalia sat there, and we sat in the chairs across from them, me across from Natalia, Blitz across from Vig.

Vig said, "What can we help with?"

I spoke to Natalia. "Do you recall when I came here with three men?" I gestured to Blitz. "He was one, then a man bigger than Vig, then another. He was short, like me, and wore brown."

Natalia nodded.

"Have you seen him? He's gone missing."

Natalia blinked, shaking her head. "Not since, no."

I turned to Vig. "He might have been out front that day I came here through the front wearing mourning. Remember? It was three, four years back, when you got raided after setting up that fight."

Vig laughed. "The cop? I remember. Cost me fifty bucks."

I would have corrected him, but I felt abashed. "I never did properly thank you for that."

"Ah, no mention it." He snorted. "No. Not seen him."

Blitz let out a breath. "Okay. It was a long shot, but if either of you see him, give him a hand, will you?"

Vig got very still. "What's he to you?"

Oh, dear. I realized how this must look. "He's not a Family man. He's a friend." I glanced at Blitz. "To us both. And we got a message he's in trouble." I shrugged. "When we came here before, we were in trouble, so I thought maybe ..."

Natalia reached over to take my hand. "If he come here, we help him. Promise."

I smiled at her, but I felt bleak. Where could he be? "Thanks."

Vig said, "What's the name?"

"Blaze Rainbow," said Blitz.

I said, "He might be going by Graham Morton." I glanced at Blitz. "That's his other name."

Vig chuckled. "I'll have my men let him in if he calls."

I felt relieved. "Thank you." Then I remembered my manners. "I hope you both are well?"

Soft smiles came over their faces, and Vig put his arm around Natalia's shoulders. "The Dealer is making a child for us. If all goes well, after the summer we shall have a son."

I gasped, delighted. "How wonderful!"

"Congratulations," Blitz said.

"I do hope all goes well," I said. "I'm very happy for you."

A knock at the door. "Vig," a man said, then he said something in a language I'd not heard before.

Vig stood, so did we all. "Gotta go."

"Yeah," Blitz said, "we best be going, too." He shook Vig's hand. "I'll be by around eleven."

Vig grinned. "Very good."

We said our goodbyes and left. Whilst on the street to the carriage, I said, "Eleven? Tonight? Who's to be watching the shop?"

"Teddy said he'd stop by," Blitz said, meaning Mr. Theodore. "And there's six watching your place at every hour." He gave me a quick glance. "I'd not leave your treasure unguarded, nor mine."

I felt foolish: of course he'd not leave his family without someone to watch over them, particularly now that Mary was with child. "Forgive me; I spoke without thinking."

Blitz snorted, in an amused sort of way. "No matter."

We got to the carriage, and my driver Zeus called out, "Where to?"

Suddenly, the man looked thinner than I recalled, his hair more thatched with white. I nodded at him, hitched my chin over at Honor, and glanced around with just my eyes.

Zeus chuckled and nodded. I went to Honor and went on tiptoe to speak in his ear. "Bryce Fabrics on 2nd, near Book."

Honor nodded sagely, then helped us inside.

On the way to Eleanora's shop, I told Blitz where we were going.

He said, "Why there?"

It was a good question. If Vig's place was a longshot, well, this was an even longer one. "Because I can't think of any other place he might possibly have gone."

The Error

Bryce Fabrics looked quite different from the windy New Years' Eve I'd first seen it over four years earlier. The front had been sanded and whitewashed, the sign updated, and the inside smelled of fresh fabric.

Eleanora Bryce-Highcard stood beside a woman, examining some cloth. The years had added a few lines to her face and streaks of white to her hair, but other than having discarded her widow's brown, she looked much the same. Joy came over her face when she saw me, but I put my finger to my lips lest she blurt out my name.

"Excuse me a moment," she said to the woman beside her, then came to us. "Dear gods, it's you!" She enveloped me in an embrace. "Have you already taken tea?"

I shook my head.

She smiled fondly at me. "Come in back and we'll get you settled."

She opened the door to her back room, and I raised my veil once the door had closed behind me.

The room looked completely different. It had been tiny before, but now seemed even more so. A wall to the ceiling with a door surrounded David's bed, whilst another surrounded what must be her and her husband's. A small wooden table sat in the center. In the left corner close by lay their stove; to the far right, the door to their back stair. The far left corner held the door to their toilet-room, which was open. Her husband Trey Highcard and her son David Bryce stood fixing a shelf over the sink.

"Look who's come visiting," Eleanora said.

Their eyes grew wide, and I believe mine did as well. David Bryce had grown as tall as his stepfather and slender, with those same dark eyes he and his brothers had shared.

Both his older brothers lay dead now: one murdered by the Bridges Strangler, the other killed trying to stop me from being sold to the Spadros Family. David looked just as I thought his oldest brother Air would have looked at that age, had he lived.

The two came out to see us. "Welcome," Mr. Highcard said, bowing low. "Your presence gives blessings to our home."

Former Constable Trey Highcard had only been in Bridges a few years now, and hadn't lost much of his Dickens accent or ways. I smiled at them both. "Is this David? How you've grown! What is it now, sixteen?"

The boy smiled, blushing, and I felt glad I'd aimed high.

Mr. Highcard said, "Almost."

I turned to Blitz. "Mr. Trey Highcard, Mrs. Eleanora, and their son David." I turned to them. "Mr. Blitz Spadros, my husband's cousin."

"Honored," said Mr. Highcard. The men shook hands.

Blitz extended his hand to David; the boy shied away.

Mr. Highcard let out a breath, putting an arm around the boy's shoulders. "Please take no offense, sir: he's skittish with strangers."

On the way there, I'd told Blitz as much as I dared about what David had gone through. I was pleased to see Blitz nod. "None taken."

"Please," Eleanora said, "sit. Davey, they've not eaten — get them their tea, please."

She went back out to the front, closing the door behind her. Without a word, David went to a cabinet beside the oven which held their tea service upon it: tea-pot, cups, sugar-pot. He filled the tea-pot from a kettle on the stove, and brought the tray to the table. Then he went to a cupboard which lay along the back of their room, and opened it. Bread, cheese, and various other goods were displayed inside. Folding a small counter out, he put a partial loaf of bread upon the counter and began slicing.

As I poured their tea, I glanced at Mr. Highcard, pitching my voice so that only the three of us might hear. "He's doing quite well."

The man nodded. "He is, I dare say quite improved."

Blitz paled, staring at his tea.

Mr. Highcard said, "What brings you to our home?"

"There's something I wished to ask David, if he's able."

David came to our table with a small basket of sliced bread, a small pot of apple jam, and a smaller pot filled with butter. Blitz and I each took a slice and spread butter upon it. Mr. Highcard said, "Davey, you remember Mrs. Spadros, yes?"

He nodded. His eyes were so dark, so like Air's, yet his gaze held a deep emptiness and pain I never wanted to see there.

Blitz put a bit of jam on his buttered bread and began to eat.

I said, "Do you recall the man who helped me find you?"

David pursed his lips, glancing away, but he nodded once more.

We'd found David in a windowless basement, in the dark, alone. Morton had picked up the boy, thin and rocking, taking him into his arms. "Since I brought you back here, have you seen him?"

David looked at me, startled, and shook his head.

I sighed. "Well, I didn't expect you to have. But thank you for telling me."

Eleanora had come in. "Has something happened?"

I turned to look up at her. "A friend has gone missing. David saw the man once, and I wondered if he'd come here. That's all."

"Well, I hope you find him," she said. She looked over the table. "Nice job, Davey — this looks lovely."

The boy smiled shyly, then went into his room and shut the door.

A bell rang out in front, and she left. Feeling a bit hungry, I ate some of the bread, which was quite good. As I sipped my tea, I noticed they only had three chairs. And Mr. Highcard wasn't eating. "We're not keeping you from your tea-time, are we?"

"Not to fret," said Mr. Highcard. The clocks outside struck half past six. "We've had tea already."

"I suppose you must have," I said.

He peered at me. "I hope you're well?"

I shrugged. Was I? I didn't know.

Mr. Highcard picked up his teacup and drank it down. "A young friend once was promoted to high position, over others who relished the power." He set the cup down. "Beware of hangers-on and new friends too interested in your affairs — they seldom mean well."

I nodded. I'd had a line of them, every Wednesday, and most fell into one category or the other.

"I'm glad you came here. I'm more glad you had the wit to disguise yourselves. But you need do better. Wear the blonde wig next time, mum." He gave me a wink and a grin.

Blitz chuckled.

Eleanora bustled in. "Finally, a chance to take breath!"

Mr. Highcard got up and offered her his chair. Then he moved towards the door to the front. "I'll keep watch."

I felt surprised at the changes. When I'd first visited here, the place was quite bare. "Your store does well."

She lowered her voice. "It's your nickel! I have so many here now able to spend a penny to make their children new clothing, or even dresses for themselves. Now I can afford to buy the fabric merchants' ends, rather than beg."

"They made you **beg**?"

She shrugged. "It felt that way. But if I can buy old discard cloth for two pennies a pound, then ..." She smiled then. "I charge a penny a yard here, and you won't find a fabric store for miles round. Them I can't sell flat yardage I cut. Squares for quilting are in demand — I match the colors and sell them as a set when I get enough —"

"Good thinking," Blitz said. "My Ma used to quilt when I was small." He chuckled, eyes distant. "She hated the cutting, could never get the pieces true straight."

"And for the bits and fluff, the paper-mill pays a penny a pound."

"Nice." I set my cup down. "Sounds as if you've found yourself a good trade."

Eleanora gave a sad smile. "I succeeded where my first husband failed." She smiled over at her second husband. "But I don't think I ever would without my Mr. Highcard's help."

Over by the door, he gave her a small bow, smiling fondly.

Their regard for each other touched me. And it was good to see David looking so well. I lowered my voice, leaning forward whilst glancing at the boy's door. "How is he, really?"

She shrugged. "You see for yourself."

"Has he ever spoken?"

"Not one word, not since that day you tried to leave." Eleanora looked sad. "He was such a bright little chatterbox before." She gazed into the distance. "At times, I wish we'd never come here." She took a deep breath, her tone falsely bright. "But then who knows what might have happened in some other city?" Her face turned determined. "No, I keep my mind on our success, on his progress. And one day, perhaps he'll be truly well."

***

I thought of David as we dropped Blitz back at my apartments, and more on the way home. This had all started with David Bryce's abduction. The Red Dog stamp on his alley wall, Morton and I finding him in that pitch-black warehouse and shooting our way out.

What had his captors **done** to him?

I envied Eleanora's strength, to be able to focus on the good as she did. All I ever returned to was the grief. So many around me had died, or were ruined, or suffering because of something I'd done —

*Broken pieces. A ball. Ma's voice, in a fury. "You destroy **everything**!"*

Where did that come from? I'd never recalled it before.

But it was true: I did.

I began sobbing. David Bryce, taken, ruined, simply to torment me for something I still didn't know I'd done. Madame Biltcliffe, shot and left to die in front of me, because I'd gone to see her. Dozens of Tony's kin, manipulated to rise up against him then murdered, because of me. A hundred more dead, defending against a mob who'd risen up due to my mistakes. My baby, crippled, possibly for life.

Even Tenni's relationship with Cheisara spoilt, because of my counsel.

The small window behind me opened, cold air spilling in. "Take heart, dear Queen," Honor said. "All is not lost."

I nodded, merely to let him know I'd heard. But I felt bleak. What hope was there? A scoundrel stalked us, backed by the highest powers in the city. Police followed him, covered up his crimes. What I'd learned about Katie from the coroner's report made that clear.

The coroner's report. I doubted Frank Pagliacci or whoever directed him intended me to see that.

Had they made an error?

Alan Pearson had gotten the report from the coroner. That meant that the man still lived. We must do nothing to put him into peril.

The Report

When I returned, I went straight to Tony. "Come with me."

He'd been working on some papers in his study, but he followed me out to the gardens. "What's this all about?"

"We must protect the coroner on Market Center at all costs — he's the proof that Katie was murdered."

Tony's face went pale, his mouth open, and I remembered I'd told him nothing of the matter.

I took hold of his arms as he staggered. "We best sit down."

There was a bench nearby. The garden lay in twilight, but the sky was still blue.

I told Tony what happened to his little sister as gently as I could.

He put his face in his hands and sobbed for a full half-hour.

I put my arm round his shoulders, holding him as he cried. When he settled, I kissed his hair. "I'm going to find the scoundrel and kill him, if it's the last thing I do."

Tony let out a bitter laugh, turning his tear-streaked face to look up at me. "I'm supposed to be the one saying that!"

I rubbed his back, kissed his shoulder. "Never fret; when he dies, you'll be there. That I promise you."

***

After a while, Tony got up and went inside. I sat listening to the birds, thinking of my own little bird under the flat stone outside my apartments. Then I went in, I started up the stairs towards my room.

"He should **never** have brought her here!" Molly, anguished.

And now I knew where Tony had gone.

I didn't hear his reply as I crept up the stairs, but Molly shouted, "What did you **think** would happen? She only wanted to **be** like her!" Her voice went on, muffled by the closed door, but I couldn't go any further.

Katie only wanted to be like me.

What did that even **mean**? She was smoking, drinking, running out in the streets, dressing like men.

I never dressed like men.

I didn't understand any of it. Now, much later, I understand what Molly meant, how Tony's mother just needed someone, anyone to cast her pain and anger upon.

But back then, I was so young. Back then, all I knew was that Molly blamed me for Katie's death, and I couldn't breathe for the grief that came over me, there on the stair.

Tony came out, his face grief-stricken and angry, and he looked utterly chagrined to see me standing there. "She's only upset. She didn't mean —"

I rushed past him into my rooms, locked the doors, and threw myself onto my bed weeping.

Molly was right. Katie died because of me.

I should have told Katie everything. I should have warned her.

I should have been her friend, not treated her like a child.

Katie loved me, and now she was dead.

Of course she was dead.

I thought then that it was good that Joe left me. Maybe now, he would survive.

***

Tony came to my bed that night, the first night in over a year. We lay together holding hands, peering at each other until Tony fell asleep.

I kissed his hands, lay upon my back. And I felt afraid.

First David, then Josie, then Katie, now Morton.

Tenni said Morton had been beaten so badly that she didn't recognize him at first. Would we find Morton ruined, like David? Maimed, like Josie? Would we find him strangled to death like Katie?

Or might we not find him at all?

I'd told everyone: *I always find who I look for*.

But my luck had to end someday. What if whoever chased and beat Morton decided to leave him in a shallow grave in the countryside? We might never know the truth.

And the longer it took for us to find Morton, the worse it'd be.

***

I woke to Tony shaking my shoulder. "Jacqui, come quickly."

Shanna hadn't been up to open the drapes yet, but pale light shone through the gap between them. "What's wrong?" I sprang up with a terrible thought. "Is Ace —?"

Tony's face had looked dismayed, but a tinge of horror came and went. "Oh, gods, no. He's fine. Still sleeping. Get up, quietly. Master Bresciane is here."

He was? What was **he** doing here?

I rushed to the toilet room, then put on my robe and slippers and hurried down the back stair after Tony.

Master Seven Bresciane stood in the midst of Tony's study as if it were mid-afternoon in the park, rather than five a.m. in Spadros Manor. "What is it?" I said. "What's happened?"

"Please," Master Bresciane said. "Sit."

I did so, beside Tony, us both behind Tony's desk.

Tony gripped my hand tightly. "You said you had bad news."

Master Bresciane nodded his strange body nod, as if bending from mid-chest. "Forgive me for being the one to tell you. But when the *Bridges Daily* editor Mr. Blackberry got the report, he contacted me at once." He turned to me. "He was most concerned that you not first see it in the papers."

"I don't understand." How had Mr. Blackberry known where to contact Master Bresciane? I didn't even know how to contact the man.

Master Bresciane took a deep breath. "Your friend Master Blaze Rainbow was found a few hours ago. He was found dead."

The Body

For a moment, the words didn't make sense. **"What?"**

Tony said, "How did it happen? Where did they find him?"

Here's how Master Bresciane told it:

Many times, when the Families kill someone, they dump the body in the river. There's a group of police they call Precinct Zero, tasked to walk the waterfront around the quadrant at night. Most of what they do involves collecting the bodies that wash up on shore before the tourists arrive for the day.

When the men made their rounds — around one in the morning, it was — they found Morton. But not washed up on shore. Shot in the chest, then tied to the enormous golden statue of Acevedo Spadros I with a sign on him: "Family Pet."

That was what one of the aristocrats called me. Tony had taken her home from her and given it to Inventor Call before he was murdered.

"The minute they saw the sign, they took it down, thank the gods," Master Bresciane said, "so hopefully no one else has seen it."

Tony let out a breath. "Good."

"They don't think he was killed there. No blood at the scene."

He'd been shot, then moved there? Why? And why tie him to the statue? There could be only one reason. "They wanted people to see what they'd done."

Master Bresciane nodded.

"We have to contact the Clubbs," Tony said. "He was living in their quadrant. We have to tell them we didn't do it."

I put my hand on his arm. "Tony." I put my hands beside his face. "Look at me. You can spare a moment to grieve. He was your friend."

Tony swallowed, his eyes going red. "He was yours, too. But we'll have no time for grief if we don't do this, now. Wars have started for less." He took a deep breath, turned to Master Bresciane. "Go to them, right now. And tell them I want to help in any way we can."

Master Bresciane gave Tony a soft smile. "I will, sir."

When he turned to go is when it all hit me. I'd seen Morton about a year ago, right outside my apartments, as I dropped him and Blitz off after Albert Sheinwold's murder. And that was the last I ever saw him.

I could never tell Morton what his help, his support, his watching my back ... what it had all meant to me. The counsel he'd given, his funny ways. He'd hang his own clothes, even though he was a gentleman of means, and always polished his shoes himself.

The main thing which always concerned him was that the Feds thought he'd killed his former business partner Zia Cashout. Had his dogged pursuit to try to clear his name led to his doom? "Zia did this," I sobbed. "I'm sure of it."

Tony put his hand on my back. "Is she the Fed who was after him?"

I nodded. "She killed that Family man. Sheinwold. Sheinwold was one of M-Master Rainbow's informants, the only one who might clear his name to the F-Feds. She's killed them both." Rage boiled up inside me, and I had an image of smashing her face in. "I **hate** her!"

Tony rubbed my back. "We'll find her, Jacqui."

"Why haven't I found her **already**?" A red-haired outsider woman shouldn't be this hard to find. If I'd gone after her with more determination, Morton might still be alive. I put my elbows on Tony's desk, my face in my hands. "Oh, gods. Blitz and Mary. Mr. Hart. Mr. Diamond. They should be told. They were his friends, too."

Tony nodded. "I'll have Ten go to the Diamonds in person."

Even after over a year since Sawbuck's back injury, carriages were painful for him. He'd have to book a private car on the train, but he'd go, if Tony asked him to.

"I'll go to Mr. Hart," I said. "He's still at his Manor, if I recall."

"No," Tony said. "I'll go. You visit Blitz and Mary." He let out a breath. "To lose a father and a friend in such a short time ..."

I nodded. It still didn't feel entirely real. Morton had been like a father to me, and now he was gone. "I'll go up and get ready. I'll visit after morning meeting."

Tony pulled the call bell for Alan, and I left him sitting there, staring at his desk.

I went into my room. The drapes were open, the bed made.

I sat on the side of my bed. How could I tell Blitz and Mary that Morton was dead?

He'd been in their home for years. He was like family.

Gods, they'll be devastated.

A soft knock, then Shanna peeked around the corner. "Oh, good, mum, you're here."

Behind her came Honor with my tray like every morning, setting it down and making to go without ever once looking my way.

I rose, moving to the tea-table to sit. "Shanna, I'll need to go to my apartments today, right after morning meeting."

"Is there something special you wish to wear, mum?"

"I'll need the charcoal one more time." The poor thing was about to fall apart, it'd been mended and patched so much.

"Yes, mum."

Shanna went into my closets.

I took a piece of toast and spread strawberry jam on it.

Shanna put my charcoal dress on the bed.

I sat feeling numb. Was any of this real? Or had I dreamed Morton was dead?

***

I stood at the door of my apartments, hesitating to knock. Signs hung on the wall beside me:

Kaplan Private Investigations

Discreet Service For Ladies

Studio for Hire — Inquire Within

Room for Rent

After I recovered from my fever, I'd told Blitz and Mary to rent out my former bedroom facing the street. But so far, no one who met Mr. Eight Howell's standards had applied.

The door opened; Blitz said, "What are you doing out here?"

"There's something I need to tell you."

Blitz shrugged. "I got word you'd be here today. I was going to fetch your mail." He opened the door wide. "But Eight'll bring it over eventually."

"I won't be here long." I moved past him, through the parlor and into the kitchen. Mary was handing Ariana wooden mixing bowls to put on the lower cabinet shelves nearby.

Ariana dropped the bowls, making a clatter. "Jacqui!" She ran to me, wrapping her arms round my legs.

I smiled down at her, then at her mother. "Sorry to cause a mess."

Mary laughed. "Never you mind. Come on, sweet pie, let's wash the bowls again."

Blitz helped Ariana pick up the bowls as I watched. They were happy, and I was set to spoil it. But Tony was right: it would be terrible for them to hear of Morton's murder from someone else.

Mary looked over at me. "What's wrong?"

"You said you had something to tell us," Blitz said. "What is it?"

I glanced at Ariana. "You best sit down."

Blitz said, "You can go play now."

"Yay!" Ariana threw up her arms and ran out of the door to the hall, and off to their rooms.

I sat, then waited for them to sit before I told them.

After Mary stopped crying, Blitz looked up at me, his eyes red. "What can we do?"

"He was living in Clubb," I said, "so it'll be up to them as far as the funeral. If they let us attend, I'll make sure they let you come with us." I took a deep breath. "If not, we'll have a memorial for him here."

Mary sounded shocked. "You think they might not let us in?"

The Clubbs had been the Spadros Family's ally for a hundred years. Something about Roy's murder seemed to have chilled their feelings towards us, and we'd not heard much from them since. "I honestly don't know. They've yet to formally accept Mr. Anthony as Patriarch, so I have no idea what they're thinking."

Blitz gaped at me. They **still** haven't? It's been over a **year**!"

I looked away. The Clubbs hadn't quite abandoned us, but that's how it felt. "I suppose we're on our own."

***

Of course, we weren't actually on our own: Charles Hart had pledged his help to us. But he was clear across the city, and he had problems of his own.

Like my friend Josephine Kerr, Mr. Hart had refused all callers after the murder of his son. But he couldn't refuse Tony's visit — to refuse the Spadros Patriarch would be to insult Spadros quadrant itself.

Tony was somber when he returned. "They're in mourning, but seemed glad to see me. Until I brought Mr. Hart my news." His head drooped, and he let out a sigh. "They must have been fast friends: the man was heartbroken."

Poor Mr. Hart. It seemed he'd suffered so much during his life. "I hope Mrs. Hart is well?"

Tony shrugged. "She looks awfully pale and thin." His eyes took on a haunted look. "But I can well understand. If my little Ace were to be murdered — and by his own man!" Tony shook his head. "I don't think I could bear it."

"We must only have people around him who love him," I said. "Who would give their lives before they saw him hurt."

Tony nodded.

"And we should begin now." I might have envied the position of Queen, wished for Tony to one day become Patriarch. But now that I saw the reality of it, the more it frightened me, especially knowing a good portion of the city wished us dead. "Let our men know him, and us know them, to see who will really be there if something befalls us."

"Good idea," said Tony. "I'll start meeting with my men, one at a time, with Ace there. How they greet each other will tell much."

The idea of my baby in meetings with trained killers chilled my soul, but these were the boy's kin. And I couldn't think of any better way to judge them. "Have Ten find out what the men say after meeting the boy. A man may dissemble in front of his King, but tell another story in his cups."

Tony chuckled. "Very good."

I felt relieved. We might live the fabled four score and ten, or we might die tomorrow. Either way, I wanted Acevedo to be safe, surrounded only by people who cared for him.

***

Later that day, Dr. Salmon came for one of Acevedo's "periodic check-ups." Moving the boy's leg, watching him at play. Tony and I tried to be there as often as we could, and it was always much the same. Asking Daisy about the boy's bowels, adjusting his medications.

But often, he'd examine me also, Tony holding my hand. Many times, the examination was painful, particularly at first.

That day, though, after I'd dressed, he asked to speak with the two of us in private. So we went to the parlor.

Tony seemed alarmed. "Is all well?"

"Well," the doctor said, "you tell me."

Tony and I exchanged a glance, and it seemed my husband felt just as confused as I did. He said, "What do you mean?"

The doctor smiled to himself. "I don't wish to be indelicate, but ... has there been any pain?"

Tony looked at me, then back at the doctor. "I don't understand."

Dr. Salmon let out a soft laugh. "Then I'll be more direct: when might we expect another heir?"

I realized my mouth lay open, so I shut it.

Tony turned red. "Um, sir ... we ... um, haven't ..."

The doctor said, "I see. You have a beautiful woman here. And a clear duty, both to her as her husband and to your Family as its Patriarch. Might I ask why?"

Tony said, "I thought we couldn't have any more children. Isn't that what you said?"

Dr. Salmon laughed. "Oh, for goodness sake. Children are given by the Dealer as a **gift**, a **result** of your marriage-love. They aren't an end in **themselves**!" He shook his head. "Young people these days —"

I could see Tony felt foolish by the way he held himself. He blurted out, "You said a man spread the infection."

"Oh," said the doctor. "That **is** what your wife's mother said, and the more I investigate the matter, the more I find it to be true."

Tony seemed to notice I watched him, and his face turned chagrined, then defiant. "I fear contracting ... this contagion. There, I said it."

He fears giving it to Gardena. Why wouldn't he just be honest?

Dr. Salmon let out a breath. "Madam, have you any fever?"

I shook my head.

"Any foul odors or discharge below?"

Tony turned red.

I said, "No, sir."

"Do you feel unwell at all?"

I shrugged. "A close friend died yesterday —"

"I'm very sorry," the doctor said.

" — but no, I don't feel unwell."

Dr. Salmon sat back. "There you have it. It's been a year since her illness. Your wife is perfectly well. You are in no danger. You may bed her, or not, as you desire." He hesitated a moment. "Assuming she's willing, of course."

Tony seemed subdued. "Yes, sir."

"I'm glad we could clear the matter up." Dr. Salmon rose. "This time next month?"

Tony sat there, eyes dazed, staring at nothing.

I rose as well. "We'll inform you should our schedules change, sir."

The doctor looked at Tony, then me. "Good day to you."

I walked him to the door, then went back to the parlor. Tony still sat there.

I didn't know what to say to the man. *Tell the truth or I won't bed you?* That seemed petty. But close to how I felt on the matter.

Why had Gardena come here, anyway? At the time, I could find no scenario in which it made sense.

But I had more important things to worry over. I went to Tony, kissed his forehead, and left him to work out whatever went on in his mind on his own.

***

Tony did not come to my bed that night, nor the night after. Which was fine with me. After the talk the doctor gave us, being in the same bed felt too fraught, too embarrassing. I didn't want to go into another round of begging him to be honest about what he was doing. I didn't want to bed anyone out of duty or obligation. Nor did I want to bed him — as the doctor said — merely to gain a child.

To be honest, I didn't want another child. One pregnancy had been quite enough.

Acevedo was a fine boy, but he preferred Daisy. And rightly so: she was with him constantly. He had someone who loved him dearly, who he loved in return.

In a way, it was almost a relief. Those who loved me tended to die; I'd not wish that on anyone.

***

One night after dinner, Jane Pearson came to me as I sat in my study. "Mum, it's about Mrs. Molly. She's hardly eaten in several days. Should I send for the doctor?"

I realized we'd not told the staff anything about Katie's murder. "She's received ... very bad news." I hesitated, not knowing what I should say, or even if I should speak of this at all. "Did you know Miss Katherine well?"

"Why, yes," Jane said. "I've been here since before she was born." She drew back a bit. "She'd changed ever so much. When she was here last. Before ..."

I nodded. Before the attack on the Manor, and all that went later. "Well, you may want to sit."

"No, mum, I couldn't possibly."

I chuckled. Being Queen had its uses. "Even if your Queen commands it?"

She curtsied low. "Yes, mum, forgive me, of course." Yet she still hesitated before sitting.

Once she'd sat, I said, "If you need to talk more about this, you may come to me at any time. But you must tell to no one what I'm about to say, not even your family."

Jane nodded, face pale.

"Miss Katherine did not take her life. We have proof she was murdered."

As Jane Pearson's shocked face crumpled into grief, I thought about Molly, alone upstairs. I didn't hate her. I didn't feel anything for her.

She never needed to threaten me. For all her life, she had Roy to use as a threat, much as Tony and Roy had used Master Bresciane.

The whole Spadros Family used them both, twin daggers raised high over the heads of an entire quadrant. I knew a small part of what had driven Roy Spadros to his blood-soaked end.

Master Bresciane seemed altogether different. I wondered what kept him at our side.

After Jane had finished crying, I warned her again to tell no one, then let her go.

As little as I wanted to, I had someone else to speak to.

***

Molly didn't reply at my knock, but I entered anyway.

She'd been sitting at her tea-table and looked up. "Go away."

I came in, closed the door behind me, and sat in front of her. "Starving yourself will not bring my sister back."

Molly stared at me, mouth open, as if somehow she'd not made the connection before. Then she scoffed, turned away to fold her arms upon the chair's back, her chin upon her arms.

"What in all this could you possibly find funny?"

Molly sighed. "Your speech to poor old Charlie." She let out a soft laugh. "His face afterwards." She turned slowly towards me, her face weary. "Your mother knew about our night together, Jacqui. She advised it."

My mind spun. "What?"

Molly smiled, an amused soft snort coming from her. "We women need connections in the city, a place to go should all in this world of men be lost. By the time I bedded Charles Hart, I no longer hated Roy.

I'd learned enough to pity him, to see he only wanted death, yet feared it like nothing else. I saw it in his eyes when he picked up Tony's gun: he chose his own destruction."

I felt stunned: Roy **chose** to die? Yet I wanted to get to the truth, her truth. Why she did what she'd done. "You feared the Spadros Family might fall."

"And I'd have done anything before I let Tony come to harm." She seemed to collapse upon herself. "That's why all this hurts so much."

I nodded. Tony had taken her deeds in the exact opposite way she intended them, striking her, stripping her of her power, making her a prisoner. And Katie ... "Katie didn't understand."

Molly scoffed. "Not at all." Her face grew sober, pensive. "But then, it seems I've never understood her, either."

That seemed to be true. "My Ma never understood me, either."

"She never wanted to send you away, Jacqui," said Molly. "You were the last link to the Dealers of old. You were the Daughter intended to bring the Cathedral into its rightful place. You were supposed to hand it safe to the Dealers of today when the question was at long last asked."

I felt taken aback. "Oh."

"I don't know everything of it." Molly shrugged, gazing at the table between us. "I'll never be one of them. But I've heard enough to know you should never have been brought here. I told Roy the same when you first arrived, and was struck for it."

That Molly took that position surprised me. "I'm sorry."

She shook her head, just a little. "I never thought you'd sign the betrothal contract. We had a plan to get you out, but we were afraid. Of many things. I could've gotten you out more than once, but I was afraid. Mostly of what he might do if we were caught. Then the day came when Roy walked in with glee on his face and your signature in his hand, and I've hated myself ever since."

I felt a huge empty stillness inside, almost as if what she said wasn't real. Then I rose. "Thank you for telling me."

Then I went into the hall, around to my rooms, and sat on my bed. And I realized: the night Air died, and the Masked Man went away for the last time, I'd always assumed Ma had been crying for Mr. Hart. But she wasn't.

She was crying for me. For all that she'd hoped would happen for me that probably would not.

And it made the words of my great-grandmother, the Eldest, now dead, more clear: *...all I see before me is a mad rush to destroy yourself, the last remnant of my line, and that I can't stand by and idly watch ...*

I was the Daughter intended to bring the Cathedral to its rightful place when the question was asked?

I couldn't think. My heart was going like a galloping horse. I couldn't breathe.

I pulled the bell for Shanna, three times. I couldn't breathe. I couldn't breathe. "Help!"

Honor rushed in, then Shanna. Shanna said, "What's wrong?"

"I can't breathe! Oh, gods." I felt more frightened than anytime in my life. I couldn't get any air. "Help me."

Shanna said to Honor, "Get the doctor." She tried to get me to lie down. "Rest, mum, you'll feel better."

I pushed her away. "No!" I feared if I lay down, I'd never get up. "I can't breathe!"

Tony rushed in. "What's happened?"

Shanna looked up at him. "I don't know, sir. She says —"

"I can't breathe!" I started sobbing. "Oh, gods, I'm so afraid."

Tony sat beside me, took me in his arms. "The doctor's on the way. Here, I'll breathe with you."

Somehow, him being there made me feel better. I put my face in his chest and wept.

The doctor got there some time later, it seemed like an eternity. But Tony just kept saying, "Breathe with me," and it helped me see I could breathe after all.

When Dr. Salmon came in, Tony looked up at him. "She's had an episode, like the one I had. Remember? During her trial?"

Dr. Salmon nodded.

I peered up at Tony; he looked blurry. "You had this too?"

He smiled at me, smoothed my hair. "I did." He said to the doctor, "I'll let you see to her."

Dr. Salmon listened to my chest and back with his device, felt my wrist, shone a light into my eyes. All the while Tony and Shanna stood watching, arms crossed.

They looked a pair, and the thought made me laugh.

This made Dr. Salmon laugh. "Well, if you're laughing, the problem must be over." He smiled warmly at me. "At least for now."

Then I felt foolish. "I'm sorry to be such a bother."

Dr. Salmon patted my shoulder. "No trouble at all, my dear." He looked at Tony. "She may engage in whatever she feels comfortable."

Alan came to the door. "Sorry to bother you, sir, mum, but Master Bresciane and Master Hogan have arrived. You said you wanted —"

I lunged forward. "Yes!" I had to hear what they'd learned.

Tony hesitated. "Seat them in the parlor; we'll be there shortly." To the doctor, he said, "Thank you for coming out at such an hour."

"It's of no consequence," the doctor said. "But your housekeeper was telling me you might have another patient here?"

"Oh," I said to Tony. "Mrs. Jane said your mother wasn't eating."

"Very well," Tony said grudgingly. "You may as well see to her whilst you're here."

Shanna and the doctor left, and Tony turned to me. "What happened before all this sickness began?"

I sat quietly, thinking. "I went to see your mother ... she told me ..." I didn't want to say it to him.

He spoke softly. "What did she say to you?"

I didn't want to tell him. I was afraid to tell him. But then I remembered what he told me that night in the meadow: *No more secrets, no more lies. That's all I ask.* "That I was never meant to be here. That she and my Ma tried to get me out but feared Roy would harm us all if he caught us. That I was supposed to be the one on the appointed day to hand the Cathedral back to the Dealers!" I began bitterly sobbing once more. "But I ruined it. I ruined **everything**, because I thought I knew better than **everyone** else."

Tony just held me, rocking until my weeping slowed. Then he pulled back, ducking his head to look into my eyes. "I don't want you **ever** to go in there again. Do you hear me? That woman is poison."

I gaped at him. "Tony! She's your ... your **mother**!"

"It's hardly been an hour since dinner. So you spent what, ten minutes with her? And I come to find you like this?" He shook his head. "She agitates every bit of peace here. You're not the only one I've come to find in a state over the things she's said. And I won't have it." He shouted, "Mr. Pearson!"

Alan came rushing up the stairs and into the room. "Yes, sir?"

"The maids must remove anything from my mother's room that she can't put on herself. They will enter only to bring in her food and take her tray. They will not speak to her, and they will plug their ears before entering. A guard is to enter with them to ensure the maid does not speak to her or allow any messages to be passed." He glanced at me. "I've had one maid come to me already with a note my mother asked to be sent." He snorted, his tone bitter. "Another guard will stand outside, door open, to observe that the guard inside is not enticed in any way. But know this: any further commotion and I will have her — and anyone helping her — put in my father's basement room. Tell the staff now."

I didn't want to contradict him further in front of Alan. But once he left, I said quietly, "We need her, Tony. She has information we need."

Tony scoffed. "You don't think I have ways of getting it from her?"

I gasped. "You would put your own Ma to the **question**?"

Tony laughed. "I hardly think it would come to that. But to answer you, yes, if she balks. This game we play is much too important to let any one card cause the round to fail." He stood, holding out his hand. "Do you feel well enough to go?"

I nodded, took his hand. "I do."

Morton had been my friend. I had to know anything the two men downstairs might have learned.

The Prisoner

As we descended the stairs, Tony told me he had given ten dollars to each of the policemen who found Morton's body and kept it quiet. He'd given twenty to the detective, telling him there'd be twenty more if he got information that helped the Families find the killer.

I imagine this made them well-motivated.

Master Bresciane and Sawbuck stood in the parlor, both looking tired and somber.

Sawbuck had been given the minimum courtesy — a few minutes in front of a curt, stern Julius Diamond, then sent on his way.

Master Bresciane said, "For a man who merely lived in Clubb quadrant, I was surprised at the depth of their sorrow at the news."

I thought over this. "For a time, Master Rainbow worked for them. And he had a way about him that touched people. He seemed to truly care for their welfare in a way that was endearing."

Master Bresciane drew back. "Then I grieve that we never met."

As we walked the two men to the door, Dr. Salmon came down the stair to Tony. Once Master Bresciane and Sawbuck had left and the front door shut behind them, he glanced at me. "Sir, there's something I must speak privately with you about."

"Anything you wish to say to me, my wife can hear," Tony said.

The doctor glanced at me again, then at Alan, who stood at his area near the door, then at Tony. He spoke so only Tony and I might hear. "Your mother. How long do you plan to keep her prisoner?"

Tony let out a bitter laugh. "So she's gotten to you, too."

Dr. Salmon blinked, giving a small shake of his head. "Nonsense. She's your **mother** —"

"Who has defied two Patriarchs, betrayed three, and shows no remorse. I could've had her killed. Perhaps I should have."

"But sir —"

"No," Tony said. Then he took a deep breath. "The Spadros Family appreciates your past service to my mother. You will continue to serve my Family as before. But from now on, another doctor will see to her."

Dr. Salmon stood there, mouth open.

"Go," said Tony. "You're dismissed."

I watched the old man leave, then turned to Tony. "Do you think it's wise to call in another doctor, when we're in such turmoil?"

"My mother is perfectly well. She just needs some time."

"But —"

"There will be no other doctors for her," Tony said, face set. "Ever. Her fate is in the hands of the gods now."

I could see that Tony would not be swayed, so I went to bed. But I felt afraid. Dr. Salmon had been our doctor for generations. And I remembered the time he told me Tony had beaten him for not revealing I'd been injured by Roy. We had few allies enough; we couldn't bear to lose any more of them.

***

To my surprise, the detective, a man named Split Freeroll, returned the next morning with a report. Whilst we were at breakfast, to be precise. "The area was well-searched: your man was murdered elsewhere. Not even a bullet-mark or a bit of blood on the statue."

Tony frowned, glancing at me. "I'd prefer you not go into detail."

"Yes, sir," the man said quickly. "Of course, sir. We did find some boot-prints leading up to the statue. We took marks of them and are looking through records to find the type."

"Good," Tony said. "What else?"

The man paled. "Well, that's it, as yet. We're trying to retrace his movements, but as yet we've not found anyone in the area that recognizes him."

Morton was masterful at disguises. If Morton didn't want to be recognized, they might search for months and not find anyone who recognized him.

Tony said, "Return when you have something useful, sir." He flicked his hand as if brushing a speck off his desk. "Good day."

Alan stepped forward. "Sir, I'll show you out now."

Once the man had left, Tony said, "I hate hangers-on. What did he think, he was going to get a twenty for telling me what I already knew?" He scoffed. "Good gods."

I chuckled at that.

"So have you heard word from the Clubbs?"

I shook my head. "Nothing in my mail."

Tony looked worried. "I don't want to miss his funeral like we had to with Master Jonathan."

I agreed. Being turned away by the Diamonds at the bridge in front of everyone ... it was most upsetting.

***

I should've known that one day we'd find Morton dead. Between his playing both sides with the police, his working for all four Families, and him being the only one left who could identify Frank Pagliacci ... well, he could never have expected to cash out. His bluffs had been called; he'd been forced to fold.

But it didn't make the pain of his passing any easier to bear.

Tony asked me to join him in his study after dinner. A fire was lit, although it was almost getting too warm for one. But I enjoyed just sitting with him, watching the fire as he read.

Alan came to us: we had a visitor, a Mr. John Selot. "He says he has a message for your ears only, the both of you."

Tony and I glanced at each other. What could the message possibly be about, at this hour?

A hooded and cloaked figure bent over a dark-stained wood walking-stick stood in the front hall, apparently unwilling to go further. He wore black; his cloak was such a dark brown that it looked close to black. Even his fine leather gloves were black. As he moved I caught a glimpse of his chin, covered by a black knitted material.

Tony said, "May we help you?"

The man said nothing.

I said, "Would you like to go to our parlor? We can speak there."

Mr. Selot's voice was muffled, low. "Is there a place we can speak without being overheard?"

Something about his voice seemed familiar.

"There is, sir," Tony said. "Follow me."

I let Mr. Selot walk ahead of me for two reasons. One, so I might observe him. "All's well," I told Alan. "You may go about your business."

I wanted to see if I might deduce who this man was.

The cloak and mask reminded me of Mr. Hart, who used to come to my mother dressed in this manner when I was small. But this couldn't be Mr. Hart — the man was taller, more slender, and he moved like a man decades younger.

Tony led us into the gardens. I didn't know any John Selot. So I had no idea who this might be.

I bent to take my pistol from its place on my calf holster and slipped it into my pocket. I kept my eye upon the man for a second reason: if he were an assassin, he'd have to reach for a weapon, or make some threatening move. If he did, I'd shoot him from behind.

Once we passed out of view of the house and into the wide meadow, Tony stopped and faced the man. "No one listens here. What news do you bring?"

The man moved a hand; I drew my pistol.

He looked back; the balaclava he wore only showed blue eyes and pale skin. His eyes went from startled to amused. "Come round, Mrs. Spadros; I'm sorry to frighten you. I mean you no harm." He dropped the cane and spread his hands wide. "See, I'm unarmed."

I came round to stand beside Tony, who looked alarmed at my gun. But I felt alarmed at this man being here. I pointed my pistol at him. "Who are you? What do you want?"

He took the balaclava off, his thick golden hair wild underneath.

It was Lancelot Clubb.

The Fiends

I cleared the chamber and put the gun in my pocket. "You **did** give me a fright. What on earth are you doing here, dressed like that?"

Lance chuckled. "I could, of course, have come here in the carriage of the Clubb Heir with all my men round me. Surely you of all people would know how ill-advised that might be."

I felt silly. Of course he had to show up this way. The Clubb Heir at Spadros Manor, after a year of silence? The frenzy in the papers over the fact that the Clubbs hadn't given their allegiance to Tony after Roy's death would start all over again if they thought some message was being sent. "I'm sorry about Master Rainbow," I said. "I know he was your friend."

Morton had volunteered to help Lance learn basic things his parents apparently hadn't taught him. Like how to tell if someone were lying.

Lance nodded soberly. "I find it hard to believe he's dead."

Tony nodded quickly, several times. "I got a glimpse of his body." He turned aside. "Dear gods, I wish I had not." He looked as if he was going to say more and decided not to, for which I was grateful.

Lance stood there, mouth open, pale in the moonlight. "Thank you for telling me," he said to Tony. "I'll make sure to inform my father."

Morton had said he was a friend of Lance's father, Mr. Alexander, and I found it touching that Lance would wish to shield his father in this way.

We stood for a moment silent as crickets chirped round us.

Lance reached into his breast pocket. "My father sends this." He handed a slim envelope to Tony. "That's about the funeral. Anyone who wishes to come with you may, of course, but —"

Tony gave Lance a sad smile. "You don't want just anyone knowing where it'll be. It'd be a prime target, all those Patriarchs in one place."

Lance's eyebrows raised. "I hadn't considered that."

Tony let out a breath. "Well, you learn to, very quickly, or you won't last long. Not in the Business." He sounded as if he knew this from experience.

What had happened to him those years I'd been gone?

Lance turned to me. "Mrs. Spadros, a Constable was detained in the matter. Several said he fought with Master Rainbow last year. On Market Center?" He shrugged. "In any case, he has an alibi to cover the time of death. But your name came up — the man said he'd been working with you and Master Rainbow on two cases. Is that true?"

Ah. "Paix Hanger?"

Lance nodded. "The same."

"Yes," I said. "He helped us more than once."

"Very good, I'll let them know this man's story checks out."

I almost laughed. "I hope he's not still detained!"

Lance's eyes went wide. "Certainly. Until we could corroborate his story. My father is willing to go to any lengths to find Master Rainbow's killers."

The vigor in Lance's voice surprised me. What power Morton had, to make so many love him! "We'll do whatever we can to help."

"There is one thing," said Lance. "What would he have liked? For his burial."

I considered it a moment. "He loved fine clothing, always in shades of brown. And he loved the Aperture." I smiled to myself, feeling moved. "He would like to be placed where he might see it."

Lance nodded. "Easily done."

I said, "What else might we do?"

"I'm sure you're doing your own investigation," Lance said, "seeing as he was your ..."

Men. "You can say it: he was my business partner."

Lance glanced quickly at Tony, then at me.

I scoffed. "There was nothing unseemly about it!" I considered the matter. "In some ways, he was like a brother to me."

Tony's gaze drew inward. He'd always wanted a brother, and the closest people to that were either gone or dead.

Lance said, "Me too." He let out a breath. "Forgive me: I had no right to cast aspersion."

I shrugged. I was a Pot rag, I was a woman, and worst of all, I was a married upper woman daring to engage in business. If Lance thought the matter odd, the rest of the city did as well.

"I've offended you," Lance said, "where I meant only to bring comfort. I'll take my leave."

He turned to go, but Tony said, "You've come such a long way. Won't you at least take refreshment?"

Lance turned a bit to his right, looking at us over his shoulder with a wry smile on his face. "No need. But I thank you for your offer." He faced us then. "I must be back before the sun, so that none of my servants marks my absence." He replaced his balaclava, cast the hood over his face, and left us standing in the meadow.

We followed, if only to let our people know we were well.

Tony stuffed the envelope into his pocket, moved his cane to his other side, and took my hand as we walked. "It must be difficult, your every move remarked upon."

Wasn't Tony's every move remarked upon? "I don't understand what you mean."

Tony shrugged, a small smile on his face. "No matter."

As we walked, I thought about Morton. He'd been my friend, my ally, a Queensman if not in vows, in practicality. We'd lived under the same roof for years, eaten together, talked and laughed together, fought together. Morton had saved my life more than once.

And now he was dead.

He'd sent a message to me, hoping I'd save his life, and I failed. I failed him, just like I'd failed everyone who'd trusted in me.

Tony handed me his handkerchief, there on the veranda. "We'll find who did this, never fear."

I wiped my eyes, but I didn't feel so hopeful back then. I'd not even found who took David, and it'd been four years now. I'd not found who killed his older brother a few weeks later, let alone the rest. Yes, we had clues, we had thoughts. We suspected Frank Pagliacci took the boy. We knew Herbert Bryce was murdered by the Bridges Strangler. I suspected Frank Pagliacci either was the Bridges Strangler, or was working with him.

But another fiend was out there, a woman calling herself Black Maria, who shot people in the chest then left them to die. Could **she** have killed Morton?

My first impulse had been to blame Zia. But on thinking of it further, I suspected this to be the woman who had shot at Morton after Marja's shooting. This woman had visited Madame Biltcliffe. Madame had described this woman to me before she was shot, saying as she died that this was the same person.

Morton could identify this woman as part of the Red Dog Gang. He could identify Frank Pagliacci as her accomplice. They'd both been trying to kill him all this time, killing at least one Diamond man in their hunt for him.

And now it looked like they'd succeeded.

I handed Tony back his handkerchief. "Thank you." Then I went up to my rooms, got undressed, and lay in bed.

But I didn't sleep.

Zia Cashout was still out there. The former Federal Agent was now working with Frank to murder every one of her informants. It seemed she wanted to remove anyone who could link her to her old life. They'd killed the Spadros man Albert Sheinwold; Morton was the only one left to testify against her.

These people were backed by the Mayor, the police, the aristocracy. They sent mobs to murder our Patriarch and burn his home.

When the Spadros Family couldn't even stop the Bridges Strangler from ravaging their own slums, how could we stop the rest?

The Spies

The morning paper had this headline blazoned across it:

DISGRACED MAYOR DEAD

Apparently the man died of natural causes, but with the company he kept, who knew for sure? He could have died any number of ways, but if the police were told to say it was natural, then natural it was.

Shanna came in. "What is it, mum?"

I let out a breath. "Mayor Freezout is dead."

"But that's good, right? He tried to have you hanged!"

I nodded. He did. But somehow I couldn't bring myself to rejoice in an old man's death, not when so many younger were dying in the city. "I can't help but think this is part of the plan."

"What do you mean?"

I sighed. Explaining it to her would take much too long. "Never mind." Then I felt amused. "To answer your question, I suppose it **is** one less scoundrel to worry about." I only wished Amelia had lived to see it: she'd hated the man.

All evidence pointed to Peter and Amelia Dewey as the Red Dog Gang's spies within Spadros Manor. It made sense, now that I look back on it.

Peter was our Stable-master: because he had to get the horses ready, every time we went out, he knew well in advance.

Amelia was my lady's maid: I had her in my confidence for almost a decade. I felt dismayed every time I considered it. What had I told her? What did our enemies now know?

The pair had good motive to harm us. Roy Spadros had violated Amelia, forced her to bear him a son, forced Peter to pretend the boy was his. Peter had tried to say he loved the boy as his own. But looking into little Pip's face, the face so like the man who'd violently defiled your wife ... a man you were forced to serve, to bow to, every day ... eventually, he'd abandoned the boy, just as Amelia had.

I hoped young Pip, far off in Paris learning to become a Chef, had finally found a way to be happy.

"Are you well, mum? You haven't touched a thing."

I peered at the tea and toast sitting before me, now cold, seeing it for the first time. "I suppose I'm not very hungry as yet."

Shanna looked at me, compassion in her eyes. "I remember a few years back when my friend was killed."

"Oh?"

Shanna nodded, face sad. "Mrs. Pearson used to take me and the other sculleries to the river on our day off. Sometimes Rob and the stable-boys would come too. That's where I met him, down at the river. His name was Bestia. He and his Papa ran a food cart there." She shook herself. "But I'm going on too much. He'd gone out with his friends drinking after work. Went out back of the pub alone for a smoke." She shrugged. "That Strangler got him."

"Good gods! I'm so sorry." How many more people's lives had been touched? This young man's father, their customers, his friends. The grief, the anger at us for not doing anything to stop it.

I wish I knew what more I could do!

Shanna shrugged. "I know you're trying, mum. You and Mr. Anthony. But a lot of people don't think so."

This wasn't too surprising. "Really."

"They think you don't care. Some say you like it, get rid of the low-cards. 'Cause we don't pay much in fees."

"Who says all **this**?"

Fright crossed her face. "No one, mum. I shouldn't have spoken."

"No, I'm glad you did. I mean no one any harm. But if people are spreading this, it had to have come from somewhere. Maybe from our enemies, the ones backing this man."

Shanna gasped, and I immediately knew I'd said too much. "People are **backing** the Strangler? They **want** him to kill us?"

Since I'd started the play, even if I didn't mean to, I'd best continue. "Yes, and they mean to use him to finish what those men started out front last year." I lowered my voice. "I believe the true target, well, besides Mr. Roy, was Master Acevedo." John Pearson had taken a dozen rounds protecting the boy with his body.

Shanna looked as if she might faint.

I knew she'd refuse to sit, and I didn't want to press her. "Grab onto the back of the chair, if you must, dear," I said. "I admit that when I realized this, I felt much the same way."

She clutched the back of the chair, looking more steady.

"If you want to leave me, you may do so. No one will harm you, I'll see to that. But something just came to me: it's unfair for you not to know what we're up against. You know what happened to Mrs. Dewey, right?"

Shanna nodded, her eyes wide, her face pale. She made the sign of the Board, her arms crossing to grasp her shoulders, and turned to bow to the North. Towards the Cathedral. "May she receive better cards next time."

I nodded. People here still bowed to the Cathedral, though it'd been sacked these hundred years. "She had cause against us. But she let that cause leave her open to bribery —"

Shanna gasped, hands to her mouth.

"— which led to betraying her Family." I shook my head. "Amelia Dewey both hated and loved me. But at the end, she chose hate."

I thought over her words, her actions, up to when she left me half-dressed here in my rooms. "She must have known what Peter did —"

Shanna nodded. So she knew that he cut the wires to the large bell before the attack.

"— yet she chose to conceal it. She thought she could escape the Family." A deep sorrow welled up inside me. "But I don't think anyone really can."

***

I had an idea, but I didn't want to do it without discussing it with Tony first. At breakfast, I said, "Might we speak privately, once we're done here?"

Tony nodded.

"It's something I wish to discuss with the staff."

Tony nodded again. "Mr. Pearson, would your people step outside for a moment?"

Alan gestured to the waiters and maids, and they all moved into the hall.

Tony continued eating as if I'd said nothing. "What's wrong?"

What wasn't wrong? "I had a discussion with my lady's maid just now. We can go into that later, but I feel it's unfair for the staff not to know the entirety of the situation."

Tony didn't change his demeanor one bit. "And why is that?"

"Mr. Howell believes there are more spies in Spadros Manor." I felt shaky. Could it be true?

Tony chuckled.

This angered me; I wanted him to listen. "You want to rule differently than your father. And in that speech you gave you said no harm can come from the truth." I took a deep breath. "If the staff knows how important this is to them, you won't have to do a thing."

Tony put down his fork. "Very well; we'll discuss it with them today." He called out, "You may return now."

He smiled and nodded at them as they entered, thinly veiled curiosity on their faces. "Be at peace, at morning meeting, everything will be revealed. Possibly more than you wished." He turned to Alan. "Everyone must be at morning meeting. Make sure they can all be seated. You may want to start calling people in at once."

***

The groundsmen, the shepherds we'd brought over from Spadros Castle, the scullery maids yawning, the stable-boys — Honor was right, almost men — all packed together, each with their own chair. Well, most — we'd had to clear the tables so some might sit atop them. Tony's men stood outside each of the open doors, peering in.

I thought Tony did a good job. He spoke of being attacked four years ago in his Party Time factory. He spoke about Crab and Duck, who betrayed us to our enemy, a man calling himself Frank Pagliacci.

A few of the women and girls looked disturbed at this, particularly the young kitchen maid I'd seen mourning Duck's death shortly after.

Tony spoke of the Red Dog Gang and Frank Pagliacci's work for them. How the man had taken a boy to lure me to them, for what reason we still didn't know. How I'd set my task over the past four years to learn who these men were and why they targeted our Family.

Many looked at me with new respect.

And I felt ashamed. Tony made it sound so noble, as if I did the Family a service, instead of betraying them all by leaving them to chase after something that wasn't even real.

"You may have read about the Bridges Strangler in the news, and how former Mayor Chase Freezout has done nothing to stop him. Your Queen has come to believe that the Mayor is — was — allied with this Red Dog Gang, and that Frank Pagliacci is the Bridges Strangler."

The whole room, it seemed, gasped. Shanna looked very pale.

"Peter and Amelia Dewey revealed themselves as spies for these men when they cut the wires to the large bell before the attack on this home, so we would be unable to call for aid. But our Queen's man believes there to be yet another." He stopped then, scanning the room. "One of you knows who that man or woman might be. Anything you know might help. No harm will come to you."

Everyone looked at each other: some afraid, some angry, some thoughtful. The maid who'd mourned Duck's death began to cry.

"I'll give you until dinner to come forward. That is all." He got up, so everyone else did, too. Then he sat. "Let's see what happens."

The maid who'd mourned Duck's death ran from the room wailing. Tony gestured to one of his men to follow. The rest broke into small groups, talking amongst themselves. Several women — Shanna and Jane included — were talking to one of the scullery maids, a girl of perhaps fourteen. She looked terrified, but the other women half pulled, half pushed her up to us.

Jane said, "This is Millie. She has something to tell you."

The Security

Millie was not a tall child, and with us sitting in our chairs on the platform, we loomed over her. I got up and squatted, so our faces were close to the same level. Then I took her hand. "Millie, dear, how long have you been here?"

She curtsied, her hands still in mine. "Three years, mum."

"And where were you before that?"

"The poorhouse. The Dealers raised me."

"I see. And did you like it there?"

She hugged herself, and I pictured her, a girl of eleven, hugging a stuffed doll. "Yes, mum. But the food is better here."

I felt amused. "Millie is a pretty name. I've never heard it before."

"It's short for Millicent, mum. One of the Dealers had just folded, and they gave me her name. When I got there." She looked uncertain. "Or so they said. I was just a baby."

"Well, Miss Millie, what news?" I glanced at the women around her. "These ladies seem to think you have something to say."

Millie hesitated.

"No matter what it is, no harm will come to you."

She nodded. "I wasn't supposed to see. But ... Zelene had a man outside. By the stables. He gave her flowers, and they were kissing."

"Zelene ... " I couldn't place the name.

Jane said, "She's one of the kitchen maids, mum."

"Oh, yes." I pointed. "That one that just ran off?" She'd been the kitchen maid left after Tony had my friends from the Pot killed for slandering him. I looked up at Tony, who sat in his chair still, watching with amusement.

He nodded. "I told them to be gentle. But she looks more grieving than thieving."

Millie's face grew alarmed. "No, Zelene would never steal!"

I patted the girl's hand. "We don't think she did. Is there anything else we should know?"

"Well, she saw me looking, and said I should never tell, that she'd be whipped for it."

I looked up at Tony, who shrugged. I turned to Millie. "I can't promise anything. But I'm happy you told me. Did she tell you anything else?"

Millie nodded. "I asked his name. He looked too fancy to be one of us." She looked up at Tony. "I thought him to be one of your men, sir. But Listy said no, he weren't. He didn't like the fellow."

Tony leaned forward. "So what was his name?"

Millie drew back, eyes wide. "Frank."

Tony leaned back. "As I thought." He called over one of his men. "Get a police artist down here. I want Zelene, Listy, and Millie to each give a description and portrait of the man. Separately, mind you."

The man nodded and left.

Millie let go of my hands and curtsied to Tony. "What's going to happen to Zelene, sir?"

Tony sighed. "It depends on whether she'll help us."

***

As I'd thought, Tony's man found Zelene weeping on her bed. Tony wouldn't let me be part of speaking to the servants: he thought both of us there might be too intimidating. Instead, he had Jane Pearson there to help him.

What they learned was alarming.

Frank Pagliacci had been hanging around Spadros Manor for some time. Peter Dewey had introduced Frank to Zelene shortly after Duck's death. The two had formed an attachment, and after I'd left

Spadros Manor, Jane had gone to Tony because Zelene had come with child, and the man hadn't returned.

Normally, a maid come with child would be dismissed. But I'd just left Spadros Manor, and Tony's men were rising up against him: Tony was in no state to dismiss anyone. He told Jane to take care of it.

"We were short on staff, mum," Jane said. "Things were in such turmoil — I didn't know who we might trust to take on. And she was a good girl otherwise. I had no idea the man was your enemy!"

So Jane took Zelene to a midwife and had the problem taken care of. Zelene went back to work, and all seemed well.

Then one day, after the problem with the trains was fixed, Frank came back. At first, Zelene didn't want to see him: it'd been several years, and she'd moved on with her life. But he started coming around once every few months. He hadn't been by since the attack on Spadros Manor ... until a week ago. That was when Millie and Listy both saw him with her.

I felt concerned. "What has Zelene told him?"

Tony hesitated. "She can't — or won't — say much. Before the child, she told him all about her day. After he returned, though, she felt unsure of his motives. She still has feelings for the man, but ..."

"She doesn't trust him." I sighed. "The poor girl."

"Well, I'll have his portrait and description shown to all my men. If he comes back here, we'll catch him."

I shook my head. "How did he get on the grounds in the first place? I fear someone has been letting him pass under our very noses." And now that Tony had tipped our hand, Frank's helper would tell Frank we were on to him.

I told Tony about what Mr. Howell had done with my apartments: no one man did a second duty within a year. All were personally verified, neither knew the other well, and he debriefed each one separately, to make sure their stories matched.

Tony sat back, mouth open. "I'm impressed. But I have dozens of men encircling the Manor. How is this to be done?"

An amusing thought came to me. "See if Master Bresciane would be willing to take on the task."

Tony didn't laugh. "Half the men would quit; the other half would flee, and we'd have to hunt them down." He sighed. "Ten will berate me for this, but I'll have to have the entire lot changed and find new men, who will keep better watch."

I doubted Frank would return, but it did make me feel better about the security here. To have the Bridges Strangler, right here on the Spadros Manor grounds! It gave me a chill.

Zelene had been very lucky indeed.

***

The next morning's news had this headline:

RIOTING ON MARKET CENTER

Apparently, all sorts of commotion had gone on in response to Chase Freezout's death. Storefronts damaged, looting, several dead.

I felt concerned about my property, the apothecary's shop that I'd been renting out these many years. So I sent a message to my tenant, hoping all was well.

Or rather, I sent Honor with a package for Blitz, instructing him to send the letter on. The Queen of Spades sending anything directly by messenger gathered nothing but attention on the recipient. And if my tenant was well, I didn't want any harm to come to him.

I'd gotten dressed for the day when Alan knocked on my bedroom door. "Mr. Anthony wishes to speak with you."

"I'll be right there." We had a few minutes before morning prayers, so I followed Alan along. But rather than going to the staff room, he stopped at Tony's study.

Alan knocked. Tony said, "Come in." Alan opened the door.

Inside stood three Apprentices, their calf-length white coats rumpled and their hair in disarray. They bowed; I curtsied to the floor.

Which seemed to astonish them. Why, to this day I don't know.

Tony seemed amused. "Come sit by me," he said. A chair had been already placed to Tony's right, so I sat there.

"These men have come to me," said Tony, "with a tale you will wish to hear." He gestured at one with his chin. "Please tell your Queen what's happened."

The tale was indeed a remarkable one: in short, Spadros Inventor Montgomery Arrow had disappeared.

The Enemies

The Inventor hadn't come down to breakfast, so his Senior Apprentice, a Master Piros Gosi, went to the Inventor's rooms, thinking the man might be ill. But he found the rooms empty. Unslept-in, with all Inventor Arrow's possessions gone.

His Apprentices had searched the grounds and questioned the men Tony had put there to guard him.

They claimed not to have seen him go.

"He's left us," one of the other Apprentices said. "Why?"

Why indeed. "Has anything unusual happened lately?"

The Apprentices looked at each other, hesitation in their eyes. Finally the Senior Apprentice said, "He's been seeing someone. For some time." He glanced away. "A woman. It's quite distracted him." He glanced at the others. "We were going to have a meeting about it, to ask if he'd preferred to step down."

Hmm, I thought.

Technically, Inventors were never allowed to marry. This had been flouted by both the former Diamond Inventor — Julius Diamond's father — and by my half-brother, the former Inventor Etienne Hart.

But our former Inventor, Maxim Call, had been most strict about it, not even allowing his Apprentices to form attachments. I'd heard that several had been dismissed over the years for doing so. "Can you tell me more about this woman?"

They all glanced at Tony, who nodded. "This was the part which I thought would interest you the most."

Good grief. So Tony already knew. Then why did the Apprentices hesitate? "Very well: proceed."

The woman had red hair, an outsider's accent, and pale skin. She was "quite comely", slender and of a medium height.

I said, "That has to be Zia Cashout."

The Apprentice flinched, murmuring to themselves. One said, "How did you know?"

"The woman is in league with our enemies," Tony said sternly, "and now they have him, along with everything he knows."

***

Tony instructed the Apprentices to go home and choose their successor. If Inventor Arrow chose to abandon them and side with our enemies, he should be stripped of his title. If he'd been taken, they could reinstate him as they wished.

Tony didn't mention the obvious: once Zia was done with him, it was likely we'd find him dead.

I hoped we would find Inventor Arrow amongst the living. He might be deluded, but I'd seen too many die in the past four years to wish death upon him.

Once they left, Tony told Alan to run morning prayers, and took me out to the gardens. Once past where anyone might listen, he turned to me. "Jacqui, this is bad."

I'd gathered that, but I felt unsure how bad he meant.

"They have our Inventor. He went willingly. The Red Dog Gang has been speaking with him for some time."

"Yes, and ..." I didn't actually understand why Tony was so upset, but I wanted to get the full picture.

"Don't you see? They **know**." His voice dropped to a whisper, as if he feared even being overheard out here. "The ray cannons don't work, Jacqui. They haven't worked since the Coup. My father used the threat of them — well, and of Master Bresciane — to keep order. To keep the other Families from attacking."

I nodded; I'd known that the cannons didn't work for some time.

He thrust his fingers into his hair. "But now the Red Dog **Gang** knows! They know any threat to use the cannons on them would be a bluff. If they pass that knowledge on to the Clubbs, or worse yet, the Diamonds —!"

I sighed. "There'd be no reason to fear us any longer."

We were at a fairly unstable cease-fire as it was. Yet neither of those two Families had officially accepted us — Tony and I — as Spade King and Queen, the rulers of Bridges. Nor had they given any reason over the year since Roy's death as to why they had not.

All had been quiet so far. But any faction which gained power inside one of the Families and were able to take over might not have the same restraint.

Was that why Mr. Clubb warned me about the Harts? Because he feared our siding with them might bring wrath upon us? Was he trying to warn me of trouble within their ranks? Or was he warning me not to trust them? Did he already know about the cannons, and fear that they'd get us in their confidence, learn the truth, and use that against us? Or against them?

Or could he have been trying to turn me against my own true-born father, the only real ally of power I might have in this city?

"Wait," I said. "This Four of Clubs, the people who hunted Master Rainbow. We still don't know who they are, where they are, or why they hunted him. They could be some disgruntled rogue group that he offended somehow —"

"Or they could be allied with the Red Dog Gang themselves." Tony stood quietly for a moment, then sighed. "I know it's not ideal, but I'm hoping to find some clue tomorrow."

The Burial

Morton was to be buried at the Clubb Family cemetery, near Clubb Manor. The morning of Morton's funeral was blustery and cool, the sky dark and threatening rain.

Acevedo was home with Daisy, the house given extra guard. If the Red Dog Gang meant to kill Ace, whilst we were away would be the perfect time to attack.

Tony and I wore the clothes we'd worn to bury Roy; Blitz and Mary rode in the back, with Honor. When we arrived, hundreds of people were there.

As King and Queen of Spadros, we had little leeway in what we might do. We were led from Tony's carriage along a golden carpet, flanked by Sawbuck and our most trustworthy men, up a flight of steps to covered seating. Away from the other Families.

"This is distressing," Tony said. "I'd hoped to at least be able to pay condolences to Mr. Alexander."

But it seemed not to be the case, at least not yet. Other than that, it was a typical funeral. Banners and incense, flowers and tears. One of the Dealers spoke at length, accompanied by Lance's older sister Kitty, now in the emerald green robe and head-scarf of the Dealers. Blessings were given over the coffin, and the crowd began to disperse. Sawbuck handed something to Tony, and spoke in his ear.

Tony nodded, turning to me. "We've been invited to a luncheon, and to the graveside after." He let out a breath. "Better than I hoped."

The Patriarchs and their wives sat at rectangular tables upon a platform a foot above the rest of the room. The tables had been moved into a very wide and shallow U.

I sat to Tony's right, which put me nearest the edge of the platform.

Sawbuck stood behind me at ground level, scanning the crowd for any threat. He'd not wanted us to attend the funeral at all, but Tony had insisted.

The Diamonds and the Clubbs sat side by side in the middle of the U, facing the crowd. We sat on the Clubbs' right. The Harts sat to the left of the Diamonds, on the far end of the platform directly ahead of us, yet neither lifted their eyes from their plates .

All wore black, and Regina Clubb was openly crying.

I'd never seen her cry before, and it felt unsettling.

The other tables began ten feet away, roped off, with one area well-wishers might enter. Escorted, of course.

The Clubbs evidently wanted no incident here.

The crowd was mostly Clubbs. Gardena and her brothers were out there, along with her brothers' wives. Cesare's wife Furuta nodded gravely to me when our eyes met.

The food at luncheon was good: sausages and pickled cabbage, sliced thin and spiced, salted fish, and a warm potato and fish soup.

I glanced to my left, at Tony. He'd also been looking out in the crowd, but at my movement, he twitched, a furtive look on his face.

Which astonished me. Had he been gazing moon-eyed at Gardena in front of everyone? And then to let himself look embarrassed at it? I'd known him almost fifteen years, and had never seen him show his true feelings in public before.

I stared at Gardena, and she blushed, glancing away. Lance Clubb sat beside her, arms crossed, face set.

What the hell was going on?

Since Tony had decided his food was of great importance right then, I settled in to endure the rest of this.

Mr. Alexander Clubb stood. "Thank you for coming out to honor Blaze Rainbow. I only knew him what seems like a short time. But he seemed a good man, and we will miss him terribly." He raised a glass with his left hand, his sleeve falling aside to reveal the brass and leather of his mechanical arm. "To Master Rainbow."

It seemed so little to say about a man who chose to be in your quadrant, to do work for you. But I had no idea what their relationship was.

I was surprised at the depth of their sorrow at the news, Master Bresciane had said. Perhaps Mr. Clubb still felt as stunned by Morton's murder as I did.

We toasted the man, our friend, and the luncheon was over.

***

I didn't have much to say to Tony right then, so we went where our escorts directed. Out to our carriage, and a short way to a large cemetery ringed with golden fencing.

Few came all this way: the Patriarchs and their wives, Cesare and Furuta, Lance and Gardena. Tony and I stood to one side as the oak-stained coffin with a brass plate for Morton's name was lowered into the earth.

I looked up at the Aperture, from this distance seemingly hanging in air. Glancing down, I saw that Lance had been true to his word: Morton was placed so he might also look at it. "He would have liked this," I said, to myself, really.

Tony came up beside me, taking my hand. "You said that before. How so?"

"Just something Master Rainbow once said." It'd been the day I'd rushed to save Dame Anastasia and my Ma from the zeppelin explosion, not knowing neither of them planned to be aboard. "He thought our Aperture a magnificent thing, said that he never tired of watching it."

Tony seemed to truly look at it then, those monstrous brass plates opening ever so slowly to allow zeppelins to enter and exit the city. "I suppose it is."

I put a penny on Morton's headstone. "May the Dealer give you better cards next time." I thought my heart would entirely break. "You were a true and loyal friend, and I will surely, surely miss you."

***

The next morning, Honor came in whilst I was up with my provisional tray, which was most unusual. "Mum, Mr. Blitz would like you to see to a situation at your apartments."

"Very well. Thank you." I wondered what this might be about.

But today was Wednesday, and I was "at home." Fortunately, I had only a few callers scheduled, but I wasn't able to leave Spadros Manor until after luncheon.

But the news was good: Blitz had an answer from Master Mike Pok-Deng, the apothecary renting Anna Goren's former shop.

"I figured anything I sent would be opened by your Mr. Howell," Blitz said. "And I didn't know what your man had to say to you."

"Good thinking." I went to my office and opened the letter.

> Dear Mrs. Spadros,
>
> Thank you for your concern over my situation. I must admit the day was distressing. Fortunately, the bulk of the violence was farther north, close to the Mayor's Mansion and government buildings. Be assured: no harm has come to your property whatsoever.
>
> May the Dealer's light shine upon you.
>
> Mike Pok-Deng, apothecary, Anna's Medicaments

I knew he hadn't changed the store's name since he bought the establishment after Anna Goren's murder, but to see her name written gave me a start.

My poor dear Anna — murdered just like her betrothed, Maxim Call. We'd never found the dark-skinned, blue-eyed woman posing as a maid who probably killed Inventor Call. Who was she? And why kill those searching for the truth about the Generators?

***

I had quite a bit of work to do, so I stayed at my apartments for tea, then went out on the front porch for a smoke.

As usual, Mr. Theodore Sutherfield sat on a barrel across the street reading the paper. I didn't know much about Mr. Theodore, other than that Blitz was his youngest brother. Early forties, dark-skinned, but not nearly so dark as Jonathan had been. A good steady sort; I felt glad he kept watch.

A man went to him and spoke in his ear, handing him an envelope.

Mr. Theodore came across the street. "A messenger boy brought this. It's not one of our usual, so they wanted to be cautious."

I took the envelope. "Thanks."

It bore the stamp of Market Center on it. The envelope was addressed with a strong, flowing hand, one I'd not seen before. I opened it, and inside lay a typed letter:

> Dear Mrs. Spadros,
>
> I have information about our mutual friend's death that may be of help. If you please, meet me at the apothecary's shop at seven.
>
> Paix Hanger

Constable Hanger, sending me a message ... **here**?

I nodded at Mr. Theodore. "This is good. When you call for my carriage, make sure they send the plain one. And please let my husband know I'll be late for dinner."

Mr. Theodore gestured at the envelope with his chin. "What's this all about?"

I smiled. "I may have just gotten lucky."

The Support

Tony sent the plain carriage, and to my surprise, Sawbuck was in it. With him were ten men on horseback, all armed.

Blitz and Mr. Theodore insisted on going along. Blitz was adamant. "What if the Constable never sent it, and this is some sort of trap?"

I said, "It could be. But not many know that the Constable knows Master Rainbow. And knows about my shop on Market Center, too?"

Sawbuck said dryly, "I'm sure dozens of people know about both."

We'd taken care to let as few know that I owned a shop on Market Center as possible, mostly to protect Master Pok-Deng. But I had to admit Sawbuck was right. "Very well. But no outriders." I might as well blow a horn to announce my coming if I brought them along.

The men on horseback looked at each other, then at Sawbuck.

Sawbuck said to them, "You lot go first, to check out the way. But do it quietly. Don't clump up, don't go down the same streets, and don't draw attention. Pretend you're out shopping. And when we arrive, get out of sight. Act like your horse needs tending, or your saddle's come loose — anything but guarding. Whistle if something's not right. Got it?"

"Yes, sir," they said, and trotted off one by one.

"Sounds like a good plan," I said.

Sawbuck scoffed. "I've been doing this since you were playing jacks in the Pot. Come on, let's go."

We got into the carriage, Sawbuck and I, and Blitz sat up back with Honor. From the sound of it, Honor was telling Blitz a story about the younger sculleries and peeled potatoes.

Sawbuck's voice broke in. "Why are we going here?"

I felt annoyed at his interruption: it was a good story. "Why did you spy on me in the Pot?"

Sawbuck snorted. "You really can't figure it out, after all this time?"

Now I felt truly vexed. "Why can't you just accept that I'm your Queen and support what I do in front of the men?"

He leaned forward. "Because I know you. Every time you've gone haring off after something, good people end up dead."

There was nothing I might say to that.

"Besides," he said, and his voice was kind, "I did support you. Support does not mean agreeing with your every word. If I thought dozens knew of what you said, others around me did as well. If I say it first, then the men won't get to muttering." He crossed his leg over his knee, leaned back to face the window. "They know they can trust me. That I won't knowingly lead them to doom."

He knew much more of this than I. "Forgive me. I just want —"

"To learn who killed your friend. I know. I've had this conversation with Mr. Anthony many a day."

He had? "So what am I missing?"

"Heh," Sawbuck said. "Never thought I'd hear you say **that**." He uncrossed his legs, leaned forward, his elbows on his knees, hands clasped. "What you may not have considered is how a Constable who's been banned from this quadrant knew you were here."

Constable Hanger had been banned from Spadros quadrant? Then I realized Sawbuck was right. How **did** he learn this?

"The fellow's as by-the-book as they come in this city, so he's got no money for spies. He barely has money for messengers."

I spoke quietly, aware that Blitz was right behind me, probably listening. "So you agree this is probably a trap."

Sawbuck shrugged. "Probably."

By this time, we'd gotten to the Pot, and all I might see was the Hedge. Beautiful — from this side.

Sawbuck said, "To answer your first question, I asked the men spying on you to tell me what you did. What you liked. Mr. Anthony wanted to know, so he might learn what to say to you."

"Oh." It felt clearer now. Tony was just a strange and quiet boy. But even then, he wanted to please me.

And I'd ruined even that.

The Hedge wasn't really even that pretty from this side. It was hideous, a symbol of this city's hate and degradation. I wanted nothing more right then to stop and command it torn down.

But if my men didn't shoot me at such a command, the rest of the city would. It'd be too much to allow Pot rags to live as quadrant-men.

To be their Queen.

Like I'd told Jonathan Diamond a few days before he died, this had to be what this was all about. That a Pot rag should become Queen of Spades, reign over the city as blessed by the gods ... The aristocrats would see the city burn before they let it stand.

And the Red Dog Gang — well, whoever their leader was — either agreed, or was willing to use that hate to further his own agenda.

Or hers, if what Dame Anastasia had told me outside my apartments was true.

The thought that a woman led them was the most puzzling part of what Dame Anastasia told me the year prior. That the aristocrats would target me made some sort of sense. But what motivation would an old woman have to spend so much time and money attacking the Spadros Family? And why now? Particularly if she were old. Why hadn't she done this decades ago, when the Families were at war and vulnerable?

If she hated me, or never wanted me to be Queen, well, she could have had me killed when I was still in the Pot, at any time after Peedro sold me to Roy.

But then I recalled the note left in Marja's hand: HE WANTS YOU.

Who was "he"?

For some time I'd thought this man to be Charles Hart — that is, before I learned he was my true-born father. Mr. Hart's actions since then led me to believe he wanted nothing but my good.

So who was it?

But then I recalled that Frank Pagliacci and Dame Anastasia had been lovers.

No, Anastasia couldn't be leading this. She'd lived right next door to us. She'd been my friend for years. She'd spoken for me at my engagement party. If she wanted to destroy me, she had so many ways along the years to hinder and harm me that she hadn't taken. It would be utterly silly of her to come to my door dressed in rags just to tell me she wanted me dead.

And Frank Pagliacci? From all I could see, he was an underling, albeit one with a taste for strangling.

Or could this "he" be some other man we'd yet not seen?

My driver Zeus must have given some sign to the guards, because we crossed onto the bridge to Market Center without being stopped.

If there was another man with enough influence over this old woman to sway her, one we'd not yet seen ... well, that seemed concerning. Who hated us this much?

I hoped Constable Hanger really was there, that this wasn't some sort of trap.

I looked over at Sawbuck, suddenly alarmed. Was the Constable himself lying dead in an alley, simply because I'd taken the bait?

Sawbuck nodded. "I hope we find the man alive. He's caused us no manner of trouble over the years, but he seems a decent sort."

My heart began pounding. I had a sudden urge to scream at Zeus to hurry.

But it didn't matter. If they wanted Constable Hanger dead, they'd have already killed him.

I put my elbow on the window-sill, disheartened, my face on my hand. "Everything I do goes wrong."

"We don't know it's gone wrong," Sawbuck said. "But you do tend to jump without looking. And trust without knowing."

"You know very little about me, sir."

"The fact that you worked with the man yet didn't know he'd been banned from your own quadrant tells me all I need to know. For an investigator, if you take a liking to someone, you seem to do very little real investigating."

"It's nothing like that —"

"I didn't imply it was." He gazed out over the water. "It's just that a year ago trusting the wrong person almost killed you. And still you have learned nothing from it."

Had I? Learned nothing?

I learned that Joseph Kerr was either stupid, unobservant of his own body, reckless, uncaring of the lives of those he claimed to love, or some combination.

Did I trust him? I never could again, no.

Did I still love him? I didn't know.

Part of me hated him. For ruining my marriage, for almost killing me, for not even having the grace to apologize. Even if it was totally unintentional, he should have at least done that.

Instead, he cast blame upon Tony, then upon me.

So why did my mind keep coming back to him?

I think now, looking back, that he and Josie and even Mr. Kerr in a way had represented a part of my home. I'd felt safe with them. We had a common bond, a shared language. They knew what it was like to grow up hunted by the police for sport, cold and hungry and without hope.

But Joe seemed to have grown callous. Where I wanted to help my people, Joe only seemed to want to help himself.

Perhaps I'd been wrong to trust him.

"You have a good mind," said Sawbuck. "A stout heart, and when it matters, you aren't afraid to do battle." He shook his head. "But until you quit taking what people say at face value, you'll never be of much use to anyone."

***

We arrived at Anna Goren's former shop — now mine, just a bit before the time set in the letter. We drove past; the street stood bare.

"Park around the corner," Sawbuck called out. "We'll check it out."

We got out of the carriage onto the street. Zeus said, "I'll circle around and meet up."

A man's voice said from behind, "That won't be necessary."

Sawbuck wheeled at the voice, drawing his revolver.

Constable Hanger took a step back, hands raised.

Early forties, dark hair and light skin, although not nearly so pale as Tony's. A steady sort of man; I felt relieved to see him. "Don't sneak up on Family like that," I said, half laughing.

Sawbuck lowered his gun. The Constable lowered his hands, then gestured with his chin. "Over here."

We followed him to a narrow cigar shop one door down. The owner stood behind the counter, nodding when he saw the Constable. We passed the man and went to a small store-room off to the left, beside the back door. Sawbuck closed the door behind us. "So you're not dead —"

Constable Hanger's face turned amused, and a laugh burst from him. "Not yet, at any rate."

Sawbuck sounded annoyed. "— so what it is we must know?"

Constable Hanger hesitated. "The matter is complex."

Sawbuck nodded.

The Constable bit his lip, looking away. "The coroner here on Market Center and I have become friends. I'd stopped in early to bring a jar of vegetables my wife had canned for him." He stopped then, head down. "I recognized Master Rainbow lying there —"

I blurted out, "Good gods!"

"Yes," said the Constable, unmoving. "That's how I learned of it."

"I'm very sorry," Sawbuck said.

Constable Hanger took a deep breath, let it out. "After the initial shock, I asked the coroner what he'd learned. He told me of the case. A fairly straight-forward case, he said: the shot to his chest killed him in a matter of minutes. Before that, he appeared to have been badly beaten, bound. Yet two things found on the body had puzzled him." At this, he brought out a business-sized card and handed it to me.

White card-stock, with a red dog stamped upon it. On the other side, it read, "I have plenty more."

The same curl-up at the "t" ... I glanced at Sawbuck and Constable Hanger in horror. "This was written by the same person who framed me for the zeppelin bombing."

Sawbuck nodded gravely. "This is proof that the Red Dog Gang and this forger are linked."

Constable Hanger twitched. "I suppose I should have suspected that the Family would already know about these people."

I sighed. He had no idea. "It suggests something else, though."

Constable Hanger blinked. "What?"

"Just consider it. If they wanted to harm a member of Clubb, or Spadros, well, they could have chosen to kill any number of people. But Master Rainbow has been kept in high regard by all four Families. Who's harmed by it?"

"The Patriarchs," Constable Hanger and Sawbuck spoke at the same time. They looked at each other, then at me.

I said, "Much like the day Roy Spadros was murdered, this is an attack on the Four Families and their rule over this city." I turned to Sawbuck. "I must tell my husband." Then I held up the card. "Might I keep this?"

"Certainly," Constable Hanger said. "His death's been deemed a Family matter, so little more will be done on it."

"Thank you," I said. "I won't forget your kindness."

Constable Hanger smiled. "And thank you for corroborating my story. Never thought I'd be sitting on the wrong side of my own holding cell."

I said, "You're quite welcome." Then I said, "What was the other thing he found?"

"Ah," Sawbuck said.

Constable Hanger sighed. "The man had been kissed. Just like Sheinwold." He shook his head. "Do you recall?"

I nodded.

Sawbuck, who hadn't been there, peered at me with curiosity.

Constable Hanger said, "It was the same, Mrs. Spadros. The lipstick. It was the exact same color."

The Mail

We sat in Tony's study, guards at every possible listening-post, as I told my husband the story.

Tony sat speechless. "So they knew he worked with all four of the Families for some time. Why kill him now? What's changed?"

"Good question." I didn't have the answer, unfortunately. "What we need is more information from the other Families."

Tony scoffed. "Good luck with **that**."

"If we knew what was happening before he was killed, though, we might be able to learn something. Anything might help."

Tony sighed. "Mr. Clubb and Mr. Diamond wouldn't speak with me at the funeral. Mr. Hart might be willing to talk, but I fear losing his son has made him indifferent to the rest of the city's woes."

"It doesn't matter," I said. "They all loved Master Rainbow — surely they'd meet to learn who killed him."

"You really think so?" Tony seemed defeated.

"I do. We all have all these secrets, but it's gotten to the point where the secrets are hurting more than helping. They're being used against us." Why hadn't I seen it before? "We must meet together, and get everything on the table. Then we'll know how to proceed."

Tony nodded slowly. "It has to be somewhere safe, where we won't be overheard."

"What about that place we met before with the Inventors? Up at the Opera House?"

"Yes, that could do. But Ten won't agree to it, and neither would the rest. It's not defensible. And four Patriarchs in one room makes for a tempting target."

"Wait," I said. "Isn't there a room like that in the Ballhouse?"

Tony considered it. "There is. It's above the Ballroom, with four doors corresponding to the four entryways. But it's a strenuous climb. The stairs go along the inside of that domed roof. They're steep and narrow." He pondered it for a moment, then he nodded. "But they should agree to it. Their people could be stationed on the landings along the way."

I recalled my half-brother Etienne Hart, the surprise on his face as his own most trusted man shot him in the head from behind. I hoped, for their sakes, that their people were more trustworthy.

"We must craft a letter," Tony said. "They must understand how important this is, and want to help."

Tony, asking me to craft a letter with him?

"Don't look so surprised," Tony said. "My mother, as perverse and wicked as she might be, was one of my father's closest advisors. In my anger, I kept myself from being like him in that way. But to be honest, I fear making a mistake. You're right: we must have them all there, and ready to reveal what they know, or this will be a waste of time."

***

We were up much of the night planning what turned out to be a simple letter. But it was more than just writing it. We had to decide how to get it there as well.

Sending a Memory Boy, while it seemed secure, had many risks. The boy might be waylaid, the letter taken from him. He or whoever he reported to might open it on the way.

Sawbuck was known to all — he could take the letters there himself. But doing so would mean days of painful carriage rides and take him from his work overseeing the quadrant.

"I wish Master Rainbow were alive," Tony said. "He'd see to this and be back the next day." Then his face fell; he lapsed into silence.

I sighed. "I wish he were alive, too. He had good counsel."

"As did Master Jonathan."

I nodded, a surge of misery washing over me. Jon would have known what to say. He'd have ideas on who might bring these. He could have brought the Diamond letter to his father that night.

Ah. "I'll visit Mr. Beloty at the Courthouse!" Beloty Diamond took over as Keeper of the Court when his younger brother Jonathan first went missing. And I'd been to the Courthouse many a time, so it might not be remarked upon. "He could bring it to his father with no one the wiser."

"Good idea," said Tony. "I'll call on the Clubbs. They might be able to refuse my mail, but they don't dare refuse me."

I chuckled. "And it's well past time I paid a visit to my father."

The Hurt

That morning, the paper read:

CORONER SUICIDE?

The coroner for Market Center was found hanging in his toilet-room night before last. Police are calling it a suicide.

His family denies any melancholy prior to this and insist he would never take his life. They did mention that he had been placed under watch by Family members, presumably for his protection, and that he felt troubled by the situation.

Candidates for Mayor have called for an end to Family surveillance of citizens. David Korol, one of our many mayoral candidates, said in his speech last night upon Market Center, "These men have lorded over us long enough! How many more deaths of good men will it take before we rid ourselves of them?"

None of the Four Families were available for comment.

"So they got to him," I said to myself. And now they'd used this murder to embolden the people against us.

This had to be a reaction to us learning the truth about Katie's death. How did they find out that we knew? We had to have another spy yet uncaught. Or I suppose it could've been innocent. If Alan hadn't proceeded quietly enough, or ...

But we'd had the report for several days. Why kill the coroner **now**? What had changed?

I made a note for Alan to look into this David Korol. Who was he, and why was he running for Mayor?

Tony and I had gone back and forth over whether I should take the Queen's carriage — making it an official Family visit — or use the plain carriage for safety. Either way, I faced several problems.

The Queen of Spadros officially going uninvited to Hart Manor was problem enough. That I went so to see Mr. Hart himself would be seen by most as scandalous.

I could say I was visiting Mrs. Hart, but all she'd have to do was deny that. I'd be in my carriage on Market Center with twenty armed men, amongst dozens who had already gotten away with murder.

My plain carriage would be only marginally safer. I still had no invitation. We'd have to wait on Market Center to be let into Hart quadrant. And as we drove through Hart we'd still be marked as Spadros Family by the horses and tack.

No one would be sure who I was until I announced myself to the guards at Hart Manor. At that point, we'd have to wait until the message was sent and word received that they would let me in.

And that wait was particularly dangerous. We'd be a target for anyone in Hart who blamed the Spadros Family for Inventor Etienne Hart's death — or anything in general.

So I did what no one would ever consider: I rented a taxi.

Blitz, Honor, Zeus, and I left shortly after dawn in our plain carriage. Zeus and Honor wore street clothes; Blitz and I wore deep red. I had on a hat with a thick veil. Neither of us wore insignia, but to the casual eye we could have been from the Memory Guild.

Since we had to drive through the city and visit the Stables on Market Center to rent the taxi, we didn't arrive at the Courthouse until well past nine.

We expected to be kept waiting until the Keeper had a break between Court cases. But as it turned out, Mr. Beloty Diamond was in his office that day. "I dislike paperwork. So I decided to make a day to get the papers done and confer with associates. Much like you ladies do when you're 'at home.' So here I am!"

I felt amused. "I'm well glad." I handed him the letter, marked: *Julius Diamond, his eye only*. "It's vital he see this tonight."

Beloty put the envelope into his left breast pocket, peering at me with his large mournful eyes. "I'm ever so sorry for your loss."

A rush of emotion. "Thank you."

"I didn't know Master Rainbow well. But from the few times he helped us here, he seemed a good sort."

I nodded. "He surely was." Then something occurred to me. "Has there been any news as to your brother?"

"Jonathan?" He shook his head. "Nothing. I only wish we'd paid more attention to him those last days. Not left him to brood at home alone." He glanced up at me. "No offense; we're ever so glad that you and your son survived."

I shrugged. I felt glad Acevedo was alive. But me?

Beloty said, "But if we'd been there with him, perhaps we could've been of aid somehow. Not make your safety cost him his life."

I nodded. Gods, did I wish that too.

He peered at me, and I felt I needed to say something. "I hope you and your family are well?"

He smiled, amused. "Quite. My third son will be born in the fall."

"Oh! Congratulations! How wonderful."

His smile turned introspective, fond. "We'll name him after Jonnie, of course." He glanced aside, eyes glistening.

I nodded, though I knew he couldn't see. When whoever meant Jon to die sent him that forged letter, they hurt a great host of others. Like this man, without any ties to me other than being born a Diamond. A man who'd only wanted to live in peace. "Well, I best be off."

Beloty turned to me, forcing a smile, and nodded. "Safe travels."

Blitz and I returned to the carriage. We'd completed the easy part: if we were stopped at the Hart bridge, things could get ugly.

Pistol in hand, I took up the speaking bell. "Drive up slowly, Zeus, and call it out so everyone can hear."

I heard Zeus chuckle, his voice tinny. "Yes, mum."

We drove towards the Hart bridge at quite a relaxed trot. Zeus bellowed, "Message for Charles Hart, his eye only."

A man replied, but I couldn't make it out.

The guard didn't even bother to look inside.

Honor opened the back window. "I didn't expect that to work."

I chuckled. "I won't claim success until we're home safe."

As soon as we crossed the bridge, the streets turned to closely laid red brick. The curbs were painted white, the lamp-posts covered in polished silver.

We passed the Hart Pot, the slums, past the street we'd turn on to go to the Kerr's home. I had an urge to go to Josie, but what we were doing was dangerous enough as it was. I'd not risk these men's lives on a whim, not again. Plus, we had no time.

And yet I wondered about Joe. Could he really not understand what he'd done? And why would he lie about it? If he wanted other women, I'd not have stopped him. In the Pot, that wasn't our way.

But not with lies. As I'd told Gardena, his lies angered me the most.

***

When we approached Hart Manor, Hart men stopped us at the corner. Even though Zeus used the same trick on them, they insisted Blitz and I get out a block away and walk. No matter what we said, they only allowed Blitz to accompany me.

So along we went, down a long, long street. Armed Hart men, flat-faced and dark-haired, went before, behind, and beside us to our left as we walked the red brick sidewalk.

Hart Manor was white, with a red-tiled roof and fixtures of silver. My half-brother Etienne Hart's fiery red carriage had been parked in front of the Manor and draped in black. Fresh flowers, icons to the Blessed Dealer, partly-burnt candles, and written tributes covered the entire street and half the sidewalk around it.

It had been almost a year since his murder! To have such devotion from his people ... "He never knew how much he was loved," I murmured, to myself.

Blitz nodded. "He was. He was their Inventor, and their Heir. It's not surprising his people might have dreamed of a return of the Inventor King —"

This startled me.

"— if in name only."

We'd stopped: the walkway had narrowed to eighteen inches wide from all the flowers there. The men stood waiting. Blitz said, "Let's get this over with."

One of the Hart men led us past the low white brick wall topped with real silver and to the silvered gates, the rest following behind.

When we gave our true names, most of the men at the front gate stared at us, mouths open. Except one, who bolted for the front door at a full run. When the door opened behind them, the rest seemed to regain their senses, hurrying us inside.

I got only a glimpse of walnut-stained wood and deep red wall hangings before Charles Hart, his lined face alarmed and stricken, came running down the stairs barefoot in a set of red silk brocade pajamas. "Good gods, why have you come? Is Acevedo —?"

I raised my veil. "Be at peace, sir. He's well." I glanced at the two men beside us, who were staring at Mr. Hart, astonished and concerned. "Might we speak in private?"

Color returned to Mr. Hart's face. "Of course," he panted. "This way."

I didn't follow. "Your wife might wish to hear this as well."

"I'll be sure to tell her," Mr. Hart said. "She's indisposed."

Indisposed? Surely she was too old for that? "Very well."

Mr. Hart led us through a long hallway to our left, past low tables filled with portraits of his son Etienne. It was clear he'd been doted-on as a boy.

Finally we reached what appeared to be Mr. Hart's study. A large, walnut-stained desk edged and trimmed in silver, walls filled with fine portraits, riding medals, horse awards.

Mr. Hart gestured to two overstuffed chairs upholstered in red leather, sitting behind his desk. "Please, sit. Might I offer some tea?"

"No, thank you, sir: we can't stay long." It wouldn't take much time for news of our visit to travel. "I only came to give you these." I handed the letter and a small silver-framed portrait of Acevedo over the desk to him.

He smiled at the little portrait of his grandson and stood it up on his desk. "Thank you." He took up the letter, read through it, then read it again. Then he looked up at me. "Are you certain?"

"Yes, sir. This is something we all must do. I only regret it's taken us so long."

He snorted quietly, set the letter down, then stood. "Give my regards to your husband."

"I will, sir."

He peered at me. "You look about as well as I feel. Terribly stricken, yet somewhat improved."

I smiled at him. From all accounts, he'd been at my side a full week after I'd fallen ill with womb fever, only leaving when the doctor said I'd survive. "A fair estimation. Please give my regards to your wife."

His face fell.

It was terribly nosy of me, but I blurted out, "What's wrong, sir?"

He shook his head quickly. "It's not my story to tell." He stood. "Thank you for coming, Jacqui." He held up the note. "And for this." He gave me a sad, fond smile, then stood, came round the desk to place a hand on my arm. "It was good to see you."

I felt touched. "You do me too great an honor, sir."

He glanced at Blitz. "Is this man trustworthy?"

I looked Blitz in the eyes. "I trust him with my life."

Mr. Hart gave me a sudden, intense hug. "My precious girl. All I've ever wanted was for you to be safe, and happy."

Tears came to my eyes, and I hugged him back. It was so much like what Jonathan Diamond had said before he died. I let go, and when he did too, I pulled back to look at him. "Thank you, sir."

He turned to Blitz, his tone menacing. "You take care of her."

Blitz nodded. "I will."

With that, Blitz and I left, making our way back to the carriage and our long trip home.

Once inside, I realized what had happened. "You already knew."

Blitz chuckled. "About Charles Hart? Yeah, I knew. Teddy told me." He shrugged. "But I'd already guessed something like that was going on."

I nodded. "Thank you."

"For what?"

"For ... I don't know. Not treating me differently." I shrugged. "I guess, for everything."

***

Past the Spadros Pot, we hit traffic on the Main Road. And I had a chance, with my veil and my clothing, to really look at my quadrant.

Here in the upper slums, people did look a bit more prosperous than before. *It's your nickel, mum.*

I smiled to myself, recalling Eleanora's words.

But people looked better-fed, the children clean, the streets bustling. Street vendors hawked cold chicken and beer on one block, a young man played a ballad on the sitar on the next. Further down, an older man stood on a box bellowing an off-key rendition of "The Gambler" to a crowd of children as we passed.

We stopped in traffic. A few feet up ahead, a boy handed out tabloids as fast as he could take the cash, whilst another boy beside him held one up in each hand, yelling: "Extra! Extra! Read all about it! Army files suit against city!"

I said, "Get that for me, Blitz, will you?"

He hopped out, gave the boy a penny. In the meantime, the carriage had moved a bit, so he jogged to catch up and get inside.

"Thanks." I took the paper from him. On the front it read:

ARMY FILES SUIT AGAINST CITY

City Cover-Up: High-Card Murder!!

The Merca Federal Union Army's Judge Advocate General, Lieutenant General Glencoe Steel, has filed suit in the Supreme Court on Hub against the Independent Domed City-State of Bridges. The Army alleges that Bridges has systematically covered up the murder of retired Major Wenz Blackwood, who ran the city's Recruitment Center until his death two years ago. The Army also alleges that their investigation into Major Blackwood's murder has been blocked at every turn, even up to the Mayor's office.

"Hmm," I said, handing it to Blitz.

"I knew that Army man wouldn't stop looking," Blitz said. "And with everything else that's been covered up by the city, it certainly stands to reason."

Particularly when it seemed clear that the Mayor's office had covered up the deeds of the Bridges Strangler as well.

***

Tony and Sawbuck had several arguments as the meeting day approached. Sawbuck was most concerned about making the crossing to the outer stair in the open, where a sniper could have us both and be done with it.

But Tony had insisted. "If we hesitate, they'll leave. This isn't up for debate. We must meet with them, and that's final."

So the day came, and Sawbuck still grumbling, we went.

I made sure my pistol lay in its calf holster, and that it was loaded. No one would harm Tony, not if I had anything to say about it.

We arrived at the Grand Ballhouse an hour before dawn, stopping at the place we'd stopped every New Year's Eve. It looked different in the pre-dawn's light.

The air was chill. The sky was clear. The streets were empty.

Sawbuck had sent men on the top of every building within a rifle's distance from the place. Five met us at the carriage, red-faced; they'd found men from other Families already at their assigned spots.

"Get back up there," Sawbuck said sternly. "And don't come down 'til you're called." Then he turned to us, chuckling. "Can't say I'm surprised."

Honor, Sawbuck, Mr. Theodore Sutherfield, and six more of Tony's men hurried us across the wide flat area and to the stair. We left three of Tony's men at the bottom of the white marble steps; the other three came up the stair with us. One of Tony's men moved past to open the door for us.

The beautiful entry chamber looked so different than when lit for New Year's Eve, plainer somehow in that thin pre-morning's light.

Sawbuck gestured to the far right: an open door I'd never noticed before lay there, only marked with "Stair."

Sawbuck looked at Tony, pain and fear in his eyes. "This is as far as I can go, sir." He went to Tony, and to the surprise of us all, grasped my husband's face in his hands, resting his forehead on Tony's. He spoke fiercely. "Be safe."

Tony's gaze softened; he put a hand on Sawbuck's arm. "I will."

Sawbuck seemed to realize then that we all stood there, and his hands dropped to his side.

Tony smiled up at him. "Don't let anyone past you."

***

The stairs were steep and narrow, gray block walls on either side up to a low ceiling lit by electrical lamps covered with clouded glass.

After some time, we reached a landing, the ceiling double high. Tall narrow windows stood at each landing that reminded me of the openings in the Diamond Country House courtyard walls. But these had glass in them; the air was cool, humid, close.

To take the next set of stairs, you had to completely turn round. The stairs then curved leftward to return to the wall of the dome. One of our men stood guard at each turn, nodding to us as we arrived. Each time, Tony would stop, clap the man on the shoulder, smile, ask if he needed anything, how he fared, or how his family was.

Tony had to be nervous about the meeting, or even afraid. But he did all he could to make his men along the way feel he was in command, and that he cared for their welfare.

My feet began to hurt; my knees and legs ached. But Tony had let me be at the table; I refused to be dealt out if I might possibly move forward.

At the last landing, the ceiling curved high above us. We'd made good time; the sun hadn't quite topped the buildings. To our left, a hallway perhaps twelve feet long and six wide went straight to an ornate set of doors. I smelled food, and even though it was well before breakfast-time, my stomach growled.

Tony stopped two paces from the doors, checking his pocketwatch. Then he turned to Mr. Sutherfield. "Teddy, you're in charge. Unless you hear me shout, or you hear gunfire, you're not to approach that door." He glanced at Honor. "You hear me?"

Both men nodded. Tony spoke to Mr. Theodore once more. "If there **is** gunfire, watch your targets. We don't want to kill a Patriarch on accident."

I gaped at him. Kill a Patriarch?

He gave me a fond smile, took my hand, and led me to the doors.

The room inside was large, some thirty feet to a side. Each wall held a wide entrance from the stair, with smaller rooms through doors along the walls for gatherings and refreshment. An electric chandelier hung from the domed roof; the room was well-lit.

Comfortable overstuffed brown leather chairs had been brought from the meeting-rooms downstairs and set around the room in a circle. Since we didn't know how many would arrive, we'd had enough brought up for the adult Heirs as well.

Tony had ordered tea-tables set up around the walls, and the side rooms readied in case we needed to stay overnight, or someone became fatigued. Food and drink had been brought up, with a man from each of the four Families assigned to wait table.

The room smelled delicious.

Rob Pearson stood by our buffet dressed in Spadros livery, a white tea-towel over his arm. When our eyes met, I winked at him, and his face turned red.

The other Families stood at the doors, peering in, as if uncertain whether we set a trap.

Tony and I entered. Alexander and Regina Clubb came in their door wearing mourning, followed by their son Lance. I was surprised to see Gardena Diamond follow him in.

Julius and Rachel Diamond came in their door. Charles and Judith Hart entered last. Mr. Hart looked out of breath. Both looked pale. But Mrs. Hart had lost a great deal of weight since I'd last seen her. When our eyes met, her gaze was weary, empty, deeply sad.

The doors closed behind them

Tony said, "Thank you for meeting us." He spoke to Mr. Clubb, who stood to his right. "We're very sorry about your daughter."

Mr. Clubb nodded grimly.

Then Tony turned left, towards Julius Diamond. "Where are your sons? Should they not also be here?"

"They feared to have us all in one place, in case of attack." He crossed his arms with a scowl. "And I am not dead yet. Say what you have to say, Spadros, and be done with it."

Tony seemed shocked. "I planned no attack!" His voice turned pleading. "Won't you sit?"

Julius Diamond looked at the room with distaste. "I can't believe I came all the way up here. You think you're some grand negotiator, going to make up for your crimes by plying us with food and drink?"

Gardena's voice cut through the silence. "Father, since you did come all this way, don't you think you should at least hear him out?"

Julius crossed his arms, not looking at anyone.

Tony sighed. "Very well. Sit, or not, as you will." He took a deep breath. "Since everyone is here —"

The doors that the Clubbs had entered opened, light spilling into the room. The sun was rising; a hooded and cloaked figure clothed in black stood in the doorway, silhouetted by blinding gold.

Then the doors closed behind him. The man put dark spectacles into a breast pocket and cast off his hood.

It was Jonathan Diamond.

But it was not.

The figure had Jon's face, his dark, dark skin, his black-coiled hair. Yet this man was Jonathan as I'd never once seen him: fit, contented, entirely well.

And my heart seized within me. This was what Jon should have been, in all the fullness of manhood, had he never become ill.

Mrs. Diamond shrieked and collapsed. Gardena took a step towards the dark figure, this pretense of Jon. But the man shook his head, speaking with a voice both rich and deep. "See to Mama."

Gardena nodded, then hurried to kneel beside her sobbing mother.

That voice. This could only be one man. "Jack Diamond," I said. "You were not dead."

The Warning

Jack Roland Diamond III walked into the room with a sardonic smile. "I watched my own funeral. Yet I am not dead."

The rest of the room burst into chatter. Julius Diamond knelt beside his sobbing wife.

I stared at Jack, remembering the man across the street at Jack's funeral procession. Add dark glasses, a cane, a slump ... that "old man" had been Jack Diamond, right there in front of me! And I didn't see it.

But Jack had changed. He no longer shaved his head; he'd grown his hair to the same length his twin Jonathan's had been. His embroidered black shirt sported a Mandarin collar with a black bolo tie held by a large black stone edged in silver. A similar stone lay in the clasp of his hooded cloak. His black leather vest and deep brown duster were of Nitivali make. Instead of white patent-leather shoes, he wore cowboy boots: black, perfectly shined, and expensive.

Tony raised his hand. "Enough. I have had **enough** of secrets!!"

Julius Diamond looked up. "You ..." He stood, taking a step forward. "You **dare** place yourself above us, silence my son, who I thought was dead, then talk to me about **secrets**?" He spat, stalking over. "I should kill you where you stand."

"Father!" Gardena said.

But Julius spoke over her: "You blackguard!" He raised his fist, throwing a punch at Tony.

Tony dodged the punch, then took the man's arm and put it behind his back, speaking softly by Mr. Diamond's ear. "This is not the time, sir. I may deserve your blow, and one day, perhaps you'll take your vengeance on me. But right now, it helps nothing."

I felt impressed: Tony's wrestling practice in the meadow with Sawbuck and his men had paid off.

Julius struggled, pinned without a way to escape. "You scoundrel! You ruined my daughter!"

Without meaning to, I said, "**What?**"

Gardena walked to him, putting her hands on the sides of his face. "Oh, Father. Yes. Tony and I were indiscreet once. But I am not ruined. I have never been ruined. Look." She glanced back at Lance Clubb, who came to stand next to her, taking her hand. "Lancelot Clubb has asked me to be his bride, and I have consented. No one is ruined. We are well, all of us, and happy."

Tony let go of Julius Diamond's arm.

Mr. Diamond stared at Lance and Gardena in shock. "My darling girl." Mr. Diamond embraced her; Mrs. Diamond ran to hug her.

"Congratulations," Jack said, and walked over to shake Lance Clubb's hand.

*Tony and I were indiscreet ... **once?***

I turned to Tony. "You lied to me."

Tony's eyes were haunted. "I did."

I shook my head. He wanted me to think he'd been having an **affair**? "But ... **why?**"

He spoke quietly, below the buzz of congratulations and tears. "Miss Gardena did come to me many a time after you left, sometimes with Master Lance and sometimes with Master Jonathan, but it was only to offer support. I thought ..." He let out a sigh. "I thought that if you had a reason to hate me it would spur you to leave, if that was what you truly wanted."

His face blurred, and I kissed him there, in front of everyone. They all stopped and stared.

Regina Clubb said, "Perhaps we should have our breakfast?"

Normally, it would be much too early for breakfast, but after that climb, I have to admit I was hungry.

Jack glanced at the waiters standing there. "I would appreciate it if what you've just learned here not leave this room. I had very good reasons to feign my death, and I'd rather not have to do it once more."

Without so much at a glance at his waiter, Mr. Hart said, "My man was chosen for his discretion."

Mr. Hart's waiter looked familiar. Where had I seen him?

Mr. Clubb said, "As were mine."

Were? Yes. Of course. Surely Mr. Clubb had dozens guarding the way up here. When — how — had Gardena managed Jack's entrance?

The Diamond waiter, an unfamiliar man of about my age, stood calmly. Our eyes met, and I realized: *he already knew.*

How did a servant know, and Jack's own parents did not?

Tony said, "Mr. and Mrs. Diamond, I deeply apologize for the harm and sorrow I have given you."

Mrs. Diamond gave Tony a warm smile. Mr. Diamond pointedly ignored him.

Jack Diamond stood aside, and neither of his parents so much as gave him a glance.

That wound is deep, I thought. *Jack must have much explaining to do.*

***

We hung back, perhaps Tony feeling as embarrassed at our public display as I did, until everyone else had gotten their food.

As host, though, no one might eat until he did, so I put one of each thing on my plate and followed Tony to the one empty table.

Tony took a hasty drink and put a forkful of food into his mouth with all watching, then once everyone else had begun, he sat staring at his plate.

I cut the unfamiliar sausage from the Clubbs' buffet. The meat inside was pale. Chicken? "Were you going to let me think badly of you forever?"

Tony shrugged despondently, shaking his head, just a little. "I've lost track of the times I've failed you, Jacqui." He leaned an elbow on his armrest, hand to his chin, gazing out over the room. "I need to do better. I need to **be** better."

I reached across the small table to put my hand on his. "Did you **really** think I would leave you and Acevedo?"

Tony glanced down at our hands, then returned to staring across the room. "I have no idea what to think."

"Tony. Look at me."

He took a deep breath, let it out, then did.

"Right now, I'm here. With you. I'm right here. Why doubt it?" I turned my hand over to gently grasp his in mine. "Why did you do it? Why ruin your reputation this way?

Tony snorted. "My reputation was ruined the moment you refused to return to me." Then he shook his head. "I can't live not knowing if you're going to disappear out a window one day and go to him." He withdrew his hand, not looking at me. "I'm sorry, Jacqui. I can't think of anything but what's happening today. If we are ever to be safe, these people must believe I mean them good, that revealing their secrets will gain them something. So we must, for once, be honest. I mean it, Jacqui. No more secrets. No more lies. Tell them everything." He looked down at his cold plate. "And I suppose I must eat something as well."

I smiled fondly at him. He never would eat when he was anxious, or upset. "Yes, I suppose you must."

The sausage was excellent. Pork, spiced with something tangy and a bit sweet that I couldn't identify. "Their Chef must be quite good."

"Oh? Whose?"

"The Clubbs." I held up a bit of sausage on my fork.

He reached across to spear some from my plate.

Surprised, I laughed.

Tony grinned at me. "If I must take charge of the situation, this seemed a good place to begin."

Tony had never done this before. What had changed? "I'm here with you because I trust you," I said. "I know you can succeed today."

His eyes dropped to the table, yet his cheeks colored, and he had a small smile on his lips. "Thank you. That means a lot to me." He ate, chewed, swallowed. "I have no idea whether any of this will work," he gestured into the room with his fork. "But I have to try." He set his fork down. "I have to believe that what they know is worth all this."

***

To my relief, Tony did finish his meal. I didn't want him ever getting so thin as he had during my trial.

Once all was done and the rest began returning to their seats, Tony stood, taking my hand, and spoke loudly. "We have plenty of time to tell our stories, but we must each do so. Patriarchs and Inventors are being murdered." He gazed at Mr. Hart. "Our Heirs are being targeted for death." He took a deep breath. "At least one killer stalks our lands, even still, and he's being backed by the highest forces in the city." He stopped for a moment, head down, then faced the room. "And now Master Rainbow is dead."

Regina Clubb wiped her eyes and turned away.

Gardena stared at him, mouth open. "You believe these things ... are connected?"

Tony nodded.

Alexander Clubb said, "I do as well."

Tony led me to the chairs, then pulled out the Red Dog Gang card Constable Hanger had given him and handed it around. "This is the mark of a group calling themselves the Red Dog Gang. It was found on Master Rainbow's body."

Everyone sat. As each handed it to the other, the reactions were illuminating. Julius Diamond looked puzzled. His wife Rachel turned the card over and over, as if trying to make sense of it. Mr. Hart handed it to his wife as if the thing were hot, or somewhat disgusting. Mrs. Hart peered at it much as Mrs. Diamond had, but as if it reminded her of something she couldn't quite place. Lance glanced at it then handed it to Gardena, who seemed more interested in the writing than the image. Jack peered at it a moment, then handed it to Mrs. Clubb. Mrs. Clubb shrugged and handed it over to Mr. Clubb, who gave it to me, looking as if he might be sick.

Tony said, "These cards have been found at the sites of various murders, including dozens strewn over the street during the attack on my home."

Mr. Clubb turned even paler, putting his elbow on the armchair, his face in his hand. Sweat hung on his brow.

Tony said, "Master Rainbow was shot, then tied to the statue of my ancestor, with the words 'Family Pet' upon a placard on his body."

This was evidently news to everyone.

"My wife and I believe Master Rainbow's death to be an attack on all four Families. Someone knew he had connections with us, and did this to give harm and dismay." He turned to Julius Diamond. "This is why I brought you here, not to become some 'grand negotiator.' My wife and I believe all this is linked." He stopped, took a breath, hesitant. "This city is being incited to turn against us, and it's been planned for at least twenty years."

Their shocked faces made me realize how very serious this was.

Tony said, "Here is my proof. After the zeppelin explosion, Dame Anastasia left my wife the apartments she lived in during the trial. These apartments had been rigged to allow those in the building behind to listen. According to City records, that building was built some twenty-four years ago."

"Whoa." Lance's face held disbelief. "How was this done?"

A laugh burst from me. "I'll have you speak with my butler; he's done a vast amount of repair to fix the matter."

Tony continued, "Beware: Dame Anastasia is **not** dead." At the exclamations, he added, "She and her accomplice knew of the explosion and escaped, I might add, without alerting anyone! Hundreds dead, hundreds more injured." He pointed at Mr. Clubb. "**Your** building destroyed," his voice turned angry, "and she left my **wife** to take the blame." He shook his head. "And with Dame Anastasia's betrayal, the vast majority of the aristocracy have turned against us." He took a deep breath, let it out. "Our Grand Ball was near-empty. Clearly they believe power lies elsewhere."

The other Patriarchs looked at each other, faces concerned.

Tony's voice turned grim. "I have no interest in negotiating. None whatsoever. I'm here to **warn** you! We have a threat, **right** here in our city, that puts our **entire** way of life into peril. And whatever any of you might think, I'm glad to have had this meeting. There is so much we each don't know, merely because no one has ever dared tell us."

The others looked at each other. Most nodded. Mrs. Clubb wiped her eyes, as did Mrs. Hart.

Tony said, "We've all had our secrets, for good reason. But our secrets are being used to harm us. Whoever our adversary is, he seems to know them all, and the only defense we have is to work together." He looked around the room, gazing for a long moment at Gardena, who shook her head slightly, then he sighed. "I have no further secrets. Who will go first?"

Silence fell, each person glancing at the others.

Jack stood. "Few of you here will like what I have to say," he gazed at Charles Hart, "but I believe I will, as Mr. Spadros put it, 'go first'."

The Tale

Jack said, "I am not as other men, I suppose in many a way. When I was very young, the random violence I saw around me sickened me. Nothing mattered, no one cared, and I was not a good child, but a cruel one. It was after I stabbed another child in rage that my playmates began to call me Black Jack."

He stopped then, his face softening as if with pleasant memory. "But then I met Daniel. Daniel was my retainer, the best man — nay, the best person — I have ever known. I loved him, in every way one man can love another." He hesitated. "And in his own way, I suppose he loved me."

He spread his arms to encompass the room. "At that time, I believed we were all friends. How innocent we were! One night, we went to meet with Charles Hart and his little granddaughter, and Mr. Hart secreted himself with my father." He turned to Julius Diamond. "Do you remember that night? It was during Yuletide, just before the New Year."

Julius Diamond looked away.

Jack continued. "Gardena was just a young girl then and loved to listen at doors. Daniel drew her away, reproving her for such unladylike behavior. Suddenly. he stood stock still for several moments, as if listening, then ran for his horse. I ran after him, calling out, but he was already down the lane. By the time I got to a horse and found him, it was only to see Peedro Sluff shoot my beloved dead."

He put his hand to his forehead. "I lost my way that night. I said things, screamed words of vengeance and hate which I have long since come to regret."

Then he turned to me. "I beg your forgiveness, Mrs. Spadros. I should have never spoken to you the way I did. You were a mere child, who'd just witnessed terrible things! It was only that night we met in the factory that I realized how much my rage must have frightened you. You were so terrified of me!"

I nodded. The horror of being tied by the man I feared most had made me so desperate to escape that my fingernails tore against the rope. They still hadn't really grown back properly.

"My brothers found me riding through the streets of Spadros weeping, Daniel lying dead on his horse beside me. Nothing about the situation made sense. How did Daniel, Roy Spadros, Peedro Sluff, and two Pot rag children —"

Tony said, "**Two** children?"

I shook my head, heart breaking, and put my hand on his.

Jack continued as though Tony hadn't spoken. "— come to even be together in the Spadros Pot? It was a chance word by one maid to another outside my door 'perhaps this ordeal has driven him mad' that I came up with my plan."

His **plan**? He had been what, sixteen?

I felt stunned: the rage Jack showed the night of Air's death was simply the devastation of a boy who had seen his first love murdered in front of him.

And the thought came: *just like me.*

At first, I didn't understand this thought. But then I considered Air, the deep friendship we'd shared, even though we were only twelve at the time. How his death had haunted me these fourteen years.

I put my face in my hands, realizing how I had misjudged and wronged Jack Diamond over the years.

"I could find no reason to murder Daniel," Jack said, "and no reason Roy Spadros and Peedro Sluff should meet. I needed to know, and I knew no one would tell a boy. Yet few people questioned a madman too closely or cared where he went, or even what he said."

Julius Diamond said, "You mean .. this ... has all been ... a **sham**?"

"I am sorry, father," Jack said. "But I was never mad."

Julius Diamond stared at his son, mouth open.

And I recalled what Jack said to me in the factory: *That is my one great fear: that I am mad, or will become so in truth.*

"From then on," Jack said, "I pretended to be mad. At first, my twin was the only one who knew otherwise." He stopped for a long moment, face downcast, hand to his chin, then continued, "But Jon had never been well, and we knew that if something should befall him then I could have need of another ally. We hadn't considered Gardena — until one day she overheard us, and we had to include her."

Gardena smiled sadly.

Lance Clubb put his arm round her shoulders.

Jack smiled at his sister fondly. "But Gardena has proved to be a mighty ally. Our plan became to encourage the rumors, fan them, make Black Jack Diamond into the most monstrous beast ever concocted. This would both make our family feared and myself free to wander the streets without being noticed." He smiled to himself, amused. "After all, a madman acting mad or going where he should not is hardly remarkable."

A few nervous chuckles went round the room. I imagined the Clubbs were highly chagrined at not knowing this before now.

"At the same time, Jon," at this, Jack chuckled, "of all people, would become the most perfect gentleman. Speak with the other gentlemen, learn their secrets. Gardena would woo the ladies, gleaning what she could there." He glanced at Gardena. "At the time, she loved my ... Daniel ... as dearly as I, and his death devastated her. She blamed herself for his death, reasoning that if she had not been at the door he would never had heard the secret which killed him. She was more than willing to see his murder avenged."

Jack took a deep breath. "I won't bore you with details; here is what we learned. I apologize for any hurt this may cause you. Mrs. Jacqueline Spadros is Charles Hart's daughter, born from his relations with one Fanny Kaplan, a brothel owner of the Spadros Pot."

Judith Hart turned white, eyes wide with horror as she glanced round, then began to cry, face in her hands.

Charles Hart sat silent, his face bleak.

I felt sorry for them both. For her, having her misery laid bare to the other Families like this must have been excruciating. She might have said she wanted the truth to come out, but to have it actually happen, in front of men, in front of **servants** ... that was entirely different. I could only imagine how horrible it must feel.

And did Mr. Hart regret me? Regret his liaison with my mother? Regret how he'd hurt his wife, his son?

Jack said, "Roy Spadros somehow learned of this. Unable to find her any other way, the Pot being what it is, he commissioned Peedro Sluff to find the girl and bring her to him. From Daniel's reaction at the door, he must have feared that Roy Spadros was to come to harm that night. I have no other way to understand it. What I don't understand at all was why Daniel cared about Roy Spadros so."

That was a good point. Under what possible circumstance might a Diamond manservant even come into contact with another quadrant's Patriarch, much less care about Roy Spadros?

Jack took a deep breath, not looking at anyone. "And I can only **guess** who hired him."

Charles Hart raised his head. "I hired Peedro Sluff to murder Roy."

I'd suspected it, too. But to hear it said ... "If not for you, I'd —"

Tony scoffed, his words bitter. "Be free of this place?"

I turned to Tony. "Of years of torment by Roy! Of the years I lost with my people." I glared at Mr. Hart, furious. "My kin **died** whilst I was kept here, for **no** good reason."

Mr. Hart looked at me, stricken. "There **was** good reason!" Then he spoke to everyone. "Roy threatened to harm little Jacqui, who was only eleven! She was blameless in the matter." He shrugged. "Peedro had done work of this kind before. No one would have suspected my hand in this." His face fell. "But I was betrayed."

Jack nodded. "And when I tried to learn the truth, you had your men try to kill me."

Julius Diamond exclaimed, "**What?**"

Jack turned to his father. "Why did **your** men try to kill me?"

Rachel Diamond gave her husband a horrified look. "**What?**"

Julius turned away. "I never told them to —"

Jack tilted his head, a wry expression on his face. "Ah, but they said you **did**. I was in your killing room, awaiting the Spadros man you'd captured to do the deed."

Tony gaped back and forth at them both

Jack strode forward, pointing a finger at his father. "But you never thought one of your men would set me **free**, did you?" He turned away. "You thought you had it **all** planned. Silence the ruined hand, then blame it on our enemy."

His father's face darkened even further. "We'll discuss that later."

Jack shook his head in exasperation.

"No," said Tony sternly. "We'll discuss it now. You captured a Spadros man. Who?"

Julius looked disgusted. "Some drunken disgraced cop. When I learned someone had freed Jack, I dumped the man back where he came from. Unharmed. I had nothing to do with the man's death."

I put up a hand. "Wait. Is this the detective who was investigating the Bridges Strangler?"

"I suppose," Julius Diamond said. "Unless you have other drunken disgraced cops around that I don't know about. If I recall, his name was Kanhu."

"Yeah," said Tony, "that's the one."

Jack fixed his father with an even stare. "You never answered my question."

Julius Diamond's face went from confusion to awareness to a sneaking fear. He glanced at me, Mr. Hart. "I'll not discuss that here, not now."

Jack set his fists upon his hips. "Either you're here to contribute or you're not. We're all adults here, no matter what you might think." He made a "go on" gesture towards his father. "Speak."

Julius blinked, seemingly puzzled and alarmed at the changes in his son. "I wish to start no wars."

Tony let out a laugh. "You think I want one? For gods' sakes, man — spit it out."

Julius sighed, shoulders slumping. "I sent spies into Spadros quadrant." He glanced at Mr. Hart, then at me, then back at him. "After you showed me her portrait. I wanted to verify who she was."

Jack said, "So you sent spies into Spadros. Why is that bad enough to want me dead? What are you **not** saying?"

I sat back, confused. "Why did you care so much about **me**? What possible reason could the Diamond Patriarch —"

"I wasn't Patriarch yet," Julius said. "My father was."

I shook my head. "Whatever. Why did you care so much about me? Why risk war to find out who I was? Why did I even come to your **notice**? Had Mr. Hart asked you —? Wait, no. I can see from his face he knew nothing of this. What was **really** going on?"

Charles Hart and Julius Diamond both fell silent, eyes on the floor.

Jack relaxed. "Perhaps I finally understand." He turned to Mr. Hart. "You see, after many years, Jon told me of the night that you brought him to the Spadros Pot to meet Mrs. Spadros when she was but a child —"

Gardena exclaimed, "Good gods, Jack, **no!**"

"— and how you promised that she would be his someday."

The Friendship

Tony gasped.

Gardena scowled. "Gods **damn** you, Jack!"

I had never heard Gardena Diamond curse. Ever.

At first, I didn't understand why Tony gasped, or what was upsetting Gardena so. I only vaguely remembered the night Jon first came to see me, back when I was eleven.

Yet realization struck like a thunderbolt. "Jon was meant ... to marry ... **me**?"

"Yes," Jack said.

"This was **not** what he wanted," Gardena said, angry tears in her eye, "and you **know** it!"

I turned away to lean on my right armrest, stunned. It all came together: the hours Jonathan spent with me, the encouragement, his deep unselfish friendship.

Jonathan Diamond loved me, all this time.

How it must have hurt Jon to know Tony lay with me, to see us together, to see me carry Tony's child — a child Jon **knew** I didn't want ... when all the time, I'd been promised to **him**!

Yet he'd called Tony his brother. Jonathan Diamond had been our best and most loyal friend.

"At the time, Gardena and I couldn't understand it," Jack said. "No offense to you, my dear, you were hardly suitable."

There was nothing I could say to that, even if I had been able to speak for the tears.

Tony pointed at Julius Diamond, voice shaking. "Yet you couldn't just **trust** the man offering his daughter in alliance with your son. You had to send in **spies**, spies who undoubtedly tipped Roy off and brought notice upon her. Whatever Roy did to her, it was **you** who sent her there."

Julius sat head down, hunched over. "I know." Then he looked at me. "I'm truly sorry. I never meant any of this to happen."

I'd never been so angry in my life. "Jon died **alone**!" I pointed at him. "My great-grandmother is **dead**!"

Tony said, "Oh, gods, Jacqui —"

Yet I spoke over him. "And I wasn't there for either of them. Can you give them back to me?"

Jack's deep voice cut through. "Why was Daniel in the Spadros Pot? How did he know to go there? Did you send him there to spy on her?"

Julius nodded.

The Diamond waiter gasped, stumbled, one hand clasping the table to steady himself.

Gardena sounded anguished. "Oh, gods."

I stared at Julius Diamond, at the fear in his eyes. He'd tried to kill Jack ... because he was **afraid** of him!

Jack's disguise had worked too well. Mr. Diamond had been afraid of what his mad son might do if he were to learn how his father had been part of driving the man he loved to his death.

Gardena looked furious. "By the Blessed **Dealer**! I **never** want to hear **another** word about our people killed back then." She pointed at her father. "**You** helped start the **war**!"

I thought Jack would rage, or fling himself at his father. But he got very still, and tears rose in his eyes. He stumbled to a chair, and sat, face in his hands.

I felt numb, drained. My friends, my family, my home ... all taken from me because of one man's suspicions. Air dead trying to save me that night when Roy met with Peedro. Jack's friend dead as Peedro took what seemed the only way to be freed from the Pot. Thousands on both sides dead in the war that followed. Me sold to Roy; Jon and I, never married as we should have been.

I couldn't look at Julius Diamond. I feared I might try to throttle the man myself.

Jack remained bent, his face in his hands. Yet his hands were cupped, only his fingertips touching his face. "So we reasoned most of this before the Grand Ball." He raised his head; tears lay in his eyes. "Your reaction, Mr. Hart, at my threat upon Mrs. Spadros gave us the truth. We understood the trap you were in, how you longed to rescue your daughter from Roy Spadros but felt unable."

Jack glanced in my direction, and without meaning to, I nodded. Jack had tried to tell me this long ago, that night in the factory.

Mr. Hart didn't look at me, his face full of grief and guilt.

"But," Jack said, "there became a problem. Someone attacked you, Mr. Spadros, and we realized the flaw in our plan. A third party wished me to take blame for their actions."

"Whoever is behind the Red Dogs," Tony said.

"Yes," Alexander Clubb and Jack said, a the same time.

The room fell silent

Tony gave Alexander Clubb a long, even gaze.

The seconds ticked by, the two men peering at each other. Neither one moved.

Mr. Clubb's face turned crimson. "I began the Red Dogs," he blurted out. "The children's gang. Many years ago. I now wish I had never done so."

Tony nodded; his tone turned bitter. "I thought as much."

I said, "I don't understand."

Mr. Clubb sighed. "I primarily wanted to undermine Roy's hold over this city. But I also confess I wished to rule over it in his stead. We hold the Aperture. To the outsiders, we speak for Bridges. Under Roy's lead, the place was becoming an embarrassment. I felt I could do better." He shrugged. "Why not try?"

Charles Hart shook his head, his face amused.

And I recalled that as Charles Hart's grandson, our little Acevedo was heir to both the Spadros and Hart quadrants. With half the city in Charles Hart's power, the others would be hard pressed to defeat him.

But then there was Gardena and Tony's son, who was the heir to Spadros and Diamond. Illegitimate, yes, but the elder.

And Diamond and Clubb were soon to be joined. If Lance adopted Tony's son and pressed the claim ...

Or if one day, Roland did. What could happen?

By birth or by marriage, Roland could one day lay claim to three of the four quadrants. And being raised by Mrs. Clubb, the woman who'd tried to use me to extort the Cathedral? What kind of man might he become?

The people of Spadros might hate me because I was a Pot rag, but they hated the Diamonds almost as much, if not more. Who would Spadros quadrant choose: Roland or Acevedo?

Or would they choose no one? The quadrant could devolve into a dozen rival groups fighting for power, just like in those terrible days of old.

Even if that didn't happen, what would happen to the Harts? Mr. Hart had for some reason not made my heritage public. But what if he did? Even if all continued well, and Roland was content to lead his quadrants, would the Hart people follow a Spadros Heir? Or would Spadros quadrant, after so many decades of hating the Harts at Roy's urging, now accept them as allies?

Any one of these scenarios could tear the city apart.

The big question was: how much of this had Alexander Clubb known when he made his plan to rule the city?

Mr. Clubb seemed somber. "Someone has been steadily taking over my people, forming false Red Dog cells, and creating havoc."

"Yes," Jack said. "I first learned of it when I discovered a Spadros boy was murdered in my quadrant." He gestured towards Tony. "With one of those Red Dog cards upon him. Another Spadros boy had been held in the cellar of my factory for no reason I could see."

With one fluid motion, Jack stood, pacing back and forth, the cloak he wore fluttering at his ankles behind him. "Several things have bothered me. Joseph Kerr inviting me to that Grand Ball. His willingness to both distract my men and call Roy Spadros from the room in order for me to get close to Mrs. Spadros —"

Julius gasped. He'd shot several of his men for not keeping Jack away from me that night.

Jack stopped, his eyes fixed on his father. "Yes. This time, my cousins were not at fault."

Julius put his head in his hands with a moan, and sat unmoving.

"Other things have happened," Jack continued, "small things, but the name Kerr kept appearing. Rumors of Joseph Kerr claiming the Red Dogs were from my quadrant. Rumors that the Kerrs were actually **bankrolling** the Red Dogs —"

Mr. Clubb and I both said, "**What?**"

Jack said, "— Then there were the old unsavory rumors about Joseph Kerr: the libertine, the gambler, the scoundrel. All rumors, no? But the thought kept sticking in my mind."

I frowned. "There's no **way** they're involved with this!"

Tony put his hand on mine and shook his head.

Jack continued as if I'd not spoken. "I began with investigating the boy who was put into my factory and the strange events which followed. First, a brown-haired gentleman wearing brown and a dark-haired maid took the boy. They shot the men who held him and terrified my workers, then left without a trace." He shook his head. "The men left dead had nothing in their pockets, and appeared to be from another quadrant. No one there claimed to know them." He kept pacing. "It took almost a year to find the boy, who lives in the Spadros slums. But his mother wouldn't talk with me, and the child was almost comatose with fear.

"Everywhere I searched I found reports of murdered boys. These boys were also from the Spadros slums: the one left dead in Diamond was the kidnapped boy's older brother. The only link between these boys is a woman that Constable Paix Hanger has put forth an extraordinary effort to find: Eunice Ogier."

Tony peered at Jack, confused.

I knew Tony recalled the name: I'd shown him Eunice Ogier's gravestone at the Spadros Country House after Roy's murder.

Jack threw himself into an overstuffed chair with a chuckle. "Miss Ogier is a maid, she is a widow, she is Romani, she is tall, she is short, she is a detective, she is a Pot rag, she is a rich woman who suddenly appears to help the poor. Half the city has some story about her."

Mr. Hart chuckled.

"When Mr. and Mrs. Spadros separated," Jack said, "it became clear that Mrs. Spadros had a business arrangement that none of us knew about. Her obvious intent was to become an independent woman of means. It took me a while to put the puzzle together, but what a surprise to learn that the elusive Eunice Ogier and Mrs. Jacqueline Spadros were one and the same!"

Most of the room gaped at me, faces shocked.

I sighed. "That Constable will be the death of me. Yet you are the better detective."

Jack rose and bowed.

Then I realized that Tony was staring at me, mouth open. "Forgive me," I said. "I suppose I never told you my aliases. I'll tell you everything later."

Jack sunk into his seat, looking weary. "Clearly Mrs. Spadros was not the kidnapper, but instead went to great lengths to retrieve the boy, putting herself in peril to do so. The closer I got to the answer, the more I was followed. A Red Dog card appeared on my step, and once, was even left in my rooms."

In his **rooms**?

"I began to receive threatening letters. Once, I was attacked by men I didn't recognize, and my men only just arrived in time." Jack leaned forward, speaking to me. "After that, I felt that **you** might be in danger. After many attempts to contact you, it seemed that the only way for me to reach you was by bringing you to me. It also seemed that the only way I would be able to learn the truth was for Jack Diamond to die."

Rachel and Julius Diamond gasped.

Jack leaned back, facing away. "Jonathan and Gardena helped set up the whole thing." He looked at me. "And as I said he would be, Jon was angry that I tricked you."

Jack then turned to his father, his face sad. "I couldn't bring you into this. I didn't know why you would send men to kill me. I didn't even know if what they said was true, or if our enemies had suborned them. It was obvious we had an enemy that could reach inside Diamond Manor, and I would rather have the target upon myself. And if you were innocent, I couldn't trust that you'd react as though you didn't know I was alive."

Julius nodded. Rachel stared at her son, mouth open, hands on her cheeks as she shook her head in disbelief.

Jack said, "After I falsified my death, I became free to move about without restriction. After my arm healed, of course."

His parents glanced at him, then me, confused.

Jack put his hand on his upper left arm. "Did Mrs. Spadros not tell you? I was shot by a ricochet when her rescuers tried to enter."

They shook their heads, speechless.

"I spent many a month at a cabin I'd built in the Diamond forest, thinking," Jack said, "until a plan came to me. For a time, I traveled, learning whatever I might about several things that puzzled me." He shrugged. "I may relate some of these later. During that time, I wore black. I let my hair and beard grow, took up a cane, wore false spectacles, began investing in property." He began speaking with a pronounced drawl. "Then I took on a Nitivali accent, returned to Bridges as a wealthy out-of-town gentleman, and retained an attorney in Clubb quadrant." His speech returned to normal. "I told him I was interested in investing in business with Mr. Polansky Kerr, and wanted to know about the man's reputation and holdings."

An arm emerging from the glare to strike Trey Louis on the head ...

"Wait," I said. "**You** rescued me. In the alley!"

Jack smiled, chuckling. "That I did."

Tony gaped at him a full second. "Then I owe you my gratitude, sir." He looked at the confused faces around us. "Dame Anastasia's great-nephew, a man calling himself Trey Louis, is in league with the Red Dog Gang. He tried to abduct her in broad daylight, with my men not ten yards away."

Surprise and horror all round.

Once the room quieted, Jack continued. "My attorney's investigations took several months, but what he learned was astonishing. While Mr. Kerr appears to be just an elderly man living with his grandchildren, he actually owns over a third of the city."

The Disbelief

Some, like me, reacted in stunned silence. I couldn't believe what I was hearing!

Others began to speak, all at once:

"This is absurd."

"How could this be?"

"This is incredible!"

Mr and Mrs. Hart simply sat, arms folded, looking bleak.

Jack held up a hand and the room quieted. "Mr. Polansky Kerr IV is registered in the city as Mr. Lans Pasha."

Gardena put her hand to her chin.

Pasha? Josie had used the name Finette Pasha once when she visited my apartments, hooded and cloaked. At the time, I'd thought it simply a name she'd made up as a way not to let anyone else know she'd come there.

"Mr. Kerr has six sons, all from different mothers. The unfortunate Master Ely Kerr," at this Jack glanced at me, "father to your friends, Mrs. Spadros, is his youngest. Master Ely told me a great deal ... once I bought him some drink."

I felt outraged. "For shame!"

Jack leaned forward. "I needed the man to talk. I had little time, I was being followed, and I barely got away unnoticed. In any case, the five other sons are registered using entirely different surnames. They each own companies which each manage and own a whole host of other companies. These own everything from the slums of Bridges to the management company for the zeppelin station."

I'd been to Mr. Kerr's home, on the borders of the Hart slums. If he were so rich, why would they live so simply?

Alexander Clubb said, "I will check into that right away."

Jack said, "None of these companies — or even the owners — are named Kerr, or anything close to it. Most are variations of King, Ruler, or Monarch, in other languages. It's clear they want their true power to be disguised."

Something tickled at the back of my memory. But I said, "Before he took him to Azimoff, Joe told me his grandfather was dying."

Alexander Clubb said, "Mrs. Spadros ... Mr. Polansky never left the city. I let Joseph Kerr pass, hoping that'd be the last we'd see of him."

I couldn't grasp what the man was saying. "Joe ... **left**? Without his **grandfather**?"

Mr. Clubb gave a relieved nod.

Why would Joe leave the city without him? Why would he leave the city without **me**? What was he **doing**?

None of this made sense. "Why are you so glad Joe's gone? What has he done?"

Mr. Clubb looked away.

I said, "If you have information I don't ... well, I'd like to know."

Mr. Clubb said, "It's not my story to tell, Mrs. Spadros. I'd not like to betray a confidence."

Mr. Hart looked clearly uncomfortable, like he wanted to speak but decided not to.

"And you," I said to Mr. Hart. "You hate Joe, too. What went on between you?"

Mr. Hart hesitated, face grim. "I'd rather not speak of it, Mrs. Spadros. It's about someone else entirely." He shook his head, not looking at me. "It's ... you truly don't want to know."

No one spoke, yet many glanced at each other.

What was going **on**?

Joe had evidently been accused of more than I thought. Something truly horrid. Perhaps that's why he felt compelled to go, with or without me. But if Joe really was accused of something that horrible, why did Mr. Clubb simply let him pass? And if he needed to leave the city that badly, why didn't his grandfather — or Josie — go with him? "What about Mr. Polansky?"

Mr. Hart shrugged, not looking at me.

Something icy touched my soul. "Has Mr. Polansky **died**? Is that what no one wishes to tell me?"

A laugh burst from Mr. Hart's lips. "The old scoundrel will probably outlive us all."

I stared at Mr. Hart, then realized my mouth hung open. "Joe told me he was dying."

Mr. Hart chuckled, shaking his head. "So far as I know, he's not sick at all."

Mr. Polansky wasn't sick ... at **all**? "I was at their **home**! I heard him upstairs, in his **bed**! Miss Josephine has told me for years that he was **dying**!"

Mr. Hart swallowed, peered at the floor. No one else moved.

And their reactions made me wonder. Josie said her grandfather was dying. Had she known what he was doing all this time?

I wouldn't believe it. "Josephine Kerr has never lied to me, ever. Even when it would've benefited her to do so. She's cared for her grandfather for years, spoken with his doctors — wouldn't she, of all people, know the truth of his condition? I can't believe she'd lie about something this important."

Mr. Hart leaned forward, peering into my eyes, "But she has, Jacqui. Or she's being deceived more masterfully than you could imagine." He shrugged. "The man's as well as I am." Then he laughed, leaning back. "Probably more so. Those stairs are a horror."

Rachel Diamond had been watching me. She'd faked the severity of her illness for many a year, even keeping the truth from her children.

I said, "Could Mr. Kerr have faked his illness, paid off his doctors, convinced Josie he was dying, while doing whatever he was doing?"

Mr. Hart shrugged. "I wouldn't put it past him."

The man was over ninety. Was Mr. Kerr actually ill, like Mrs. Diamond, but faking how sick he was? Many ailments didn't show until near death.

Or had Mr. Kerr faked being ill entirely?

Yet if I were to believe Jack Diamond — which I wasn't sure I did — Mr. Kerr oversaw great wealth.

I knew a bit about what overseeing great wealth entailed just from the conversation I'd had with Sawbuck after the museum opening. The only way Mr. Polansky could be doing all that he'd done was if he had dozens of lackeys we'd not yet seen carrying out his commands.

And if Mr. Kerr had only **pretended** to be ill, that explained that fool of a doctor tending Josie when she got the women's fever a year earlier. The man probably wasn't a doctor at all — just someone paid to tell Joe and Josie that their grandfather was dying.

My stomach knotted. When Josie was truly sick, Joe must have called for the man because for all those years, they'd trusted him. That so-called "doctor's" incompetence almost got Josie killed!

But if Mr. Kerr wasn't sick, he would've known from his lackeys that Josie was desperately ill.

That man let Josie almost die, without saying a word! I sat back, stunned. "This is unbelievable." I couldn't believe a man would risk his own grand-daughter's life like that.

And I recalled what Joe had said about his grandfather, several years back: *the man is a monster*.

Joe told me his grandfather had beaten them, terrorized them, blackmailed him with threats of killing me.

Joe left the city without his grandfather. So either he'd given up on him, found out his grandfather had lied to them, or both.

Lance Clubb said, "So Polansky Kerr owns companies, and he's an extremely good liar. I don't see how this relates to any murders."

Jack said, "The whole establishment, down to the most wretched slum tenement, is coordinated by a Miss Finette Pasha."

Josie had said she managed her grandfather's affairs. I now saw why she'd been chosen, rather than her twin. Joseph Kerr was an utter wastrel, a scoundrel, a cad.

But for her to be in charge of all **this**? It seemed incredible.

"Everything goes through her," Jack said. "Including a rather large sum paid to the family of one Stephen Rivers, a boy who was found murdered in the Diamond under-tunnels on Market Center."

Mr. Hart's jaw dropped. He leaned forward, a stunned expression on his face.

I felt both appalled and astonished. "This makes no sense. Why give money to **them**?"

"That I don't know," Jack said. "But the boy's uncle was a worker in one of their companies and may have threatened to go to the police if someone didn't pay up." Jack paused. "Which is disturbing, because it meant that Stephen said something that the uncle felt linked the Kerr family — or, should I say, the Pashas — to the boy's murder."

"Or perhaps was the cause of it," Julius Diamond said. He raised his head to peer at Jack. "Where's the uncle now?"

"Dead," Jack said. "Found in the river. The rest of the boy's family has disappeared — hopefully they left the city alive."

Josie can't possibly be involved with this. "How did you learn of it?"

Jack grinned. "Kind words to a spinster teller work wonders."

Lance said, "So they paid off a boy's family." He leaned forward, glancing around. "What aren't you saying?"

"Forgive me, Master Jack, but this may help." Tony glanced at me, then back at Lance. "Whilst looking into Master Rainbow's murder, one of my men met up with a Constable who's been involved in the investigations into the Bridges Strangler. They've spoken extensively on the matter. This Constable claims the marks on this boy Stephen Rivers' neck match those of the other victims exactly."

Gardena gasped.

Tony hesitated. "And I had my man go over the coroner's records for Master Rainbow's case." He looked around. "At the risk of being indelicate, it appears he'd been bound ... and ..." He let out a breath. "Someone tried to strangle Master Rainbow, perhaps a day before he was shot."

I stared at Tony, appalled. To torture a man, then shoot him?

Tony nodded. "The marks match those of the rest."

Mrs. Clubb began crying, putting her head on Mr. Clubb's shoulder. He put his arm around her.

The grief returned, and I got out my handkerchief. Master Rainbow didn't deserve this sort of end.

Mrs. Clubb began to wail, sobbing, "Oh, gods, poor Blaze ..." and her husband held her to his chest, rocking her.

Many looked aside.

I felt annoyed at her display. Why did this **upset** her so? Had she and Master Rainbow formed a friendship he'd never told me about?

Odd, but in character. Making friends seemed to have come easily to him.

Once all quieted, Lance said, "So we have proof of Lans Pasha — or this Finette Pasha, but I assume it was at his command — paying the family of a boy killed by the Bridges Strangler." He leaned back, hand to his chin. "It could be a coincidence, I suppose. But it is interesting, in light of that exposé series in the *Bridges Daily*. It said Mayor Freezout covered up those crimes, even to the point of intentionally hanging the wrong man." His eyes narrowed. "And now we have proof the Strangler still hunts — another victim, and a high-card to boot. So ... this Pasha fellow and Freezout could be, what, partners?"

"So it appears," Jack said.

My mind went blank. Polansky Kerr ... and Chase Freezout? Did Mr. Kerr know what Mr. Freezout planned to **do** to me?

This couldn't be true. I leaned forward. "This is an inferior line of play. How many people in the city use the name Lans Pasha? How many use the name Finette? Are you certain Mr. Polansky and this particular Lans Pasha are the same man? Is there any proof whatsoever that this money came from the Kerr family?"

"I can show you what my attorney found," Jack said calmly.

I would not be deterred. "Someone named Finette Pasha might have signed checks, but that doesn't prove it was Josie!"

Those sitting around the circle looked at each other.

"And do we know what the money was **for**? Perhaps Mr. Kerr gave the money to this family to **help** them. We can't know until someone speaks with them."

No one said anything. Mr. Hart shook his head, looked away.

Why were these people so ready to believe evil of the Kerr family? I crossed my arms. "So far, Master Jack, I've heard nothing but gossip and conjecture."

Jack said calmly, "I'm sorry you feel this way."

I scoffed. "Do you have anything **else** to say? Any **others** here to give grief to?"

Jack only sat watching me, his eyes sad.

The more I saw of this man, the less I liked. I stood, feeling weary. "Then I suppose it's time to tell my tale."

The Gentleman

I took a deep breath, unsure how much to say. I'd learned too many puzzling things. So I decided just to give them the facts, as I knew them. "I began my investigator business when I was sixteen, some ten years past. I specialize in missing persons."

I'd feared no one would care about any of this, but the others appeared interested in my story. "I met Blaze Rainbow in the Diamond Pot whilst searching for a missing boy named David Bryce. This was over four years ago, just after the New Year. At the time, Master Rainbow called himself Morton."

Mrs. Clubb twitched at that, but kept silent.

"He asked us to use the name Graham Morton if we were ever questioned about him at the inquest." I held out my hand to Tony, whispering, "The card?" Once I had it, I held it up so all might see. "There was a stamp exactly like this upon the wall where the boy had been taken."

The rest looked surprised at that.

I said, "Later, Morton came to Spadros Manor dressed as a gentleman, claiming he was an investigator named Blaze Rainbow who lived in Hart quadrant."

Mr. Clubb appeared startled, but he also kept silent.

I wondered what Morton had told **them**. "He'd been working with a red-haired woman who he first called his maid, then his sister, then his business partner: an outsider named Zia Cashout. He and the woman lied, first claiming she was deaf, but then clearly she was not."

To my surprise, the room watched me intently. "Master Rainbow and I worked together to find the boy. During that time, Master Rainbow told me he had an employer he refused to identify. This employer had started a children's gang called the Red Dogs —"

Again, Mr. Clubb seemed startled by this, yet didn't speak. Why was he startled? He already **said** he started the Red Dogs.

Taking a breath, I continued, "— yet the gang was being infiltrated, and falsely blamed for kidnapping and murder."

Mr. Hart said, "Murder?"

Morton said he'd worked for Mr. Hart. If Morton worked for Mr. Hart ... wouldn't Mr. Hart **know** this? But I nodded. "Yes, the strangulations of at first David's older brother, then other children. Some were in the Red Dogs themselves." I shuddered. "Stephen Rivers was one."

"Wait." Gardena seemed perplexed. "So you believe these Red Dog children were attacked by the Bridges Strangler."

"Yes." Taking a deep breath, I went on. "The group calling themselves the Red Dog Gang is now entirely made up of adults."

I didn't want to get off the subject too much, so I forced myself to focus. "Master Rainbow said he had been tasked by his employer to learn who these people were and find some way to stop them."

Tony and Mr. Clubb looked confused.

I didn't know how much to reveal. "Master Rainbow said Zia Cashout told him that she knew a man in the District Attorney's office who could help. She arranged a meeting in some restaurant."

Tony snorted. "I **knew** Rainbow wasn't a Bridges man!" He shook his head. "To accept help from the District Attorney's office? In public? He'd have to be out of his mind."

The Dickens accent when he was ill — but not anything like Trey Highcard's, more like Zia's. The unusual words he'd use sometimes ...

Why hadn't I seen it before?

Who **was** Morton? And where was he **from**?

Heart pounding, I continued. "Master Rainbow told me he met with them. Five were present: Master Rainbow, Miss Zia, a man claiming to be a police detective named Jake Bower —"

Both Julius Diamond and his son Jack gaped at me.

"— the man claiming to be from the District Attorney's office, who called himself Frank Pagliacci —"

Tony let go of my hand, shaking his head in disgust.

"— and a young woman secretary, dark of hair and pale of skin, who they called Birdie." I stopped for a moment, to recall what Morton said. "Frank Pagliacci told Master Rainbow he had an informant who would tell Master Rainbow what he needed to know — if he met with me first. Mr. Pagliacci also told Master Rainbow that he had **faked** David Bryce's kidnapping, and was using this false kidnapping case to lure me to the meeting."

Lance let out a laugh. "Sounds implausible at best."

"Well, I thought so too. Why not just speak to me directly? And I know the boy's mother. She's suffered terribly."

Tony took my hand.

"Master Rainbow went along with this story, he says — said — because he trusted Miss Zia's judgment in the matter." I took a breath, feeling shaky. "But Master Rainbow was deceived. Apparently when he sent a message to this Mr. Pagliacci, the boy returned saying the office had been cleared out."

Murmurs filled the room.

I tried to keep the images of death and blood in that factory basement from my mind. "We rescued the boy. I shot a man who I believe to be Frank Pagliacci. But I later learned from Dame Anastasia that he'd survived."

Nods around the room. Lance said, "I recall from your trial. She was this man's lover, was she not?"

"She was." I took a deep breath. Dame Anastasia might say she had regard for me. But she'd done so much to betray me that I just didn't know what to think. "A few weeks after we'd freed the boy, Master Rainbow came to us beaten, collapsed upon our doorstep, claiming the Feds were after him. He said he'd been chased by them the entire time, and that they exploded his boat as he slept in it."

Mrs. Clubb gasped.

I turned to her. "You might have read about the explosion at your marina in the papers." Then I addressed the room once more. "We kept Master Rainbow in our home until he was well, and he helped me stay safe during the zeppelin explosion."

Tony broke in then. "While he stayed with us, I persuaded him to speak of his employer." He gave the Clubbs a quick glance. "I allowed him to stay with us in exchange for acting on my behalf in the matter of my son."

Gardena crossed her arms, obviously unhappy that Tony mentioned him.

There were no questions; clearly everyone already knew about Tony and Gardena's son Roland. Except, apparently, Rob Pearson, our waiter for the day, who gaped at us, eyes wide.

The rest gave me surreptitious looks; I shrugged. "I want only the best for the boy; he's blameless in this matter. What is he now, eight?"

Tony didn't look at me. "Nine."

Julius Diamond growled, leaning forward with anger in his eyes. But his wife Rachel put a hand on his arm, and he relented.

I continued. "But I didn't believe Master Rainbow's story about the Feds, and neither did my husband. Exploding boats and chasing someone around the city sounded more like Frank's men to me."

Mr. Hart snorted in amusement.

"Master Rainbow told me some time after this that he believed his employer had betrayed him to his enemies —"

Mrs. Clubb said, "**What?**"

Tony frowned, puzzlement on his face.

I nodded. "— and he wished to learn why. After I left Spadros Manor and the trial ended, I allowed him to rent a room at my apartments."

Mrs. Clubb leaned forward. "What was he like there?"

I wondered what her interest was in the matter. "Kindly, always a gentleman. Well-liked. A good investigator. Very helpful, particularly in the matter of getting clients to pay." Then I hesitated, searching for the right way to say this. "I always did feel, though, that at times he was doing something other than what he claimed. The address he gave in Hart quadrant was false, for one. At the time, I thought only that he had yet to trust us with his true home. But once after he'd been living in my apartments for some time, he said he was off two weeks fishing, and he wasn't a bit tanned."

"Heh," said Mr. Hart.

"I never wished to press the matter. I regarded him as an older brother, perhaps even a father. He always gave good advice."

Tony seemed downcast. Mr. Hart put his hand to his chin. Mrs. Hart crossed her arms, face set.

"He'd had a number of attacks against him, and so I warned him — for his own sake — to leave my apartments as soon as possible once I returned to Spadros Manor. I thought his enemies might not dare to attack with me there, but ..."

I looked round: everyone seemed fixed on my story. Except Mrs. Hart, who was looking aside, apparently lost in her own thoughts.

I sighed. "But once he moved to Clubb, I rarely saw him. He mentioned being roughed up by Hart men at one point, the other by Clubbs. But the last time I saw him, he seemed well." The thought of Morton, dead, made me feel ready to cry.

I didn't want to do this. "My husband has commanded me to reveal all. Perhaps some of this might help." So I told them everything: growing up in the Pot, being sold to Roy, the beatings, the terror. Being forced to marry Tony whilst being in love with another. I didn't name Joe. But I admitted I went to the zeppelin station after the inquest intending to leave the city. How Jonathan Diamond and Morton took me instead to Clubb Manor, and how Mrs. Clubb had tried to use me to blackmail the Cathedral.

Everyone, even Mrs. Hart, had looked most uncomfortable during my story, almost angry. But at the last, Mrs. Clubb looked as if she'd had a revelation.

I said, "I suppose you all know the rest. I've continued my work, returning home after with the Dealer's help Mr. Spadros and I made a son." Who was now forced to live his young life in pain. I took a deep breath, feeling the eyes upon me. "I've done everything I can to learn about this Red Dog Gang and why they kidnapped little David Bryce. We identified the owner of the apartments behind mine once we learned they'd been used for listening — a Mrs. Roberta Bird. No one is registered —"

"Ah," Lance said. "Birdie."

I nodded. "Indeed." Weariness washed over me. "I've had nothing but trouble over this," I gestured at the Diamonds, "as have you."

"I knew it was a mistake for her to go to you," Julius Diamond said. His wife put a hand on his arm, but he shook it off.

I smiled to myself. I'd told her that when she arrived, but it would help nothing to say it. "I truly apologize for the harm my home brought to yours."

Julius Diamond crossed his arms, looking away.

He would never stop hating me. "This Birdie is now going by the name Black Maria —"

Many looked at each other in alarm. Black Maria was another name for the Queen of Spades.

"— and has taken over a children's gang I used to belong to in the Pot called the High-Low Split. There are indications that the false District Attorney's man Frank Pagliacci is consorting with both Black Maria and Zia Cashout. These people used the uprising we had in Spadros some years ago to attack us, then murdered our men as they fled to safety."

Stunned horrified faces all round.

"I tell you this so you'll understand what kind of creatures we face." I took a deep breath, feeling shaky. "Frank Pagliacci has been described as brown of hair and skin, charismatic, well-dressed, and 'very good-looking.' He seems to be the connection between the Red Dog Gang, the High-Low Split, our rogue Spadros men, various tabloids, and the aristocracy. By introducing him to the aristocrats, Dame Anastasia did us more harm than you know."

I didn't yet know what Dame Anastasia's game was. Last I'd seen her, she'd been roaming the streets dressed as a fishwoman. "But from what I've observed so far, Frank Pagliacci isn't intelligent enough to mastermind this conspiracy against the Families, nor to actually run a city. No, I believe him to be their dummy —"

Tony nodded. "Master Jonathan and I agree."

Both Mr. Hart and Mr. Clubb leaned back, hand to chin. Mrs. Diamond sighed.

It felt a bit jarring to hear Jon spoken of as if he were still alive. "So if Frank Pagliacci is not the leader of this cabal, who is?" I gripped my hands together to stop them from shaking. "Dame Anastasia seems convinced that this Red Dog Gang is run by a woman. I'm not sure I believe her. The aristocracy is definitely involved. But a **woman**? In **Bridges**?" The idea seemed ridiculous. "I believe a very old man runs this. He has to be old, to know all the things he knows."

Mrs. Clubb leaned forward eagerly. "Like what?"

I scoffed quietly. "Perhaps if you give me a chance to speak ..."

She crossed her arms and looked away.

I refused to cower: I was Queen, just as much as she was. "Deeply personal, hurtful things. Things only someone with decades of spies inside a Family's Manor might know." I gestured at Mrs. Clubb, who had stopped looking away. "You might do well to check your own home. Have you received any threats?"

She stared at me blankly, mouth open.

I ignored her. "I have thought about this for some time, trying to deduce the structure of this group. First we have a Director, some very old man. Below him are Frank Pagliacci, Zia Cashout, and the young woman secretary, this 'Birdie' woman who now runs the High-Low Split." I took a deep breath, trying to focus. "Master Rainbow was shot at by 'Birdie' at least once. I'm certain either Birdie or Zia forged the papers brought forth at my trial."

Mr. Hart and Tony nodded.

I held up the card. "This is the proof. That writing on the back is the same as that used in the forgeries. And two of the murders — including Master Rainbow's — had a kiss-mark on the cheek in Zia's shade of lipstick."

Mrs. Clubb gasped.

"Good gods," said Mr. Clubb.

I nodded. "So several groups stand against us: the Red Dog Gang, the High-Low Split, the aristocracy, and for a time through former Mayor Freezout, even the District Attorney's office."

Mr. Hart sighed.

Thank the gods Thrace Pike is District Attorney now, I thought. He'd have nothing to do with these scoundrels. "All conspiring against us."

Something else tickled at my mind ...

Jack Diamond held up a hand. "Wait." He glanced at Gardena. "Don't you remember? Oh, gods, it was when we were children! You overheard a woman say something about Pasha —"

"Yes," said Gardena. "I thought I'd heard the name before! Some of the aristocrats, the old women, were telling each other that ..." She put her hand to her chin, looking down. "Old Pasha's going to set things right. Straight. Something like that."

"Wait," Julius Diamond said. "I recall my father telling me the same thing." He looked at me. "Jon told him."

Jack leaned forward. "Don't you see? I don't know ... I was ... perhaps eighteen at the time."

And he was Jon's twin. Jon would've been one and thirty this year, had he lived.

"Good gods," Tony said. "The aristocracy was plotting against us even then!"

I was missing something ... "Wait." I turned to Mr. Hart. "They forged invoices against us both. But we never learned what they stole from **you**." I tried to recall the list ... "A ladies' shop, a button shop, a paper company, mining supply, and oh, a place called 'Open Stakes Trainers'. What was that one?"

Mr. Hart shrugged. "Horse training for circus shows. They could get a horse to do just about anything."

"Did you ever learn what horse? What they taught it to do?"

"No," said Mr. Hart. "I'd sent a man there to get the information on what was purchased, but he never spoke with the trainer." He gave a quick nod. "I'll see to these myself."

"Good," Tony said. "It might help us figure out what their real game is."

I shook my head. That wasn't it. "Their game is subtle. From what they've done, their Director must be entirely charismatic, extremely wealthy, and more cunning, I fear, than any of us. I've spent thousands of hours, years of my life, lost more friends than I can count to their murderous hands."

I glanced at Tony; he took a deep breath, then nodded.

So I faced them all. "I have proof Katherine Spadros was murdered. I believe they were responsible."

It was Rob Pearson this time who faltered, looking as if he might be sick. For the rest? Murmurs, tears, and much glancing away.

I broke in. " But I don't think we've seen their real play yet. And I fear it." I took a deep breath. "Whilst I will keep trying to hunt the Red Dog Gang until my dying day, I am only one woman." I reached for Tony's hand; he gave it. "We are only one Family. We need your help to stop them. That's why we're here." I sat, feeling grieved.

Mrs. Clubb broke the silence. "You're a Memory Girl."

I peered at her, confused. "What do you mean?"

She beamed. "Your conversation with me at our Hotel was over four years ago. You were deeply drunk, after almost dying of alcohol withdrawal. Yet you related it to us today near word for word." She shook her head, tears in her eyes. "If only you'd been born in Clubb!"

Instead of the Spadros Pot.

I took a deep breath. This explained some things.

Feeling shaky, I turned to Mr. Hart. There was one question remaining: if Morton wasn't a Bridges man, why would Mr. Hart hire an outsider? "So ... Blaze Rainbow was **your** man. **Right**?"

"No," Alexander Clubb said sadly. "In a way, he was ours."

Tony gave a slight smile.

He knew this already. "Your man?" I glanced between Mr. Clubb and Mr. Hart. "But Morton told me he worked for the Harts."

Julius Diamond said, "He told me he worked for Mr. Hart, too."

I stared at Mr. Diamond, astonished.

As did Charles Hart. "Julius, he told me he worked for **you**!"

Tony laughed. "Now you see why I called us here."

"I'm glad to be here," said Mr. Clubb soberly. "You see, I have a story of my own." He leaned back, an elbow on the arm of his chair, hand to his chin. "Mrs. Spadros, you've made quite the impassioned speech. But I have to point out that there is someone who directly benefits from all that's gone on. You."

Tony raised his hand. "Now wait just a minute —"

I looked around. "I don't understand."

Mr. Clubb said, "You conveniently left Spadros Manor just as your husband's cousins attacked him. With the trial, and later, living on a lower street, you endeared yourself to a great many in the city. The people say you are the one Family member who truly understands the city's woes." He smiled, but it was unpleasant. "You conveniently arranged to be absent at the time of the most recent attack on your home." Mr. Clubb's expression said he knew exactly where I'd been. "With the death of Roy Spadros, you remove a player who has caused you nothing but trouble and pain. If not for the heroism of your butler and your husband's cousin, you would've also extricated yourself from an unhappy marriage, a troublesome mother-in-law, and a child forced upon you."

I felt so stunned I couldn't speak.

"And now, you're Queen of Spades." He nodded sagely. "An excellent play."

Tony turned to gape at me.

I felt horrified. "**No!** I had **nothing** to ... How could you even **think** that?"

Mr. Clubb said, "Was today's meeting concocted in that factory the night you and Master Jack Diamond met two years past? Does this explain the interference with my son's courtship? The repeated attempts to pair your husband and his sister ... so they might be elsewhere when you began the round? Is this place," he gestured around him, "a trap?"

I began to feel frightened. "**No!** Why would you **believe** that?"

Mr. Clubb leaned back. "I don't. Or I wouldn't be here. But these were the arguments made by my advisors, who vigorously warned me against this meeting."

I stared at him. His **advisors** were discussing ... **me**? I felt mortified.

Gardena peered at me. "Wait. Go back." She leaned forward. "My brother Cesare told me after he took over the quadrant that you thought another spy worked against us, a man as yet uncaught." Then she turned to Mr. Clubb. "By your wife's reaction, Master Rainbow is someone very important to you."

Lance put his hand on hers, but she shook it off. "No," she told Lance. "One day, you may bid me silence as my husband. But today,

I'm a free woman. And I speak for Diamond." She turned to Mr. Clubb. "Now, sir, you must tell us the truth." She glanced between Mr. and Mrs. Clubb. "You're on a first-name basis with Master Rainbow —"

Ah. She'd caught that, too.

"— and by Mr. Anthony's reactions and statements here today, I suspect Master Rainbow has worked for you all along. If Master Rainbow **did** work for you, why was he telling everyone else he worked for someone **different**?" She leaned forward. "Had you sent him to us as a **spy**?"

Mr. Clubb looked chagrined. "We never sent him anywhere. Ever." He took a deep breath. "Master Rainbow didn't actually work for us. He never worked for us. He worked for the Feds."

The Revelations

The room erupted in outrage.

I didn't blame anyone for their reactions. Morton, a man I'd known and trusted for four years, was secretly an **enemy**? I thought I might be sick.

Julius leaned forward. "You betrayed us to the **Feds?**"

Alexander Clubb snorted. "Hardly."

Mrs. Clubb held up a hand. "Please. Perhaps I should explain."

Julius Diamond leaned back, crossing his arms and legs, looking away. "You damn well better."

Mrs. Clubb glanced at him, giving an amused snort. "Very well." She took a deep breath. "Our city is chartered as a garden city, a city of culture. Since the overthrow of the Kerr Dynasty, our city has drifted from its charter. So it's been on a probation of sorts. The Feds demand reports; the Cultural Correctness Committee demands reports. As the guardians of the zeppelin station, and more to the point, the Aperture, it's fallen on the Clubb Family to have to deal with these people."

Mr. Hart laughed. "Oh, that's rich. My grandfather **hated** that your father took it! He always said he wished he would've thought to get the Aperture instead of the Racetrack." He pondered for a moment. "But I think he was happier with his horses."

Mrs. Clubb shook her head slightly and sighed. "Except for a brief period when the city lay in chaos, the Feds didn't actually object to the Coup. If we'd have returned to our charter, they wouldn't have even become involved. They didn't object to the division of the city, nor to the brothels, the infighting, nor even to the manufacture of Party Time. In the rest of Merca, Party Time is perfectly legal."

Lance chuckled.

Mrs. Clubb gave her son an amused glance. "But two things did garner their attention: the Spadros Family's numerous attempts to smuggle alcohol to Chicago —"

This surprised me. *Alcohol?*

Mrs. Clubb said, "It's illegal there, just as Party Time is here." She took a breath. "They'd been importing Party Time back, in trade. Well, the Feds **hated** that! They viewed this as disrupting the peace just as much as importation of weapons or tech. But then there was the chaos after the assassination of Acevedo Spadros II," she looked around, then said, "the grandfather of Mr. Spadros here."

"Father," Tony said. "He was my true-born father, though I have no memory of him." He glanced around, chagrin on his face. "I suppose I had a secret after all."

Julius looked at Tony with astonishment. "Wait. You mean, your **mother** and ...?" The man seemed entirely scandalized.

Tony shrugged. "I only recently learned this."

Julius Diamond covered his mouth with one hand, his eyes wide and horrified.

His wife Rachel chuckled softly to herself. It looked to me as if she'd known the entire time.

"In any case," Mrs. Clubb said, "when things became quiet after Roy's admittedly excessive retribution for his father's death —"

Good gods. Roy knew Molly and his father were having an affair; he'd murdered his first-born son after the boy revealed it. Had Roy orchestrated his own father's death? If so, killing the men he'd persuaded to do it was a fine way to clear the board.

"— the Feds decided to watch, seizing any illegal shipments they discovered. And when the Diamond-Spadros war left the city's powers equally split —"

"Wait," I said. "They weren't before?"

Julius let out a bitter laugh. "No, we owned most of your western mid-card area. We lived there in peace." A spasm of grief crossed his face. "Until Roy came through and slaughtered them all, for 'daring to defy him'. My father gave the territory away to keep Roy from sending assassins after my daughter."

I stared at him, shocked. No **wonder** the Diamonds hated Roy!

Mrs. Clubb continued. "When they received news of a fifth group whose purpose was to sow chaos in the city, the Feds sent undercover agents to investigate."

Tony snorted. "And you let them in."

Alexander Clubb said, "We knew someone aboard the craft was with the Feds —"

"Zia Cashout," I said, feeling bitter.

"Wait," Julius Diamond said to me. "You knew the identity of a Fed inside the city all this time and never told us?"

Fear struck. "I'm sorry! There was so much going on at the time ... Morton told me she was a Fed after the explosion. Before the inquest! No one knew I was an investigator. I feared my husband. I feared what Roy might do to me if he found out I'd had a business behind his back. I never dared tell anyone." I felt angry at myself. "When I learned she'd been a Fed, I should have gone to Mr. Blackberry right then, told him to print her name and description, and —"

"He wouldn't have," Alexander Clubb said. "That would've told the Feds we knew she was there."

Regina Clubb said, "And inciting death on a Federal Agent would've gotten the city taken away for sure." Her tone turned sneering. "You're **way** out of your league here."

Gods, how I hated that woman.

"But until we caught him," Alexander Clubb continued, "and found the proof, we had no idea that Blaze was with the Feds as well."

I felt a shock: they'd been on a first-name basis ... with a Federal Agent! "You should **never** have let Zia Cashout in the city."

"What would you have us do?" Alexander Clubb said. "We didn't know the identity of the Fed, only that she was one of the three hundred or so aboard. So we had no choice but to let her in."

Mrs. Clubb said, "The communication we had with them after the incident with the surface-to-air missile — which, I might add, was not our doing — was very clear. Allow all traffic in and out, no matter how we might feel about those aboard. Or seal the city."

"Hmm," said Mr. Hart. "So they tried to frame us even then."

"What does he mean," I said, looking at Tony, "seal the city?"

"Nothing in or out," Charles Hart said. "They'd close the Aperture on their end. No commerce, no visitors, nothing. Left to stand or fall on our own, without help. A siege, if you would call it such, until we submitted to their governance. Then, our charter would be revoked. Our people would be hunted down, forcibly removed, and spread amongst the other cities. The city under the dome would be razed and given to another group."

Mrs. Clubb said, "Apparently there's a waiting list."

I knew they could take the city, but ... "Can they **do** that?"

"They have before," Mr. Clubb said.

I said, "So M-Master Rainbow already knew about the Red Dog Gang?"

Alexander Clubb said, "Apparently so. Not by that name. But he knew we'd been having trouble." His gaze turned inward. "I should have suspected him then."

"I never suspected him," Mr. Hart said. "He never made any inquiry that I recall."

Julius Diamond shook his head. "He seemed more interested in befriending us than gathering any information."

"I often wondered why he was here," Tony said. "But other than his interest in the Generators — and, well, the Pot, I don't rightly know."

"Heh," Alexander said. "My men caught him trying to call outside the city a day or two before his death. He had his badge and call codes in a compartment in the heel of his shoe!"

Tony laughed.

I said, "No wonder he was so interested in his shoes! I rather thought him a dandy, but ..."

Julius laughed.

Lance seemed annoyed. "All this about the man's shoe is quite amusing. But this is **terrible** news. We trusted a Federal **Agent**! He was in the call room **once**. But how did he know where it was? Had he been there **before**? What did he **tell** them —?"

The rest of us looked at each other, appalled.

Lance said, "What **evidence** did he collect? What can they now **prove** against us? Are we in **danger**? Are they planning to **arrest** us? What can we do to **stop** this?"

The Ally

I had no idea what we were going to do. Even our most trusted ally had secretly been plotting our downfall this whole time.

Mr. Hart said, "It seems incredible that the Feds haven't reacted to Roy's murder."

"They probably don't know," Mr. Clubb said. "I ordered a news blackout in the quadrant until your husband was well."

That this actually worked seemed unlikely. It'd been over a year. Surely a tourist would've brought the news to someone.

But it sounded as if taking quick control of our quadrant made the Feds feel things were calm enough for them to watch, rather than act.

I glanced at Tony. We'd been very, very lucky.

I turned to Mr. Clubb. "What will happen now?"

Mr. Clubb said, "We knew Blaze must have some private way of identifying himself to his people. So we convinced him to give us the information in case he couldn't return at the appointed time, which he agreed to do."

I said, "I'm astonished he trusted you so. What was there to stop you from killing him and pretending he was still in the field?"

Mrs. Clubb looked angry and hurt, but Mr. Clubb put his hand on hers. "She doesn't know, Gina." Then he hesitated.

But before he might speak, Mrs. Clubb broke in, voice shaking. "I was born Regina Morton, in the Little Ireland section of Dickens. Blaze Rainbow was my youngest sister's son." She took a deep breath. "Graham Morton was my older brother. He turned in his cards twenty years ago." She smiled to herself. "Graham doted on Blaze; they were inseparable —"

Mr. Clubb said, "We would never have harmed him."

I felt chagrined. "I apologize. I am truly sorry for your loss." Then I recalled what Eleanora told me Zia had said to her. "Did you know Zia Cashout? She was from there as well."

Mrs. Clubb shrugged. "It's a big place. And I've not been there since my brother's funeral."

Tony twitched, drawing back as he let out a surprised breath. "But they knew Master Rainbow was your kin. They **had** to have known." He thrust his hands through his hair. "They **used** him to get her into the city!"

And Morton was new at ... being a Fed, I suppose. He didn't know what he was doing — he even said so. "Now he's dead, probably at her hand."

I sat staring at the floor. He thought the Feds had betrayed him. He wanted only to clear his name.

I felt torn. He was a Fed. He was my people's worst enemy.

Yet he'd been my friend. He'd lived in my home. He'd saved my life time and again.

What should I do?

I looked at Mr. Hart. "Albert Sheinwold. You said some time back that you'd look into his disappearance."

Mr. Hart blinked. "Did I?"

"You did. Master Rainbow had asked me to search for him. Sheinwold had some information Master Rainbow felt might clear his name to the Feds."

"I don't understand," said Mrs. Clubb.

I turned to Mrs. Clubb. "Master Rainbow told me the Feds thought he'd killed Zia. In reality, she'd taken up with Frank Pagliacci and killed **every** one of Master Rainbow's informants — **except** Sheinwold. But the Feds didn't believe Master Rainbow's story." I took a deep breath, feeling shaky. "Master Rainbow felt he needed to prove Zia was false. He'd gotten an affidavit from Albert Sheinwold that he thought would do that."

What happened to it?

Mr. Hart said, "Oh, yes. I remember now." He shrugged. "Sheinwold was a Spadros man, a Detective Constable with a temper. He'd been accused of sending boys to kill two other Constables. When those boys turned up dead —"

Mrs. Diamond gasped.

Mr. Hart turned to her. "Yeah. Strangled." Then he faced the room. "Sheinwold was demoted, had a sloppy work attendance for several months, then one night he disappeared." He sighed. "He always claimed he'd been framed for the attack on the Constables. This suggests he was right."

I felt bleak, remembering Morton's reaction to Sheinwold's murder, and what it all implied. "Sheinwold's dead. Strangled."

Mr. Hart shook his head with a sigh.

"I don't feel as if the question about Master Rainbow was answered," said Gardena. "What happens now?"

Mrs. Clubb shook her head. "Blaze was interrupted whilst reporting. They have to suspect we know his true nature. And we don't know if the Feds sent a second Agent out of suspicion at his ties with us. If there are any further disturbances, or if Blaze didn't trust us ..." Her eyes filled with tears.

"What she means," Mr. Clubb said, "is that we are in grave trouble. We must find this murderer of children, this kidnapper, this man or group of men who wish to disrupt the city, and do it soon. Or else we may not have a city much longer."

I felt alarmed. "Surely they can't blame **us** for what these men do!"

Julius Diamond had been sitting with his elbows on his knees, eyes downcast. He looked up at us. "But we **are** to blame. We so-called Patriarchs have been squabbling over our toys while the building falls apart around us. My own children have put me to shame ..."

"Mine too," Charles Hart said softly, gazing over at me.

Judith Hart shot to her feet. "And my husband has shamed me for the last time. I have the lot of you as witnesses to his confession of adultery." She glared at Charles Hart. "I will next see you in court."

The door shut loudly behind her.

I thought of poor Katherine. *She doesn't know the half of it.*

"I don't trust that woman," Gardena said.

Nor did I. But someone needed to speak with her. As the daughter of the Bridges Grand-Master, she had to know much that could help.

Mr. Hart let out a sigh. "This is my fault. She's known the truth about Mrs. Spadros for some time, yet she had no preparation for Master Jack's speech. I've let her be humiliated in front of you all." His face changed, as if he'd come to some decision. "For years, she's begged me to tell the truth." He took a deep breath, let it out. "I should have told someone long ago."

I said, "Told us what?"

Mr. Hart hesitated a long time. "Polansky Kerr has been blackmailing me."

The Deed

He's as well as I am.

What was happening?

I remembered how Tony rushed us out of Polansky Kerr's home the one time we'd both been there. *I got a terrible feeling*, Tony had said. *I feared taking tea with them.*

Mr. Hart leaned forward, elbows on his knees. "The last words of the man who shot my son were, 'He warned you what would happen if you told her.'" Mr. Hart shook his head, face pale, eyes red. "I killed my boy, as sure as if I pulled the trigger myself."

I stared at him, appalled. He believed Polansky Kerr had Inventor Etienne Hart murdered because Mr. Hart told me I was his **daughter**?

But Mr. Hart **hadn't**! And at the time, I hadn't known who the man who killed my brother even referred to.

And then I remembered Josie.

Josie had admitted she wasn't in love with Etienne Hart; I'd never seen her even look at a man, not once. But she saw her betrothal as the play to get her family out of poverty. She'd worked so hard on her dress, her wedding plans.

And then her grandfather had the man **murdered**?

By all accounts, she'd been devastated by Etienne's death. I only hoped she didn't know what her grandfather had done. What would happen to her if she learned the truth?

Alexander Clubb leaned forward. "You actually think Polansky Kerr had your son murdered in front of you?"

Mr. Hart sighed. "I'm sure of it."

Lance said, "They're in your quadrant. Why haven't you had the Kerrs rounded up and shot?"

Everyone else in the room looked at me.

Except Mr. Clubb. "It was put before the Commission after Inventor Hart's murder." He turned to face me. "And again, Mrs. Spadros, after you fell ill."

I gaped at him.

Alexander Clubb gave me an even gaze, speaking gently. "At first, your husband felt that since he'd had Mr. Polansky's grandchildren in his home and been to Mr. Polansky's home in return, that he wanted more proof of the man's involvement than the words of a madman." He glanced away, then back. "The second time, your husband dissuaded Mr. Hart from taking action — out of regard for you. Your feelings for the grandson."

Joe.

So everyone knew.

But ... Tony **dissuaded** him? After **everything** I'd done?

Why?

Mr. Hart looked away. "And short of kidnapping — or assassination — it'd be difficult to detain Polansky Kerr even if we did have proof."

Lance scoffed, leaning forward with a new energy, excitement in his eyes. "So let's kill the bastard and be done with it!"

Mr. Hart shook his head, then spoke to Jack. "He's more powerful than you imagined. He owns property, farmlands, whole villages out by the Rim. And I've seen him speak. The aristocrats hang on his every word about 'restoring the city.' They love the man with a passion you wouldn't believe." He glanced over at Lance. "I'm glad to have been dissuaded. If I would've had him killed, I'd have been dead by nightfall."

Lance drew back in hesitation.

I stared at Mr. Hart, stunned.

He shrugged. "We all would. Dead, or in a cells, every one of our secrets in the tabloids." Mr. Hart sighed. "He has the Chief of Police in his pocket." He said to Lance, "He's encouraged the aristocrats to gather armies of men loyal to them." He shook his head. "Most are ours, bought off after minor irritations were stirred into secret hate."

Now it all made sense. I thought of how easily Frank Pagliacci was able to get onto the Spadros Manor grounds. How easily Katie had gotten out of Spadros Castle. Even how they'd gotten a Red Dog Card into Jack Diamond's rooms. Men we thought were ours had to have been helping them all along, even if by simply looking the other way.

Mr. Hart said, "Mayor Freezout and Mr. Kerr have been — or I guess, were — business partners for some time. He bankrolled Chase Freezout's bid for District Attorney —"

Tony leaned forward. "You're kidding."

"I wish I were," said Mr. Hart, appearing disgruntled. "He used my money to do it."

Tony said, "Sir, we must know what this blackmail is about if we are to help."

Mr. Hart froze. "This endangers more than just me."

Mr. Clubb leaned back. "We and our men are the only ones here." He glanced at the waiters and spoke in a warm and gentle tone. "If any of this is revealed, I will personally put the four of you to death."

Julius leaned forward. "Now wait just a —"

"I'm sure it won't come to that," said Mr. Clubb, as if discussing luncheon. He smiled at the waiters, who stared at him in terror. "Right?" He turned to Mr. Hart. "Please, sir, tell us what happened."

Mr. Hart seemed to slump in on himself. "The Cathedral wasn't always owned by your mother, Mrs. Spadros. A brutal and wretched man had taken the place and made it his. On the outside all looked well, but ..."

It came to me. "You went to Mr. Kerr to get the place for my Ma."

He nodded. "I did." He leaned forward, elbows to his knees, hands steepled in front of him. "I paid — quite a lot, I might add — for the man to be killed, for the title to transfer to your mother." He snorted. "I was such an innocent back then. I thought he would do the deed and it would be over with. Yet it put me in his debt." He took a deep breath. "Turns out the man was a son of one of the aristocracy, from 'under the table'. Also turns out the man worked for Mr. Kerr."

A laugh burst from Lance. "He murdered his own man for money."

"Not only money — the chance to hang it over me. I can see the headlines now: 'Charles Hart murders aristocrat's son to give Cathedral to his whore.'" He smiled to himself. "But I'd do it again in an instant." He looked at me. "Fanny carried you, and the man had threatened her." He scoffed quietly. "She never could keep quiet, not even to save her own life."

Tony snorted. "Sounds about right."

I said, "Surely that can't be all?"

Gardena drew back. "That sounds entirely enough."

I shrugged. "Why?"

Tony put his hand upon my arm. "With Mr. Kerr's testimony, Mr. Hart would be jailed for murder. Mrs. Hart would've been forced to leave the city in disgrace. Mr. Etienne would have been thrown into scandal, scrutinized by the police for his part in the matter." He glanced around. "Your brother might never have been become an Inventor!" He took a breath. "Hart quadrant would now be in the hands of," he waved his hand around, "whoever survived the battle that would surely have followed. The Cathedral would have been seized by the city." He shook his head. "The women — including your mother — would've probably been evicted to live on the street, unless the Dealers stepped in."

I stared at him, appalled.

Mr. Hart hung his head. "I had to sponsor Polansky Kerr into the quadrant. I must pay him an enormous amount every month. More, since he's learned you know I'm your father. And Etienne is dead."

Because of me. "This is so unfair," I said to him. "You never told me a thing; Jack told me, there in the factory the night of the fire."

Julius glared at Jack, who shrugged.

I said, "I know you can't speak of these matters. I understand now. But why can't you just tell everyone I'm your daughter?"

Mr. Hart began to tremble. "And lose you, too?" Mr. Hart's eyes turned red. "You want me to publicly humiliate my wife? Make a —" He suddenly stared at me, aghast.

"You can say it: Pot rag." I felt ready to cry. "That's what this is all about, isn't it? These aristocrats, all these factions. This city. They'd rather see Bridges burn, see Bridges fail, even see Bridges handed over to the **Feds**, than have a Pot rag remain Queen of Spades."

No one said anything.

I faced Mr. Hart. "Well, I'm here, by the gods, and by the Dealer's hand, sir, you made me. So you have two choices: keep silent and let the cards fall as they may, or speak."

Mr. Hart sat stock still, shame radiating from him.

I felt sorry for the old man. "Acevedo is your Heir now, or haven't you considered?" Then I recalled Tony's words over breakfast. "Acevedo needs you, if only to prepare his people for him."

Lance spoke gently. "Well said."

Mr. Hart took a deep breath. "I will consider it."

Everyone sat in silence.

Mrs. Clubb said, "Perhaps it's time for luncheon."

This amused me: she perpetually wanted to direct matters.

Tony nodded at Rob, who directed the other waiters. More covered warmers were brought in; the smell of good food hung in the air. Then Tony rose. "Please, help yourselves."

We all got our food, went to tables. Tony began to eat.

But I didn't feel much like eating. "There's one thing I must know."

Tony seemed surprised. "What?"

"You've had the chance to kill Joe a hundred times already. After all that I've done to you, why would you care one bit about my feelings?"

Tony sat quietly, looking at me with sadness. "I don't know how or why, but Joseph Kerr has a hold on you none of us understand. A hold that not I nor Jonathan nor anyone has yet been able to break. If I were to kill him, the only thing it would accomplish is to make you hate me." He leaned back, glanced away. "Everyone thinks I'm either weak, or a fool." He scoffed. "Even my cousins raised against me when I refused to kill him. They said I was unmanly, unfit to lead." He put his elbows on the table, leaned forward. "But everything inside tells me I need you." He shook his head. "A Memory Girl, in my very home! But Mrs. Clubb is exactly right." He nodded sagely. "You're a brilliant woman, a strong woman." He chuckled. "You lack wisdom, perhaps, but that'll come with time. What I'm saying is that you have the ability to become a Computer, perhaps one of Bridges' finest." He straightened, gazing to one side. "I need you working for **me**. But if I'm to win you to my side, I'd rather it be done fairly. Because you find me worthy. Not because the man you really love is dead."

The man you really love ... I felt as if he'd stabbed me in the heart.

There are days I've wished he would have.

"You best eat," Tony said, a wry smile on his face. "We have quite a day ahead of us."

The Collaboration

Luncheon done, we all gathered once more. The little I'd eaten sat like a lump in my stomach.

It was put before the Commission ..

Everyone thinks ...

Your husband dissuaded Mr. Hart — out of regard for you.

I thought I might be sick.

Tony said, "Is there anything else we should know?"

I said glumly, "The Magma Steam Generators are failing."

Jack raised his eyebrows. The waiters looked afraid.

The Patriarchs and Mrs. Clubb nodded. Yes, that made sense: they had to know.

Gardena leaned forward. "Failing? In what way?"

I took a deep breath, trying to stop my voice from shaking. My stomach from turning. *You're a Memory Girl.* "I am no Inventor. But my understanding is that this entire city is a mechanical construct. In the pilings which anchor the city far below, there are tubes that use the earth's fire to create steam. The steam turns enormous generators which power the city. Maxim Call showed me the piling under Spadros Manor several years back." *It was put before the Commission!* "He told me that these tubes are deteriorating. Inventor Call believed that without drastic action — which as far as I know, no Inventor knows how to accomplish — the city will eventually stop."

"Oh," said Gardena. She pondered this a moment. "So?"

They all knew about Joe.

I forced myself to focus. Not to cry.

Then I recalled what my apothecary friend Anna Goren had told me when I'd asked the same question. "We'd be left with no power, no lights. The rivers would stop running." I had to make them understand. "We've all seen the chaos that just the train stoppage caused!" Then it came to me. "But if the power failed whilst the Aperture lay shut ..."

Mrs. Clubb's mouth fell open, and Mr. Diamond put his hand on his face.

"... the Feds wouldn't have to do anything against us at all."

The room went silent.

Mrs. Clubb leaned forward. "We've approached the Dealers numerous times on this matter. They won't even discuss it. Even my daughter Kitty changes the subject." She looked at me. "Does anyone know why?"

So she knew I was one of the Dealers' Daughters ... but I wasn't sure what influence with or knowledge I might have about the Dealers themselves. They'd never once given us in the Pot anything but disdainful neglect. Well, except Kitty Clubb, but that was before she truly joined them. "Our former Inventor, Maxim Call, said once he'd sent spies into the Cathedral."

Most everyone in the room gasped.

I felt annoyed at the Inventor for what he'd done, even then, years after his death. "But I'm not sure how that relates to the Dealers."

"The Dealers see the Cathedral as sacred," Tony said. "They didn't come out and say such, but I could tell from the way they spoke of it. Inventor Call's act might have offended them beyond repair."

Julius Diamond shook his head, scoffing. "To send spies into the **Cathedral** ...?"

"It was **not** upon my order," Tony snapped. "The man acted on his own." He leaned forward. "So what do we **do**?"

This is why I had traveled here. I stood, the heavy chair scraping across the wooden floor. "We all have our own men, our own spies, our own resources. Use them **together**. Instead of spying on each other, fighting each other, stealing from each other, let's **find** these scoundrels and put an **end** to them, once and for all!"

"Hear, hear," Lance Clubb said, and there was a general nodding of heads. Which surprised me, as most of the room was male, but miracles do happen.

Suddenly feeling conspicuous, I sat.

Tony leaned back. "We must have a central place for information and a unified plan of attack. I have no particular talent in spycraft, but I would be willing to coordinate this endeavor."

"Excellent," Mrs. Clubb said. "Mrs. Spadros will be a mighty ally."

I peered at her in confusion, surprised at her support.

Mr. Clubb said, "I will, of course, send anything I believe to be relevant. But if you have need of any of my people or information, you have only to ask."

I felt sure they'd figure out a way to use whatever they learned to their advantage, but Tony nodded serenely.

Jack Diamond said, "I'll continue my investigation of the Kerr family. If proof of their crimes is what you want, I'll find it for you."

I felt suddenly afraid. "Beware, sir; Major Blackwood had been investigating Mr. Kerr, and now he and his lawyer are dead." Major Blackwood had to have been investigating Mr. Kerr — there was no reason at all to have brought Joe and Josie into it.

Jack looked more than a bit alarmed at this.

Charles Hart sat quietly, head down. "I sponsored Polansky Kerr into this city. I allowed him to gain power, and I may have unwittingly enabled his attempts to overthrow our **entire** way of life." He shook his head. "I'll find the truth."

Gardena said. "Isn't Joseph Kerr running for mayor?"

Mr. Hart chuckled. "Along with half the city."

I felt suddenly out of breath. *Joe?* "Where did you hear that?"

"It's in yesterday's evening news," Lance said, producing it. "I brought one for the drive here." He shrugged. "I thought this would be a dull affair."

I burst out laughing. *Hardly.* My heart felt as if it would pound right out of my chest. "May I see this paper?"

I hurried to Lance, who handed it over; I returned to my seat to read it.

The list took four pages, laid out in alphabetical order by last name. I rushed to find Joe's name, hands shaking, only then realizing I'd held my breath.

Everyone was watching me. Sheepishly, I also looked for Frank Pagliacci's name, yet didn't find it.

Of course: now that he knew the Families were searching for him, he'd use a different alias.

I scanned the pages, my mind racing. "One of these men is the Bridges Strangler, I feel certain of it."

"Hmm," said Mr. Hart, in a tone both pensive and disturbed.

Tony made a despairing sound, turning away.

This man would have the backing of the aristocrats, the Chief of Police ...

He owns whole villages, out by the Rim ...

The entire area under the dome voted for Mayor, and the Four Families' influence wasn't nearly so great out in the countryside. If Polansky Kerr had as much power as Mr. Hart feared ... the Bridges Strangler might become our next Mayor.

But **why**? Why would Mr. Polansky work with, support, nay, even encourage, a fiend like Frank Pagliacci?

I felt angry. "Mr. Kerr has pretended to be a friend to the Spadros Family, a friend to Mr. Hart, all whilst plotting our downfall."

Then something occurred to me. When Trey Louis tried to abduct me, he claimed he was bringing me to Frank because I was in danger.

Frank and Mr. Kerr were working together. Mr. Kerr was calling the play; Frank was Mr. Kerr's dummy. Could Frank only be luring people in, and Polansky Kerr be the actual Strangler?

I'd never considered that before. Mr. Kerr was so old ... but then who would guess an old man might do **any** of this?

But in any case, once Frank Pagliacci — under whatever name he used — was Mayor, how could we remove him? No Mayor had ever been successfully impeached, and the office was held for life. What havoc would the man wreak on Bridges before this was done?

The Accord

Jack Diamond's implication that Polansky Kerr IV took the Red Dogs children's street gang away from Alexander Clubb to use for his own purposes made at least some sense. From what I'd seen so far, each thing the Red Dog Gang did disrupted the city, with the goal, it seemed, of one day overthrowing the Four Families.

Mrs. Clubb said, "Polansky Kerr has ample means, and he evidently feels the time is now." She let out a bitter laugh. "Who else has better cause to hate the Four Families but the heir of the King? I don't know who his parents were, but one of them had to have known the first Polansky Kerr, possibly even his father King Taylor. Those men were their father and grandfather." She took a deep breath, and her voice shook. "Our ancestors put King Polansky's head on a spike, murdered his family, destroyed their whole reason for being, razed their home, forced them to flee into squalor ..." She shook her head. "Revenge over something like that can travel **very** far."

I said, "But why kill young men? Why attack and torment **me**?" That last part made no sense whatsoever.

Mrs. Clubb shrugged, shook her head. The others appeared just as puzzled as I felt.

I barely knew Mr. Kerr. I was just a Pot rag, dragged into the Spadros Family against my will. I'd never been — or even wanted to be — a threat to him. But the Red Dog Gang had attacked my home, murdered my friends, even tried to murder my Ma. What could I have possibly done to Polansky Kerr to earn **this** much rage?

Then I felt horrified: if Polansky Kerr really took over the Red Dog Gang ... could he have orchestrated David's kidnapping?

"Jacqui," Tony said. "What is it?"

I turned to him. "I can find no reason for Mr. Kerr to take David Bryce from his back stair. If Polansky Kerr IV owns a third of the city, was partners with Chase Freezout, has the police on his payroll, and the fervent love of the aristocracy ... why send men to kidnap an outsider boy? What was his interest in luring me to that basement?"

The others shrugged, shaking their heads.

"Wait," I said. "One of those he had murdered was a woman who helped raise me. Her name was Marja."

Tony nodded. "I recall. She was a friend to Master Joseph and Miss Josephine."

"Yes," I said. "She was Mr. Polansky's housekeeper. Remember? At the racetrack. They complained no one would help in her murder."

Tony nodded. "What about her?"

I said. "Black Maria shot her, the same night she shot at Master Rainbow. I found Marja on the street, dying —"

Gardena gasped.

"And in her hand was a note. Part of it said: HE WANTS YOU." I looked around. It had also said: YOUR FED WILL BE DEAD SOON ENOUGH. "But why? Why would Polansky Kerr IV possibly want or need ... **me**?"

No one there had an answer.

I considered the matter. He'd had six sons with as many women. Could a man of his advanced age possibly want a seventh?

I suppose it showed the charisma this man had that instead of being repulsed at the thought, I was intrigued. The man I'd met that New Year's Day four years before was quite good-looking, even at almost ninety. But ... if he were as rich as Jack Diamond implied, he could have anyone.

And something else bothered me: how in the world did Polansky Kerr IV know Frank Pagliacci? Why send ...

Wait, I thought. I sat back, recalling the day we found David Bryce, what happened as we rushed to escape.

Gardena said, "What is it?"

"I **assumed** it was Frank up there on the platform above the factory warehouse floor. I shot a man I believed to be Frank." Just like I'd assumed the man in white was Jack Diamond. "But I never directly asked Morton about it. Morton had met the man, could possibly have glimpsed him, recognized his voice."

Tony let out a breath. "I've considered this. Master Rainbow could identify them all."

Morton seemed to believe Frank's men were after us there at the last. "But if he did recognize Frank up there, why did he never say so?" Why had he never shown a bit of interest in pursuing David's kidnapping further?

And why, after four years, was Constable Hanger — of all people — still investigating it?

I needed more information.

Lance shrugged. "Does it really matter?"

For an instant, I felt annoyed with him. It mattered to **me**!

Then I began to feel uneasy. "We should be moving on before our enemies learn of this meeting. This would be a tempting target."

Julius Diamond completely ignored me. "I'll find any further Feds. Alex, if you need assistance we stand ready to help."

"Thank you," Alexander Clubb said. "Although we'll both be busy preparing for a wedding."

Julius beamed. "That we will."

Feeling bitter, I gazed at Julius Diamond, remembering the day he refused to let us attend Jonathan's funeral.

Mr. Clubb said to Tony, "I'll bring the information we have on Mr. Kerr and the Red Dogs to you. And I'll instruct my Inventor to focus solely upon the Generator problem." He turned to me. "She would very much like to speak with you."

I imagined she did. "So we all know what to do?"

"What will you do, Mrs. Spadros?" Mrs. Diamond said.

I was surprised — and alarmed — at the relevance of her question. Did she suddenly trust the rest of us? Why?

Then I realized everyone in the room — with the exception of the waiters — probably already knew. Once little Roland had told Lance his grandmother was well, Lance was sure to have told his parents. "I plan to do what I intended all along: learn exactly who kidnapped David Bryce and murdered his brother, and most importantly, why."

I had to know what happened to David Bryce. And it seemed that he'd never be able to tell us.

Frank Pagliacci's statements, if it had been him up on that shadowed platform, seemed too little reason to go to the trouble he had to take the boy. "I feel that once we know that, the rest will become clear."

They all nodded, their faces showing that they didn't understand. But that didn't matter.

Dozens of people had to have been involved in the events surrounding the kidnapping: Morton and I killed six getting David out of that basement. Someone had to have gotten the boy food, moved him, made sure guards and factory workers were distracted as they did so.

In Jake Bower's letter, brought to me after his death, he'd confessed to being one of those men. My only hope was that over four years from when we rescued David, there were others who still lived.

Why hadn't I accomplished more all this time? Why had I let myself become so **distracted**?

Or was this exactly the reason our enemies had thrown so much our way? To keep us distracted until all was ready to defeat us?

This thought made me afraid.

Tony stood. "Thank you all for coming. Have a pleasant, safe journey home."

There was scattered applause as the meeting broke up into small groups, talking. Lance returned to the Diamond buffet. Alexander and Regina Clubb held each other, Regina's head on her husband's chest.

I sat numbly, overwhelmed by what I'd learned, drained from all the emotion.

But I had to think. This might be the only chance I had to speak with these people before they scattered to their quadrants, hidden behind pomp and protocol.

Polansky Kerr IV had to be the Red Dog Gang's Director. He owned land, buildings. Much of the city. He had wooed every one of the powers already against us ...

I suddenly remembered the tabloids. The *Golden Bridges*, the "People for a Better Life" pamphlets. He'd used them against us, too.

Something Tony had said once came to me: *we rule here at the sufferance of the aristocracy.*

As much as I hated the woman, Mrs. Clubb had been right about Polansky Kerr's motive to hate us. If the aristocracy loved and supported him as much as Mr. Hart said ... and if their hatred of the Pot (and by extension, me) was that great ... well, then Mr. Kerr had all the help he might ever need.

But what was his end goal? Did Mr. Kerr want to take over and use the aristocracy to declare himself King Polansky II?

It didn't matter. I had to think. We had to stop him.

What had I actually learned? Mainly that Polansky Kerr was a lying scoundrel and Morton was a Fed.

I wasn't sure how to feel in either case.

But I also learned that Jack Diamond believed Joe and Josie were helping their grandfather overthrow the Four Families.

This seemed ludicrous.

First of all, because I remembered how embarrassed Joe and Josie seemed when Mr. Kerr had gone on about restoring the city. Why be embarrassed if they had the same goal?

But this made Joe's bid for Mayor ... interesting.

The Mayor had from the beginning been opposed to the Royalists. Did Joe run for Mayor to challenge his grandfather? To stop him from causing me more harm?

If so, it suggested he knew at least a little about what his grandfather was doing. Could that be why he'd been so adamant about speaking with me alone?

I began to regret refusing to speak with him privately. But by now he was in Azimoff, doing whatever it was he was doing, and I might never see him again.

My eyes fell upon Charles Hart. He sat alone, bowed over, elbows on his knees, seemingly lost in his thoughts.

I felt a surge of affection for the old man. Yet I hesitated to obey the urge to go to him. He'd lost everything because of me; I'd not give him more grief, not now.

Jack Diamond sat watching me.

I immediately went to Gardena, pulling her aside from where she stood beside Lance. "I have treated you coldly, cruelly, seemingly without reason, and I am sorry. My husband —"

Her face softened. "Did exactly as I asked him to."

I took a step back. "I don't understand."

Gardena moved forward to take my hands, very much as I had taken Josie's that day at her grandfather's home long ago. But there was little joy in her tone. "I saw how unhappy you were, how much you longed to be free. I would rather lose your friendship entirely than see you trapped in a life you hated. Tony wanted to take the blame himself, but I said no. I felt compelled to make amends for ... many things," she said, "and this was my way."

I let go of her hands and hugged her. "I am so very happy for your betrothal." And in spite of everything, it was true. I put my hands on her cheeks, peering into her face. "Do you love Lance?"

Gardena smiled to herself. "With all my heart." She took my hands from her face and held them. "I needed someone I could talk freely with, to be myself with. Lance has been all that and more." Her face glowed. "My parents and brothers are happy with a good match; the gods have blessed me with a good man." Then she let go of my hands and sighed. "I'm so sorry Jack told you about Jon." She shook her head. "You were exactly right in what you said. He's only given you more grief, on top of everything you've been through. I will never, **ever** forgive him."

"No, Dena." I put my hand on her arm, feeling moved. "No." As much as I hated what Jack had done in other matters, I wouldn't break apart his family. "Don't ... please don't be angry with Jack." He'd been the only one to tell me the truth. "He's given me a gift. Everything Jon's done makes perfect sense now."

Jon loved me. And it made perfect sense that he was dead.

Gardena gave me a thin smile; I could tell she was still upset with Jack. "Very well."

Lance Clubb came over, taking Gardena's arm. "Please excuse us."

I smiled at her fondly. "Go, join your admirers."

Then Jack Diamond came to me, offering his arm. "May I speak with you a moment?"

Jack looked just like Jonathan, but ... he was not. His presence in the room felt entirely different.

"Certainly." I took his arm with an odd feeling, but without hesitation or fear.

Gardena glared at Jack, who ignored it.

Tony gave me a brief glance then resumed talking with Mr. Clubb.

As Jack and I strolled towards an empty tea-table, I said, "You wear black well."

Jack smiled, but it never reached his eyes. "Daniel liked me best in white. But once I was 'dead,' it seemed like a liability."

The pain in his voice said it all. "I understand."

He stopped, faced me. "I would never have taken you, nor would I have used chloroform, had I known you were with child."

I nodded. Then I remembered the horrors of that night, and anger surged within me. I took a step back. "You had Jake Bower burned alive. **Why?**"

"Oh, gods. You didn't tell —! No, of course not. Otherwise he would surely have said something."

I stared at him. Jon never told him of our conversation?

Jack sounded far away. "The ghost of Jack Diamond **did** visit my brother the night he died."

I felt numb. "So **you** were with him in the end."

"I was."

Whilst I lay that night bearing Acevedo, bleeding almost to death, Jack Diamond, of all people, was with Jon as he died.

Gods, how I wished it'd been me there with Jon. Grief flooded through me, and I fought to keep it at bay. I would not cry in front of this horror wearing my Jonathan's face. I wouldn't.

Jack said, "Mr. Bower had tried to blackmail my sister, impersonate me, frame me for all sorts of crimes. But more than that, I was desperate. I was hunted." He took a deep breath. "I had to make everyone believe — really believe — that I was dead. I thought killing Mr. Bower was what my father would have done. I needed someone, anyone. And my brother Cesare gave him to me." He put his hand on his forehead. "I didn't know what else to do."

I didn't know if I could forgive him. No one deserved to die like that.

Jack said, "But there's something I wished to tell you." He took my arm, leading me to a tea-table, where we sat. "Please don't berate yourself about Jon. He loved you more than I've ever seen anyone love another. He wanted desperately to be with you." For a moment, he got very still. "Yet he once said how grateful he was that things turned out as they did, because he never wished you to be burdened with a widow's life."

I felt as if my heart were breaking. It took a while before I might speak. "So he knew he had little time."

Then I felt foolish. Of course he did.

Jack smiled, but his eyes grew moist. "Yes. I was with friends in the country one summer when rheumatic fever ran through the city. Jon had stayed home, and contracted a severe case, which badly damaged his heart." He looked away. "They say once we had the skill to treat such things." He sat quietly for a moment, then nodded. "In any case, yes — he knew his time was short." Jack turned to me. "Spending it with you as he could made him happy, and for that I thank you."

Grief rushed over me. "Jon was better to me than anyone." He was the one man who understood me, who'd been by my side through everything. The man who deliberately gave his life for me and my child. Who loved me more than anyone could have ever expected anyone to.

And I'd never, ever see him again.

Jack sat with me until the storm passed.

And I thought: *how strange it is to sit across from a man who looks so much like the man I might have married, if the world had been a different one.*

"There is one more thing," Jack said. "I'd almost forgotten! During my travels, I was attacked in my rooms by a woman I believe to be with the Dealers. She tried to stab me! If your investigations take you there, be on your guard."

This startled me. The Dealers, **attacking** people? "What did she look like?"

"She reminded me a bit of your late Inventor: brown skin with eyes of light blue. In her early forties, I'd say."

I nodded. This sounded like Miss Nola Rank, the woman posing as a maid who we suspected had stabbed Maxim Call. And possibly Anna Goren as well.

So Miss Nola Rank might be with the Dealers. Interesting.

Jack peered at me for a long moment. Then his shoulders suddenly relaxed. He leaned forward, thrusting out his hand: palm up, fingers gently wide. "We've both lost someone we love." His fingers curled ever so slightly. "I don't know if you can ever forgive me for what I've put you through. But my dearest wish is for us to be at peace."

I drew back, staring at Jack's outstretched hand, his quietly patient face, Jake Bower's screams echoing in my mind.

Mr. Bower had worked for Frank Pagliacci.

But he'd tried to help me. He'd begged me for help at the end. And I failed him.

I didn't know what to do.

So I shook Jack's hand. If Jack Diamond would leave me alone until I could take my vengeance on him, on everyone who'd gone against me ... well, that was all I might hope for.

The Agreement

I saw Mr. and Mrs. Clubb chatting with each other across the room, and there was one last thing I needed to do. "Excuse me."

I went to them. "I wish to apologize. I feel I broke our agreement."

Mrs. Clubb blinked. "Which agreement?"

I felt ashamed. "I promised not to interfere in Lance's courtship. But I did." I looked up at them, blurry with my tears. Jack didn't want to hurt me. Jon had loved me. He **loved** me. "Why did you still help?"

Mr. Clubb looked down for a bit. When he once more gazed at me, his eyes were red. He spoke quietly. "Because you loved our Nina."

I didn't know what to say.

"No one ever speaks of her," he said. "Because she took her life. But we loved her. We **loved** her. And clearly, so did you."

"I did," I sobbed. "I did. She was everything to me."

I took out my handkerchief, but before I could get it to my eyes, Regina Clubb — of all people — gave me a swift intense hug, then walked away.

Alexander Clubb spoke softly. "I'm sorry for what happened at the hotel. Regina is a brilliant woman, a strong woman. A good woman," he smiled to himself. "The best. But dealing with people is her weakest suit." He shook his head. "I was vexed when I learned she'd tried to blackmail you. That was never my intent, and it only turned you against us."

I nodded, wiped my eyes. "Forgive me, my husband has probably already asked you this, but —"

"Why have we failed to acknowledge him?" He chuckled. "Politics, my dear, that's all. You see, Diamond and Clubb will ally soon." He took a deep breath and looked away. "But our alliance with Spadros quadrant during Roy's slaughter of the Diamond people will never be truly forgiven. Perhaps if we seem to have broken our ties with you, then one day they may accept my son's child as their Heir."

I nodded, finally understanding Tony's moods, his frequent trips to Diamond quadrant. On top of everything Tony had lost, he'd been forced to give his little Roland to the Clubbs. It'd been the only way he could save him.

And yet the Clubbs were silent for so long. It must have been excruciating for Tony not to know what sort of reception his son might face. He had spent what little time he could with his child, all the time praying he was doing the right thing.

I felt glad to hear Mr. Clubb wanted to have the boy as his Heir. Roland looked like Tony, yes, but he also resembled Gardena in many ways. And if Gardena said he was Lance's true-born son, and Lance agreed, well, there was nothing anyone else might say to it.

Alexander Clubb smiled down at me. "It's all about the future of the Families. There's nothing more important to any of us than for our Families to survive." He held out his hand. "And I'd like nothing more than for us to be friends."

I blinked back tears as I took his hand. "I'd like that as well."

He released my hand. "Perhaps we might have luncheon together one day, once all this blows over. Maybe a boating trip?"

I smiled up at him. "I'd like that."

Tony spoke from close behind me. "Jacqui?"

"Forgive me," I said to Mr. Clubb.

"Go on, my dear —" Then he cried out, clutching his head.

Everyone turned to look.

Mr. Clubb staggered, gasping. "Oh, gods, it hurts!"

He collapsed into my arms, and if Tony hadn't been close by, Mr. Clubb and I would've fallen to the floor.

Mrs. Clubb cried out, "Apoplexy!"

Everyone rushed over.

I stared at her, then at Mr. Clubb, who sagged in Tony's and Mr. Diamond's grasp. Mr. Clubb's face drooped on the right side, his arm and leg on the left dragging.

Mr. Hart rested the man's mechanical left arm upon his chest, then cried out, "We must get him to a doctor! Guards!"

The guards from all four Families ran in then, guns drawn.

Mr. Diamond waved them off. "He's taken ill! Help us get him to his carriage."

It took us all at various points to get him down the narrow, winding stair — he was a tall man, and heavy. Regina Clubb sobbed the whole way. Gardena followed, carrying Mr. Clubb's top hat and cane. Some of the guards ran ahead, alerting Mr. Clubb's carriage, I presume trying to determine the closest doctor.

But by the time we got him downstairs, Alexander Clubb was clearly dead.

The Ordeal

As Mr. Clubb's men rushed him to his carriage, Lance, Regina, and Gardena followed more slowly, holding each other, weeping.

Jack had returned to help his mother down that long and winding stair. Once she was safety outside, he stood gazing over the scene, his dark spectacles and hood on once more.

Tony came to stand beside me, staring out at the carriage as it raced away. Tears ran down his face in front of everyone. "So passes a good and gentle man." He took my hand. "He's done everything he could for my son, and more."

"Oh, Tony," I said, my heart full. "I didn't know you cared for Mr. Clubb so."

He let out a bitter, despondent laugh. "No. That's not it. That's not it at all." He took out a handkerchief, wiped his face. "Do you know who was after Master Rainbow? The Four of Clubs were Mr. Alexander's **grandsons**! Near to Master Rainbow's age, the older three, and the younger one, to ours. They caught the man, beat him, hounded him." He shook his head. "Mr. Alexander claimed he never wanted this, even when he learned the man was with the Feds. He'd planned to keep Master Rainbow safe. To send him back to his people, for his wife's sake." Tony's face fell. "But he never told Master Rainbow." He took a deep, shuddering breath, let it out. "Blaze Rainbow must have thought they meant to kill him. And in his terror, Master Rainbow escaped." He gestured broadly in front of him. "And out here, somewhere in this cold, cruel city, he found his death."

He turned to me then, desolate. "I don't know if I can **do** this anymore, Jacqui. I never wanted any of this."

I never wanted Morton dead. I never wanted Mr. Clubb dead.

I never wanted anyone dead.

"But I know I must," Tony said. "I'm all that's left of my Family."

His tone, so bleak, so hopeless ... it surprised me.

Then he took my hand. "Tell me about Nina."

I blinked, surprised. "Nina?"

"Yes. Forgive me, I overheard your conversation with Mr. Clubb, before ..." He sighed. "He said you loved his Nina. Who is she?"

I smiled to myself, feeling the heat rush to my cheeks. "Nina Clubb. His daughter. I suppose you might say she was my first love." Then I felt desolate. "She died long ago."

Tony had been staring at me, mouth open. "How ...?" He looked the most perplexed I'd ever seen him. "But you ... love Master **Kerr**."

Now I felt confused. Then I realized what he was saying and a laugh burst from me. My Ma had been right. "You can desire anyone you wish, didn't you know?"

Tony seemed to realize his mouth lay open, because he gave a start and closed it. Then he began to laugh bitterly, as if he couldn't help himself. "Oh, gods, Jacqui. I have been so ... unutterably cruel. I won't ever ask you to forgive me." He glanced away, then spoke earnestly. "I should **never** have agreed to Miss Gardena's plan."

At first I didn't understand.

It must have showed, because Tony said, "Blitz told me of how Master Kerr threw the story of 'my affairs' in your face." He shook his head. "I've brought shame and disgrace upon you, when you've suffered so much already." He turned away, still holding my hand. "So much. On my account."

He feels guilty for all that Roy did to me. "Most of this was not your fault."

He turned to me with a sad, bemused smile, his face downcast. "So I've been told." He let out a sigh, there as we stood on the steps of the Ballhouse, our men keeping a respectful yet wary distance. Then he let out a weary laugh. "Ten will berate me for standing out here like this."

I smiled to myself, expecting any moment to see Sawbuck storming around the outside of the huge building.

Tony relaxed his hand so we held each other by one finger only. "Everything about this ... about us. It's been completely wrong. So wrong, no one would believe it even if I wrote it down. And oh gods, my poor **Jon**! How horribly cruel I've been to him." He sounded completely lost. "I thought him to be a **man**-lover! The things I told him ... Oh, gods, I never once guessed the truth." He sighed. "It's all gone wrong, all of it." He swallowed, hesitated. "I don't know if I can ever trust you. I don't know if I can ever ... love you ... after everything."

Relief washed over me. He was, for once, being honest.

"But can we **try**? Can we begin again?" He shook his head, just a bit. "I need you, Jacqui. I need you. And we have Acevedo to think of. He needs you, too. He's just a baby, and his life has been **so** hard. I think he knows we love him, but he needs us to also love each other."

I considered this. And I didn't see any reason to hide anymore. "I do love you, Tony. That's what's made this whole ordeal so difficult. I didn't want to love you, even from the first night we met. If you would've been foul, or horrid, or uncaring, if I could've hated or despised you ... my life would've been so much simpler." I smiled at him then, amused. "So yes, I will try, too."

Our eyes met, and a feeling came to me, one I'd only ever had before with Joe. Well, and once with Jon. As if we were looking into each others' souls.

Then Sawbuck came around the building, looking ready to fight someone. I laughed, entwining my fingers into Tony's, relishing the beautiful feeling of his hand in mine. I didn't know if I could do what I needed to either. But I had to try. "I won't leave you, sir: not ever again. We'll fight these scoundrels together." I smiled up at him. "And if Ten berates you, he must berate me as well."

The Mourning

I held Tony's hand on the long carriage-ride back to Spadros Manor, feeling grieved

We'd all lost so much. We'd all lost so many.

We still didn't know who murdered Katie.

We had a possible name. I should have known Katie would return to Frank Pagliacci, who I thought probably was the Bridges Strangler.

We had a pretty good guess as to who was supporting Mr. Kerr and his Red Dog Gang — the city, the police, the aristocracy.

So we had a serious problem. Even the *Bridges Daily*'s exposé series on Mayor Chase Freezout's backing of the Bridges Strangler hadn't made the aristocracy abandon him. And by Mr. Hart's accounting, with every atrocity they loved Mr. Polansky even more.

We needed proof, not guesses, if we were to overcome them.

That night, Tony came to my bed, and we lay together weeping for some time. He never left that night, or any of the nights to come.

***

Clubb quadrant lay draped in black, mourning a man who'd been their Patriarch for almost sixty years.

The funeral parade wound throughout every part of the quadrant, thousands weeping on every block. Almost a hundred attended the graveside memorial: his closest men, his children, grandchildren, great-grandchildren. Those of us from other quadrants stood a bit off, near the aspens, allowing his family to have their peace.

Cheisara Golf and her sister Karla Bettelmann — two of Mr. Alexander's many granddaughters — were there. A thin man with large eyes and dark curly hair stood beside Karla — that could only be Mikhail Bettelmann.

And Tenni stood beside Cheisara. When she saw me looking at her, she smiled.

So things between them had improved after all.

As the casket was lowered, Regina Clubb, Lance, Gardena, and little Roland cast golden flowers into the grave. Once Roland cast his flower, he looked at me through the moving crowd, his face bleak and wet with tears. And I realized how much he'd loved the man who'd wanted to be his grandfather.

He looked to Tony; Tony opened his arms. Uncaring of who watched, Roland ran around the grave and to his father, weeping.

Tony crouched down to hold him, smoothing Roland's dark ringlets. "My dear boy. My poor dear boy. I love you so much."

Lance stood watching, grief and fear and sadness mixed.

Tony glanced up at me, then at Lance, and he stood. "I hear your Mama and Master Lance are to marry."

Roland looked up at him, and nodded.

"Well, that's wonderful!" He leaned over, speaking quietly. "Now you'll have two Daddies. Some boys never have even one."

That made Roland laugh.

Tony tousled the boy's curls and brought him back to his mother. It was a foolish thing Roland did, in front of the people who'd probably been part — even if by their silence — in wanting his father-to-be dead.

But I suppose we're all allowed to be foolish sometimes.

I left a penny on Morton's headstone as I looked up at the Aperture that Morton loved so well. Might it one day be used against us?

The Feds knew we were onto them. They knew Morton was, if not dead, held captive, all their secrets with him.

The Feds had to be preparing a move against us, if only to retrieve their man. And now the Red Dog Gang had turned the Army against the city as well. What could we do? How could we stop them?

***

After the Clubb quadrant's forty days of mourning, Lancelot Clubb and Julius Diamond publicly announced an alliance between Diamond and Clubb. They also announced Lance's betrothal to Gardena Diamond. The announcements were met in both quadrants by a full week of stunned silence.

Our former Inventor, Montgomery Arrow, was found the next day. Shot through the heart, crimson lips upon his cheek, like so many before. I wondered what information Zia Cashout had gotten from him before he died.

Tony had been right about one thing: his mother Molly just needed some time. After several weeks of moping in silence, she took up finger-knitting. She told everyone she planned a woolen bedspread for Acevedo's wedding chest.

Acevedo was just a baby. So we smiled and gave her whatever thread she asked for.

I planted the daffodils Rachel Diamond had given me in front of Spadros Manor that fall. And I pictured them blooming the next spring. Their white petals, their golden centers ... they made me think of Lance and Gardena.

And sitting on the grass beside my front porch, my snipers upon every rooftop, I recalled Mrs. Diamond asking what I would do that day at the meeting

At the time, I had only the most general answer. But now, I knew: I had to help Josie. Because surely when this came out, she'd be blamed for everything.

Josie loved her grandfather. She'd supported him. She'd handled her grandfather's business, she'd signed the checks. She'd probably even gone to the bank for him.

What a horror she'd face when she learned the truth!

To our people, harming a child brought an immediate death sentence. Even as leader of the High-Low Split, Josie had **never** ordered the murder of a **child**! Josie would never have condoned David's kidnapping, or Stephen Rivers' murder, or any of the rest. She'd have done **anything** to stop it!

And, after she'd been forced to live in poverty her entire life, to learn her grandfather owned all this **wealth**? The magnitude of that betrayal **alone** could kill her!

And as much as I despised what Joe had done to my life, he surely was no kidnapper. And it was inconceivable that he should go along with a man who was strangling children!

Joe must have learned the truth. That had to be why he decided to run for Mayor, so he might bring all this to light. So he might stop his grandfather, before more people were hurt.

... the way things are here, I don't think I want to come back.

Had Joe already tried to oppose his grandfather and found the man too powerful? When I abandoned him, had Joe given up?

For a moment, I felt dismayed. But then I gathered my resolve.

I had to learn who kidnapped David Bryce so I might clear Josie's name. And I had to do it quickly, before she got caught up in her grandfather's deeds the way I'd been caught up in Dame Anastasia's.

I didn't want her to go through a trial like I had. At the time, that had been one of the worst experiences of my life.

Mr. Hart said he wanted to learn the truth.

But Jack Diamond said he wanted to prove the Kerr's guilt. That meant Jack already thought the three of them guilty.

Jack was, in my view, likely to find Mr. Polansky's guilt. And when the recriminations began, Joe and Josie would go down with their grandfather.

Joe and Josie might be jailed, or killed, or even sent back to the Pot.

I couldn't let that happen.

Joe had done me so much harm. At times, I even wanted Joe dead. But I didn't want him to suffer for something he could've had nothing to do with.

And Josie! This sweet, beautiful woman, who'd already spent everything she had on her wedding, only to lose her betrothed to murder. To learn what a monster her grandfather was alone might kill her. That she should then be brought out into the public eye to face scorn and scandal and threats of death? The thought was too terrible to bear.

I had to prove their innocence before any taint of Mr. Kerr's plot came onto them.

And if it meant going up against Jack Diamond, that was what I felt fully prepared to do

~~ This ends Chapter 10 of the Red Dog Conspiracy ~~

235

The Jack of Diamonds
Part 11 of the Red Dog Conspiracy
Now Available

Acknowledgments

My thanks go to Julian White, Dawn Wilke, Hope Gerhardstein, and Lenka Trnkova for beta reading *The Four of Clubs*. I'd also like to thank Andy Loofbourrow and Rebekah Brown for help with line editing, playing card terms, and wording during some key moments.

Thank you also to my street team, The Commission, without whom this book might not have made it into your hands.

Special thanks to my Patrons, whose monthly financial support makes this series possible:

Julian White

Melissa Williams

Laura Prime

Michaelene Alston

Cristina

Danielle Barnes

Rachel Heslin

Phoebe Darqueling

By Wilson

Follow the Red Dog Conspiracy on Patreon

patreon.com/red_dog_conspiracy

About the Author

Patricia Loofbourrow is the NY Times and USA Today best-selling author of the Red Dog Conspiracy steampunk noir crime fiction series. She has been a professional blogger, author, and editor since 2000 and began writing novels in 2005. Her first published novel, *The Jacq of Spades*, released in 2015 and has sold over 20,000 copies worldwide.

A native of southern California, Patricia Loofbourrow has lived in central Oklahoma since 2005 with her spouse and three children. You can see all her books (and learn more) at pattyloof.com.

Note from the Author

Thanks so much for reading this far! If you like this series, please leave a review where you bought this.

www.ingramcontent.com/pod-product-compliance
Lightning Source LLC
Chambersburg PA
CBHW030748190726
48285CB00003B/751